The Good Ol' Days

Donald O. Clendaniel

Evergreen
PRESS

The Good Ol' Days
by Donald O. Clendaniel
Copyright ©2006 Donald O. Clendaniel

All rights reserved. This book is protected under the copyright laws of the United States of America. This book may not be copied or reprinted for commercial gain or profit.

ISBN 1-58169-206-4
For Worldwide Distribution
Printed in the U.S.A.

Evergreen Press
P.O. Box 191540 • Mobile, AL 36619
800-367-8203

Dedication

*To my son, Donald,
and my daughter, Karen Sue*

CHAPTER 1

Tadd Tobin's freckled face cracked into a smile, which accentuated his deep brown eyes sparkling with mischievous delight. "Come on, Gandhi," he yelled at me. "Let's get over to the church before somebody else beats us to it."

It was eleven o'clock, December 31, 1938, and we didn't want anyone but us to ring the church bell that hung in the rickety old tower. We had piles of special things to do, and this was one we particular looked forward to. Since we were little tykes, Tadd and I always rang the church bell every New Year's Eve at midnight on the dot. It was like a secret ritual for us.

Tadd and I were close buddies because long ago in the Camp Ground woods we made a pact to be true friends all of our lives. We had seen in the movies how the Indians did it, so we followed their example. Tadd had a pocketknife that was a beauty. The blade sparkled in the sunlight like a flare throwing off colored flames. He pricked his wrist, not too deep, and then he pricked mine (which seemed like it was a bigger gash than his). When the blood began to trickle out of our wounds, we put our wrists together to let the blood mingle. We took the solemn oath that Tadd fabricated right out of his fresh thoughts: "From this day forward, I, Tadd Tobin (and me, Gandhi Reed) are blood buddies, and we will never tell any of our secrets to nobody but always tell the truth to each other. Otherwise, may lightning strike us dead and cause our bellies to bust open and spill our insides, including our hearts, right on the ground."

So, you can see how serious we were about being buddies. By the way, my real name is Marshall Reed, but everybody calls me Gandhi. I got stuck with the name when I had lost most of my front teeth and they said my mouth looked like the famous guy in India who wore sheets. I didn't mind the name.

As we pulled the rope that rang the bell loud and clear in the belfry, Tadd said some words that sent shivers up my spine even though it was covered with a heavy set of long underwear, a flannel shirt, two wool sweaters, and a heavy mackinaw.

"Gandhi," he said, "I can just taste the sweetness of summer in my mouth. Can't you? And what about our big project—our raft?"

I could see in my mind's eye a beautiful raft floating lazily on the Elk River. If there was one thing we wanted more than anything else, it was to build a raft and sail her out to the bay, ten miles away. Nothing, but nothing, would stop us from doing that.

All the time, be it fall, winter, spring, or summer, he was savoring the smells, the sights, and the sounds of summer. I guess you could say he had a summer attitude. To be around him gave you a good feeling all over, like getting up from the table after a great Thanksgiving dinner. Why, even in the dead of winter, he would look at shorn trees and declare that the naked branches were just waiting to put out their buds that would bloom into satiny leaves.

Tadd's question about my tasting the sweetness of summer in my mouth dangled in front of my mind, waiting to be answered. Now, I am not for lying, that is, too much, but I had to tell my buddy the truth so I said, "Honestly, I can't taste nothing but them onions that Mom put in the meat loaf for supper."

"Ain't you got no imagination, Gandhi?" Tadd shot the question to me quick-like, and his eyes pierced it right through my skull.

I took a tighter grip on the bell rope, squeezed my eyes tight together, and tried hard to taste in my mouth the juice of an apple or the smoothness of a cold glass of lemonade.

Tadd jolted me from my reverie when he slapped me on the shoulder saying, "What in the tarnation are you doing?"

Before I could speak, I belched and that ruined everything.

"Honest, Tadd," I replied remembering our oath, "All I can taste is them onions."

We buttoned our coats, forsook the darkened church and stalked out into the still, cold, black night that hurtled big flakes of snow silently and slowly to the ground. Already snow hid the ground with a thickness of six inches.

Tadd and I trudged homeward without a murmur escaping between us. As I turned down the street toward home, Tadd called out to me through the clouds of snowflakes, "See you in the morning."

"See you," I replied without lifting my head. I quickened my pace, anxious to get home and shed my wet clothes. My tired bones ached for the feather bed that waited for me.

DAYLIGHT FILLED THE WINDOWPANES OF LEWISTON, and the whole town began to stir for a fresh start in a new day. After breakfast, Tadd and I met on the church corner, our usual meeting place, and made our way through the unshoveled snow down the hill toward the pier where Capt'n Lacey's boat was docked.

Before we went on board, Tadd hollered, "Hey, Capt'n. It's us." The foredeck hatch yawned open. Capt'n Lacey's head appeared in the opening, his face wreathed in a smile as he invited us aboard with a wave of his hand. Comfortably situated inside the cabin of the old fishing boat, Capt'n Lacey took two cups from the rack and filled them with hot, steaming coffee. This was a silent ritual of long standing for us three. Capt'n Lacey always treated us like grown-ups and never talked with us like we were fourteen-year-old kids. "Well, men," he began, "what be you up to today?"

I took a small sip of the black coffee in my mug. We all drank our coffee black because Capt'n Lacey said men never used cream or sugar in their coffee. Tadd spoke up first 'cause his mind was always churning with all kinds of interesting thoughts.

"Thought we'd go sleigh riding on the hill. You know the pond is froze over, and after the kids slide down the hill a few times you can glide right out onto the pond. That is, if somebody has cleaned off the snow."

"Sounds like it might be a heap o' fun," agreed Capt'n Lacey.

I volunteered a question, "Why don't we get going now, Tadd?"

"Wouldn't be any fun yet," Tadd retorted almost in disgust. "We'll wait till the kids have the hill packed down real good. Then, it will be freer and faster sledding."

Tadd always had been a wise thinker, and many were the times I wished I could think thoughts like he could.

Capt'n Lacey eyed Tadd. Approval was written in every wrinkle of his face. We sat cross-legged on one of the bunks as the Captain busied himself about the cabin. It took a long time to drink one of his cups of coffee. It was always hot and extra strong.

The Captain looked straight at Tadd and observed, "Tadd, my boy, you have the makings of a successful man. You have a good head on your shoulders, and you use it. Yes, sir, you'll get on all right in this world. Mind you, I hold no truck with a man who's a conniver. To really win in this world, a man has to have a stout heart and sticking power. You've got both."

There was a breath of silence while Capt'n Lacey lit his pipe. When thick puffs of smoke began to circle around in the air as if they would push right through the cabin to topside, the Captain propped his feet on the rim of the pot-bellied stove and spoke reflectively, "When a man truly desires to do something or be somebody without being burdened by the trouble of acquiring it, then he ain't no more than a snake in the grass. He is a weakling of the lowest order." Neither Tadd nor I said anything for we knew that the Captain wasn't finished with his advice. We had been around him enough to tell when he had more to say. He continued, "Anything worth having is only to be got by paying its price. If you don't earn it, you don't deserve it."

"What about the air we breathe?" Tadd asked.

Now that was just like Tadd. His quiver was always full of searching arrow-like questions.

Capt'n Lacey drew deep on his pipe like he always did when he needed time to meditate on his answer. "There are such things like begin born, breathing, loving, searching for happiness that is God-given. You see, the Almighty starts us out with the fundamentals, but it's up to the individual to do the fishing if he expects to get anything on his hook."

Our coffee mugs being empty, I asked the Captain if we could fetch him anything from the store that he needed. "That's right considerate of you, Gandhi. Let me take a look." To receive such a compliment from a man like Capt'n Lacey made me swell up inside with pride like a bullfrog about to croak.

He ripped off the corner of a brown paper bag, wet the lead end of a stubby pencil with his tongue, and wrote out his order. He needed a tin of tobacco, a bag of beans, two pounds of sugar, and a side of bacon.

"Take this over to Mr. Mason's store and tell him to put it down to me. I'll pay him later." He handed the paper to me, which proved he trusted me. Honesty was a virtue that Capt'n Lacey emphasized, and both Tadd and I upheld that belief. In our town, business deals were done on a handshake. People trusted one another. In fact, we didn't have a key to the front door of our house. It was always unlocked, and there was never no trouble.

After we delivered the Captain's store goods to him, we headed for the hill next to the pond, figuring that the kids would have packed the snow for some mighty good sledding.

We took fresh heart at the sight of the mob of kids sliding down and climbing up that hill. Neither Tadd nor I owned a sled, but that made no difference to us. It was no trouble to borrow a sled for a ride, that is, providing you pulled the empty sled up the hill first. We sledded up and down that hill until our bellies were sore, our feet sopping wet, and our fingers, noses, and ears almost frostbitten. It was a great day.

LATE THE NEXT AFTERNOON, Tadd and I moved in quick steps toward our secret cave. Only we knew its whereabouts. It was truly camouflaged and no grownup had ever seen it. About a quarter of mile down stream, the creek made a sharp right turn. To the left, a little slip of water meandered back into the thick, matted part of the woods.

As we came near to the pier, we began running and stirred the snow like a horse galloping on a parched country road. With deft movements, I untied our skiff while Tadd fetched our hidden oars. Without a word, Tadd pulled the oars that moved us into our secret cave.

Inside, the cave was cold and damp. But with some paper, a few dry corn cobs and chunks of slab wood, the cave was lighted and warmed in a jiffy.

"What did you do this morning, Tadd? I missed seeing you about."

When Tadd looked at me, there seemed to be a mysterious stirring in him. "Gandhi," Tadd commenced, "I had a frightening experience this morning. I was riding Niter (that was Tadd's Uncle Scank's black three-quarter horse that Mr. Scank used to deliver papers) over yonder behind the Camp Grounds. You know the place." I nodded my head.

"Well," continued Tadd, "As I was riding Niter slow-like—for I didn't want him to slip and fall and cripple himself—I thought I saw a brick fence ahead of me."

"A brick fence!" I chimed in. "I ain't never seen no brick fence back there."

Tadd affirmed, "Yep, that's what I said, a brick fence."

"Was it a mirage?" I asked him, sensing the mystery of it all.

He shook his head vigorously. "Nope, it weren't no mirage. I seen it with my own eyes. While I was trying to figure out what it was, all of a sudden Niter reared to his hind feet. I slid into the snow and that black horse ran off in four directions."

"A horse can't run off in four directions even if it has got four feet!" I said incredulously.

"Well, maybe two directions then," Tadd answered, which seemed more plausible to me. "Anyway," Tadd went on, "I got up and ran after him. After a bit, I coaxed him to me with an apple I had in my pocket. I went back to the fence, much to Niter's dislike, and tied him to a sapling."

"Then what did you do, Tadd?" I asked, wanting him to get to the point for he always was one to go around Robin's barn to get to anything.

Tadd spoke right smuglike, "I climbed the fence and what do you think I saw?"

Tadd's words glowed into flames that ignited my heart. A chill slid all the way down my backbone as I yelled, "What?"

Tadd's eyes narrowed into a slit and said, "A graveyard."

"A graveyard..." I could only whisper the word.

"Yep, a graveyard. And right in the center was a brick building about the size of two outhouses."

"Did you look inside?"

"Gandhi, will you please hush and let me tell it to you?" His voice had begun to betray disgust at my impatience. I closed my mouth and let him go on without a peep from me.

"Of course I went in," he continued, "but it weren't easy. It was black as pitch. I couldn't see a thing, but I felt this here ladder. So I backed around and started to go down it. I went down about four steps when it dawned on me I weren't going to see nothing anyhow."

"Didn't you have no matches on you?" I couldn't refrain from asking that question.

"Nope, Not one. When I started back up that there ladder to get out, something grabbed my back pocket. I tried to move two different times, and it wouldn't let me go. It was a squishy, lumpy thing with protruding arms. Probably a rambling monster. I went as limp as a wet leaf on a log."

In the dead of winter, I found myself perspiring all over just listening to Tadd. "What did you do?" I asked putting another stick of wood on the fire.

"I jumped out of there with all my might and rode home on Niter as fast as he'd run." Tadd slowly shook his head. "It was an awful experience."

Tadd must have noticed the question marks in my eyes for he turned his back to me, lifted up his coat, and showed me his hip pocket. Sure enough, the lefthand pocket was ripped clean from his pants with only his underwear showing. That was evidence enough for me. All I could say was, "Whew! What a day!"

Tadd responded, "Yeah, quite a day."

We sat there for a time just thinking. Then I had a thought that floated on the wings of a fanciful idea. "Tadd," I said, "let's you and me go back there after supper."

"Naw, that wouldn't be no fun."

"Why?"

"Mostly 'cause it'd be too early. You see if it was a monster, and I ain't so sure it weren't, he might be resting about the time we got there after supper. But..." and Tadd began to churn on the idea like it was his own, "if we'd go there about midnight, I'm sure he'd be awake, and we could see him."

Tadd had a thinking head on his shoulders. Capt'n Lacey was right. "Sure," I said, "you're right. Monsters don't mill about before midnight."

"Right," agreed Tadd. "Now, not a word of this to nobody." We shook hands with our secret grip.

"Let's get going," Tadd spoke as he got up and began throwing sand on the fire.

We rowed back to the pier, tied our boat, and made our way home.

It being Friday night, Pop had been paid and was drunk as usual. He cursed me good and proper for being late since I had answered "out" when he asked me where I had been. I didn't say anything during supper, but Pop mumbled all the time, cursing his boss and that cold, dust-filled button shop. Mom didn't say anything for she always seemed tired, having worked hard in the sewing factory.

I went to bed early, but I didn't dare go to sleep. When the old clock in the living room struck eleven, I knew it was time for me to start moving. I pulled my corduroy pants over my long underwear and put on my heavy wool shirt. My coat and sweaters were hanging on the back stairway door. Luckily, I slept in the rear bedroom. I crept like a cat down the back stairs, lifted my sweaters and coat from the nail, and went up to my room. My high-top boots were by my bed. I laced them, trying not to breathe too hard. I listened for any stirrings in Mom and Pop's bedroom. There were none. Silently, I lifted my bedroom window, which I had soaped before I went to bed so it wouldn't screech. It worked like a charm. I gently closed it all but an inch from the sill and let myself down the old walnut tree to the snow-covered ground.

I made my way to our appointed rendezvous and waited on the cellar doors behind the church. By and by, I heard a soft bobwhite whistle. I knew it was Tadd.

We made off down the hill behind the church, which led on to the mill pond road. It wound around to the entrance of the old Camp Grounds. For the first time, I spoke. "Did you bring a flashlight?"

I couldn't see Tadd's face, but I knew he looked at me as if I was crazy.

"Sure I did," he said in harsh tones. "How did you expect to see anything if I didn't?"

I was at a loss for words so I said, "I just wondered."

The woods grew thicker as we left the Camp Grounds, but Tadd and I had been there so often that it wasn't any trouble to us.

"As often as we've been in this here woods, it's strange we ain't seen this dilapidated old graveyard before."

"Yeah, it's mysterious-like." Tadd agreed with me for a change.

We trod this way and that. Tadd flashed his light in all directions, but we saw no brick fence.

Tadd pulled out his Mickey Mouse watch. "We've been searching over an hour and ain't seen a thing. I know I'm in the right place." He put his watch back in his pocket and pointing his flashlight in a northerly direction said, "Let's go this-a-way."

I was beginning to get cold and sleepy. I whined, "Are you sure, Tadd, that you saw that graveyard here?"

"Sure, I'm sure. Didn't I show you my torn pants?"

But by now I was becoming doubtful for he could have torn his

The Good Ol' Days

pants climbing a barbed wire fence. "Let's go home and come back another time," I pleaded.

"What ails you, Gandhi?" Tadd asked, flashing the light in my face. "Ain't you got no adventuresome spirit? Suppose Columbus was like you? Why, we'd all still be furriners."

"You're right, Tadd. I'm with you."

"There it is," Tadd shouted, "the brick wall I told you about!"

I was beginning to think that my idea wasn't so hot after all. My stomach began to ache and I told Tadd so. He only told me to keep quiet or my head would ache if the monster heard me. This notion all the more convinced me that we were where we ought not to be. I pulled Tadd's coattail to tell him I was going home. He jumped a foot high. For a minute I thought he was going to hit me with his flashlight.

He whispered, "We can't back out now. We're too close to our investigating. Now, you wouldn't leave me out here alone, would you?"

He knew I wouldn't do that, so we inched closer to the brick wall. Slowly, we made our way along the wall until we came to the broken, rusted iron gate. Tadd flashed his light quickly on the brick building. The door was wide open. I hugged Tadd and whispered right into his ear, "Do you suppose the monster is out walking around?"

Tadd didn't seem to mind my hugging him for he whispered right back into my ear, "Naw, he's probably been out to get something to eat and gone back in for the night." As an afterthought, he whispered, "Guess he forgot to close the door."

We didn't move but stood fixed on the spot like scrub trees transplanted deep. Finally, Tadd took a step, but my legs seemed frozen. He grabbed my arm, and I leaped to his side. With uncertainty, we shifted our weight from one foot to the other, moving forward in a very cautious manner. I noticed the flashlight in Tadd's hand beginning to waver like an outgoing tide. He put both hands on the light, but it didn't stop its quivering.

I whispered another question, afraid of Tadd's answer, "Are we going down the ladder?"

"Guess...so." Was his shaky reply.

At last we stood by the open door. Stealthily, Tadd shoved his flashlight inside at arm's length as if someone might grab the light and we would have a chance to run. I guess he flashed it all around, but I didn't see a thing 'cause my eyes were shut tight. Tadd put his arm around me and tugged me toward him. I almost fainted or guess I did, for I have never fainted before. But I am sure I was close to it that very minute.

"Come on," Tadd said in a loud whisper.

I opened my eyes to see him getting ready to go down the ladder front ways. I looked behind me but only saw pitch blackness. We picked our way down the rickety ladder. A dank, foul odor encircled our gloom. My eyes were opened wide now and as Tadd flashed the light along the brick walls, we saw the ends of caskets with name plates on each of them. It was an eerie sight. One slot in the wall was empty. Tadd must have had the same thought I did, for when I saw his face in the reflection of the flashlight, he shook his head. This showed me that we both thought that was the bed of the monster.

Just then there was a sudden, loud crash above our heads. It was all I could to swallow my heart back down in its place. Tadd flipped off the flashlight. My stomach felt like something was eating away at my innards. I took in big gulps of stale air that gave me the hiccups. Tadd turned and jumped at me. He shook me and I lost my hiccups. We breathed long, slow breaths. Silence hung on us like snow to our coats. I imagined I heard bones rattling, but I couldn't speak for my tongue had swollen and become fastened to the roof of my mouth. Any moment I expected to see the green bulging eyes of that squishy, lumpy monster at the doorway, blocking our escape. I just knew he would eventually devour us alive, clothes and all. I started to cry to myself and then I remembered Rev. Thompson saying in one of his sermons that God hears all prayers, no matter who says them, as long as the one who prays is sincere. I never felt more sincere in my life. I said my prayer aloud, "Dear God, please get us home safe. Amen."

God must have heard it for He made Tadd flick on his flashlight and start up the ladder with me right at his heels. Outside the brick house, Tadd flashed his light in all directions. Seeing nothing like a monster or skeletons walking around, we ran harum-scarum in a southerly direction toward the Camp Grounds. It seemed we ran for a good hour, although I guess we really didn't, until we stopped to catch our breath. I was completely exhausted and even Tadd appeared winded. Tadd shone his light on a building directly in front of us and it was the old, faded, yellow tabernacle—the Camp Grounds at last! How much more bravely we walked out through the woods onto the road that wound 'round the mill pond.

Before we parted to steal back into our bedrooms, I asked Tadd, "What time will we meet tomorrow?"

"About noon."

"Okay," I said, "let's make more plans about our raft." He nodded his head and we went back to our homes still a little shaken by our adventure.

SATURDAY WAS ALWAYS A BUSY DAY in Lewiston. Farmers from the surrounding countryside came to town to do their shopping. After lunch, Tadd and I just stood around downtown to see what we could see. There was always something to feast your eyes on if you knew where to look.

Like this day, Topsy, a likeable, rotund woman came by the post office measuring her way with slow, struggling feet over the packed snow and ice. All of a sudden, she slipped on a bare spot of ice, and her feet sailed over her head like a small flock of scared geese. Her petticoats fluttered in the breeze, and she landed with such a thud that her red bandanna came clean loose from around her head. She grunted a loud guttural sound and just lay there.

Tadd and I laughed when she had fallen for it certainly was funny to see a woman as fat as Topsy laying on her back. Why I do believe that her dress could have been re-sewn to make a pup tent for four Scouts to sleep in. But when Topsy didn't move and just lay there, Tadd and I ran over to her. What puzzled us was that many folks came by, laughed, and walked on.

Tadd and I tried to help Topsy to sit up. Tadd pulled and I tried to push. By this time, a crowd had begun to gather, both men and women. They just stood there and looked and laughed.

When Tadd became angry, he would say words that cut right through the skin to the bone. Holding onto both of Topsy's arms and still pulling, he turned to the crowd as bitter tears began to well up in his eyes. He wailed, "What ails you grownups? Ain't you got no religion? I hate you all. I hope I never grow up!"

Mr. Jones and two other men moved toward us. They gently lifted Topsy to her feet and helped her into the post office. Mr. Jones returned and said, "Now, Tadd, don't hold no grudge toward us. It was such a funny sight seeing you and Marshall (he never called me Gandhi) tugging away at a load too big for you to budge that we wanted to enjoy ourselves for a spell. Will you forgive us?" He was truly apologetic, and his words and manner seemed to soothe our feeling.

By this time, Tadd had cooled off considerably. The frostbitten air could have had a little something to do with it. He began to realize, maybe for the first time, that it is easier to put squeezed out toothpaste back into the tube than trying to take back something you've said and wished you hadn't. It appeared to me that he was having difficulty tying his thoughts together, and this was something new and strange for Tadd.

Finally he stuttered out, "I'm sorry, Mr. Jones...and...and everybody." He didn't even look up, but kept his chin buried in his coat-covered chest and walked on toward the pier. I followed.

AFTER WE HAD BOARDED THE MARIE TOMAS II, (that's the name of Capt'n Lacey's fishing boat), Tadd poured out his mixed up heart to Capt'n Lacey. When he had unfolded to the Captain all the happenings of the forenoon, Tadd blurted out, "What makes older people so hard to understand, Capt'n Lacey?"

Capt'n Lacey struck a match on the seat of his britches as a pensive look crept over this face. By and by, he spoke. "Well, son," he began, looking straight into the bewildered eyes of Tadd, "when a feller be-

The Good Ol' Days

gins to put on a few years, life for him stops being an anticipation and he settles down to live in its realities. So, when he gets an opportunity to laugh a bit, he takes it."

He puffed on his pipe awhile to let his words sink in. Sometimes, the Capt'n would speak in words that had to be thought over for a long time. Today was one of those times, at least for me.

He continued, "You see, boys, when you become a man, you take off your rose-colored glasses and look at life with the naked eye. It ain't always so pretty because there's a lot of misery in the world and suffering and a whole lot of transparent pretense. Life can paint some mighty ugly pictures if it falls your lot to have to look at them. I'll tell you now, even the happiest life is a tangled yarn."

He did it again, mixing up words of good sense with a clincher that tickled your fancy but didn't do a thing for your gray matter. Oh well, that's what the Captain said and it must have been right and made sense or he wouldn't have said it. But sometimes, he used words like storybook characters.

"You boys did a good thing today." The Captain drew deep puffs on his pipe. "Kindness don't cost nothing and buys everything. You never go wrong by helping the other feller when he's in need."

"But I did something wrong, Capt'n Lacey," Tadd broke in the stream of one-way conversation. "I lost my temper."

"Well, any man worth his salt would've done the same thing you did, my boy. Usually, though, when a man loses his temper there ain't nothing left in him but a fool. Now, mind you, son, I ain't calling you no fool. I'm just saying that generally a man is a fool to lose his temper."

I piped up with an observation. "If a man don't lose his temper once in a while, why, he ain't got no gumption!"

"Right you are," the Captain agreed, nodding his head.

And then he turned and looked out the starboard porthole. "Boys, something ain't right." We knew what he was about to say was serious for he furrowed his eyebrows smack together by squeezing his eyes closer to his nose. Capt'n Lacey continued to speak, "This old crick has been acting up of late. She's been saying things I don't like. All my life has been spent on these waters and I ain't seen the likes of it before."

"A crick can't talk, can it Capt'n Lacey?" I asked, but wished I hadn't after I saw the look on Tadd's face.

"Not in words, maybe," he answered, "but nature has a way of letting us know things if we open our eyes to it."

"What do you mean she's acting up like you ain't never seen before?" Tadd couldn't hold back his questioning either.

Capt'n Lacey stood up, chuckled and said, "Don't you boys pay no mind to what I just said. You see, I was talking out of the top of my head. It weren't nothing important anyhow."

We put on our coats, buttoned them up tight to keep out the frosty air, said goodbye to Capt'n Lacey, and trudged off downtown again. You see downtown Lewiston sat right on the bank of the Elk River with its stores and businesses. On the south, west, and north sides of town, the homes of the people who lived there were perched secure on the small hill that surrounded the town in the shallow valley. The east end of town was where the Elk River turned into a crick. It was spelled creek, but everybody—old and young alike—in town called it the crick.

Mr. Jones spied Tadd and me ambling down by the movie house. He called out, "Hey, where did you boys get off to? Topsy wanted to thank you."

"We went down to see Capt'n Lacey." It was Tadd who answered him.

"That rum hound!" Mr. Jones shot back. "You boys had better stay away from him. He'll get you in a peck of trouble."

Fire flew into Tadd's eyes as they seemed to throw off wild sparks, but he kept his tongue from flapping by keeping his mouth shut. I could not hold back speaking on behalf of the man we loved and held in the highest respect. "Capt'n Lacey is one of the best men in the world. Even if he does have the habit of drinking now and then, I ain't never heard him speak ill of nobody. And besides, we have a code among us that when he's in his cups, we know and don't go near. He don't want us ever to see him that way."

"Just the same," Mr. Jones barked, "he's in his dotage and the Lord only knows what he might do."

Tadd and I hurried to get away by pretending we had somewhere we had to go. When we were out of earshot of Mr. Jones, Tadd turned to me and said, "I hate that old Mr. Jones. Talking about Capt'n Lacey like that. He just don't know. I hope I don't have to speak to him ever again."

"He's full of fudge and I don't believe a word he says," I agreed. As an afterthought, I added, "He's just jealous 'cause he don't know as much as Capt'n Lacey."

"Yeah," Tadd added and then he whirled at me, "but you didn't have to tell him one of our secrets."

"I didn't tell him any secret."

"You might as well have."

"You mean about the code?" I asked.

"Yeah, about the code."

"I didn't tell him what it was," I continued.

"We'll have to think of something else," Tadd spoke reflectively, settling the cogs of his brain into motion. And to be sure, he would come up with something. He always did.

You see, our code was this: Capt'n Lacey always told us in his sober moments that he did not want us to come around when he was drinking. To let us know when he was in his cups, he tied a red slip of cloth to the pulpit of his boat.

"Should we go back and tell him about it now?"

"Naw, let's think on it," Tadd reassured me as he threw me a smile and patted me on the back while we made our way down to pond road to see if anybody was sledding on the hill.

I could never understand it, but I always got soaking wet right through to the skin every time we went sledding. Of course, there were the usual spills and rolls in the snow banks. Come to think of it, lying in the soft blanket of snow was a rather delicious feeling like floating in a low-flying cloud. If you closed your eyes, you could imagine all kinds of things. And when the wind of heaven brushed against your face, you somehow knew that the blue dome sky was the roof of your real home.

Well, being all wet and everything, Tadd and I decided to go home, get dried out, and wait for supper.

THE NEXT DAY WAS SUNDAY. Unless we were sick, Tadd and I always went to church. The big, white church sat solidly on top of the hill with its slender, but tall finger-like, steeple pointing right up to God in heaven. The bulletin board out front announced each Sunday's sermon. In bold black letters the sermon title for that Sunday read: **JESUS, THE DEAD CARPENTER PREACHER**. Underneath the title were the words **EVERYONE WELCOME!** And then in smaller letters was the minister's name: Rev. David Conner Thompson. I'd never heard anyone in town say an ill word against Rev. Thompson; no one, that is, except the heathen, and they said plenty, but we shut our ears to their remarks.

Sunday was always dress-up day, and that was the only reason why I could truly say that I hated Sunday. The starch in my white shirt collar scratched my neck, and my only tie was like a tightening noose around my neck. It gave me a creepy feeling that I was being outfitted for the gallows.

Capt'n Lacey never went to church nor heard Rev. Thompson preach, but he always told Tadd and me that the preacher ought to comfort the afflicted and afflict the comfortable. That made sense to me.

Tadd and I sat in our usual place, and we both turned around to see if Topsy made it this Sunday. She never missed church and always sat in the right front pew of the balcony. Sure enough, she was there and somehow we felt satisfied that she was.

Rev. Thompson was a slow starter in his preaching, somewhat like a well-trained racehorse getting off slowly but picking up speed as he went on. And so along about the middle of his sermon, he picked up steam from somewhere and then to the end of his sermon, he pounded out each word right forceful. Those pulpit Bibles were made of good stuff 'cause they sure took a beating, especially from Rev. Thompson.

The Good Ol' Days

It was quite evident the men singers in the choir were chosen more for tone than looks. It appeared to me that the women were the main underpinning of the choir, especially when they all had to strain for those high notes. But they were a faithful lot and sang a different anthem every Sunday. I guess it was a different anthem, for to tell the truth, I couldn't remember which was which.

It seemed to me this particular Sunday that Rev. Thompson had swallowed an English grammar book for he used so many modifiers that Tadd and I completely lost the subject and the verb of every sentence. And before he had pronounced the benediction, he had lost me back there in the thick undergrowth of his sermon. Yet, this didn't bother me for I figured we're not supposed to understand grownup sermons. I thought that when I grew up I'd understand them and that would be time enough.

Rev. Thompson wasn't quite so long-winded that Sunday, or maybe he was more hungry than usual. At least, we got out of church almost on the dot of twelve. Good thing, too, for my stomach was beginning to growl like a grizzly bear because I hadn't eaten since last night's supper.

Sunday was a slow day. The sun seemed to drag its feet on this day as it walked its orbit from east to west. I found myself wishing and praying that it would move a little faster so that Monday would arrive and Tadd and I could do things.

That afternoon, we walked along the road out by the Camp Grounds. We talked about our raft, the kind of timber we would use, the galvanized nails, the fifty-gallon oil drums to keep her afloat, and the cubbyhole to store things.

"How long are we gonna stay on our trip, Tadd?" I asked.

"Don't know," Tadd answered, reflectively. "I suppose as long as our rations hold out."

We stretched the silence between us as far out as we could and then I broke it. "What do you suppose our moms and pops will say?"

"Ain't going to tell them," Tadd quickly answered, much to my complete satisfaction.

CHAPTER 2

The snows had melted and the March winds were blowing a gale, breathing fast to dry up the muddy fields and watery roads. Of course, it was the time for kite flying.

Tadd lived next to a house that had been vacant for years. An old horse and buggy doctor had lived there once. No one in town would dare buy the place because everyone knew it was undesirable to live in. The old doctor had committed suicide there, and it was days and days before anyone found him. Some said that when he was finally discovered, the meat on his bones was beginning to rot away. And that isn't all. It was not a secret that every closet in the old house was full of dead baby bones since women went there when they didn't want babies and the doctor just stacked them all up in the closets. At least, that's what Tadd told me.

But behind that old house was a huge barn, and we used it for our clubhouse. All told, we had six members and everyone had been initiated into this secret club. Tadd was elected the president. I was elected vice-president, but I never did get to preside at any meetings. Anyway, this day we were all present. Tadd was presiding.

He was wearing his official attire, which consisted of a grass sack around his shoulders and a plumed hat which Pop once wore when he played in the town band.

"The meeting of the Wandering Knights will come to order," he intoned, important like. We all stood and then sat after he was seated on his orange crate chair, painted blue.

"I have a popping idea!" he exclaimed. We all turned and looked at one another wondering what he was going to come up with.

He continued, "The first storm we have we'll fly a kite with a key tied in the middle of the string."

"What for?" asked Burrous Scull, one of our members.

"Ain't you done no reading?" Tadd asked in disgust. Burrous shook his head sideways, and we all knew he was telling the truth. Tadd was a good president for he explained things when anybody didn't understand.

"Well," he began, "a long time ago a great man by the name of Benjamin Franklin was an inquisitive sort. He was always getting into things. You might say he was a kid with a grown-up body for he was always wondering about things and experimenting. Just like us kids. And he weren't skeered neither. One day he decided to find out what lightning was so he flew a kite during a storm and discovered it weren't nothing but electricity flying loose in the sky. So you see that's what we're going to find out come the first real storm."

Hunter Pettyjohn, another member, spoke up, "Ain't that dangerous, Tadd? Why we're liable to be blown clean off the face of this earth if'n we try such a dang fool trick 'specially if'n it's sharp lightning."

Tadd smiled like he was full of all the wisdom in the world, "Naw, we won't. Didn't kill old Ben Franklin, so it won't kill us."

Levin Mustard was the next to speak. "If it's all the same with you, I'd like to be counted out of this here daring experiment."

"Why don't you take a vote?" I asked and it seemed to meet with everyone's approval.

"Good idea," agreed Tadd. "This here club is a democracy just like our government. All in favor, raise your right hand."

Two hands shot in the air, Tadd's and mine. Disappointment was written in every freckle on Tadd's face, but our club was democratic and he wasn't one for disobeying the rule of the majority. Quick as a flash, he banged his fist on top of the barrel, which served as his desk and declared, "Meeting adjourned."

The members filed out one by one and went home; that is, all but

Tadd and me. I broke the icy silence by suggesting, "Why don't you and me do it, Tadd?" Just 'cause the members are against it, don't mean you and me can't do it. Free country, ain't it?"

I guess I was what you might call ugly, but I knew from the look on Tadd's face that I satisfied his heart if not his eyes. He smiled and his eyes gleamed over at me.

"Gandhi," he spoke with real feeling. "You're the best buddy in the whole wide world."

We immediately began to prepare for the eventful hour. After tying long pieces of string together, we had enough to make two large spindles. Then we ripped tiny strips of cloth from an old sheet we had in the clubhouse for special purposes, and what could be more special than flying a kite during an electrical storm? Everything in readiness, we carefully laid the kite, the tailpieces of sheet, and the string in a safe place.

"Come on, Gandhi," Tadd said, "let's check the cave."

We walked down the hill with quickened steps toward the pier. Tadd got the oars out of their secret hiding place while I untied our skiff. We didn't talk while Tadd pulled on the oars. I've found out that between such good friends as Tadd and me there is a sort of secret communion even when we're silent. We beached our skiff, and I tied her secure.

"Look here, Gandhi," Tadd called out to me. He pointed to the water line past the oak tree stump. "I ain't never seen it that high before."

I joined him to get a better look. Sure enough, the crick water encircled the stump. "Well," I reminded him, "it's high tide and besides, the rains and melting snow has got to flow somewhere."

"Guess you're right," was his casual reply.

There was a foul odor inside the cave, and moisture clung to the damp earthen walls. We removed the brush from around the opening as much as we could so the air could flow inside and wring it dry.

"Should we light a fire?" I asked.

"Might as well."

After I got a small fire going in our special fireplace in the cave, I

The Good Ol' Days

emerged and joined Tadd on a fallen tree limb nearby. It was peaceful and quiet, which we both relished. Here away from everybody and everything was a place where you could let cheerful thoughts slip into your mind and set them floating around for a time before you talked about them. It was almost like being in church. Finally, I said, "Tadd, wouldn't it be nice to just live here the rest of our lives?"

"Sure would," he replied. He didn't speak for a minute but then said, "Remember a while back when Rev. Thompson read from the Bible how God had a mess of rooms in His mansion?"

"Yeah, I remember," I answered, but not absolutely certain whether I remembered his exact words.

"Well," Tadd went on, "it seems to me that this here woods must be one of God's rooms 'cause I can almost hear His voice right here in His outdoor mansion."

I shot a glance at Tadd to see if he was going to go off on one of his fanciful spells as he was wont to do now and again. He must not have seen me looking at him for his eyes were fastened on the treetops.

"See them tall green pine trees here," he pointed to a clump of pine trees laden with cones. I stretched my neck to get a good view. He continued, "They're God's fountains spilling over with happiness. They're happy 'cause all they have to do is stand here and soak up the sunshine and rain."

"What do you suppose He made trees for besides to build houses and boats and to bust up for firewood?" I wondered out loud.

He threw me an answer that made a lot of sense, "I guess God made trees to sweep the sky clean of dust."

We got up and walked around in the woods behind the cave to see if we could find any dry wood for the fireplace. The ground was all sheeted with moss while green turkey beard shot up through the wet, dead leaves. The east wind began to stir.

Tadd cocked his head to one side and said, "Listen, sounds like the junior choir chanting in the treetops don't it?"

I couldn't hear any singing, but I agreed with him anyway because he was always hearing and seeing things that I never heard or saw.

Here and there we picked up some dry sticks as we wandered

deeper into the woods. Of course, we were so familiar with those woods that if we got lost, the very soles of our feet would have told us where we stood. We must have searched longer than we thought, and we talked about everything. When we arrived back at the cave, the sun had sunk deep in the west, a warning sign for us to get home for supper, quick.

Tadd put out the fire while I began dragging the brush and limbs to cover the mouth of the cave. We rowed back to the wharf and walked up the hill.

At the top of the hill, Tadd called out over his shoulder as he headed for home, "See you."

ANOTHER DAY BROKE SILENTLY OVER LEWISTON, a day like I have never seen before. It was daytime, yet the clouds were so thick and heavy and black-looking that you could have easily mistaken it for nightfall. Even on our way to school, the people round about talked in muffled tones. It was a nasty looking day, promising ominous happenings.

During history class, Miss Stumps, our teacher, called out my name, "Marshall Reed," she commanded, "come before the class and recite the Gettysburg Address."

I was not one for talking before people, let alone kids of my own age and in school. And to make matters worse, I didn't know all of it anyway. I marched slow-like to the teacher's desk, shivering all inside, but hiding my fears with a calm face. With much prompting from Miss Stumps, I finally got through it. After school, Tadd told me my face was like chalk. And that wasn't like me at all because everybody knew that I normally had a much darker complexion.

It commenced to rain on our way home from school so we started to run. By the time we reached the millpond hill, the bottom seemed to fall out. The rain was a frog strangler, and the sky darkened even more. All of a sudden, sharp lightning cut clean through the raindrops and currents of thunderbolts rumbled overhead. I looked at Tadd. He was smiling from ear to ear.

"This is it," he yelled. "Grab your raincoat and boots, and I'll meet you."

Mom and Pop were at work so there was no one home to say I couldn't go. I changed my wet clothes, strung them over the back step's railing to dry, and put on my old clothes. When I arrived at the church corner, Tadd was there with the kite, string, tail and all under his coat. He passed me the string and tails to carry under my raincoat, and we headed toward the school grounds. The rains subsided somewhat, but the wind kept its steady pace.

We reached the schoolyard by following the path through the woods that wound around the millpond. Tadd and I hovered close together while we tied the tails onto the kite and secured the string to its corner post made of balsam wood. Gently, as if he were launching a new boat down the rails, Tadd began to run down the schoolyard all the while letting out the string as he ran. Like a swan taking flight, the kite fluttered and fussed and rose skyward. It was a sight to behold. When she was sailing a good fifty feet in the air, Tadd called, "Come here quick, Gandhi. Hold this string." He gave it to me, reached into his pocket, and brought forth a good-sized key. He tied the key with a short piece of string and then attached it to the string on the kite.

"Now, let me have it here," he said and taking the string from me that held the kite. He slowly fed out the string as the whirling wind took it up to even greater heights.

The rain changed to a drizzle, but the storm grew worse. Long streaks of lightning flashed across the black sky followed by claps of thunder that could have ripped open the earth beneath our very feet. To put it mildly, I didn't like that experiment one bit.

Tadd's wet face was flushed with glee. Mine was covered with wet goose pimples. He beckoned to me, "Hold onto the string with me. We want to do this adventure together, don't we?" At that moment, I wasn't too sure he was using the right pronoun. "Come on, now," he said, jerking his arm toward me.

Before I took hold of the string, I asked him, "Suppose that there lightning does strike that key and it comes down into our bodies and kills us dead. Who'll visit Capt'n Lacey or look after the cave…or…preside over the Wandering Knights? Suppose we're killed and nobody finds us and the buzzards come to eat us. Suppose..."

Tadd cut right into my supposing by saying, "Ah, shut up, Gandhi and take hold of this line. You ain't skeered, are you?"

Now, no red-blooded American boy would admit to being scared, so I reached out both my arms and grabbed hold of the string like I was going to pull in a line with a man on the other end clinging to a life preserver.

There we stood, both of us holding onto the string for dear life with our eyes glued on the key dangling in mid-air while the lightning spit fire all around us and the thunder bolts rattled our teeth in the sockets of our mouths. Still, the lightning did not strike that key.

After holding on for an eternity, it seemed to me, I asked, "Do you suppose that Ben Franklin did it this away?"

"Sure he did. There ain't no other way."

"Well, I'm for going home. And right now," I said with finality.

Tadd was discouraged as well. We didn't say anything but slowly began to wind in the string around the corncob spindle, and the kite came down with such force that it smashed into tiny bits. It was a disheartening sight, but Tadd said there would be other kites and other storms. We gathered up the remains of our experiment and threw it all in the woods as we set out toward home.

THE NEXT AFTERNOON near the church corner, Tadd met me with the lines of laughter scribbled all over his face. "Gandhi, I have a brilliant idea."

"What?" I asked, wondering about this new idea that whirled in his mind.

"You know them warts on your hand?"

"Yeah."

"Well, do you want to get rid of them?" Tadd inquired with a sparkle in his eyes.

"Sure I do."

"Then today is the day."

By now, I was growing cooler to his brilliant idea for it involved me and not him, and that could spell trouble—for me.

"Well, come right out and say what's on your mind," I inquired anxiously.

"You know Chicken Johnson." This wasn't a question from Tadd for he knew that everyone in town knew Chicken Johnson. She was the old witch that lived in a hut in the swamp behind the Squire's office. It was the spookiest place in town.

My defense flew up like an iron gate. "No, you don't, Tadd Tobin," I said, throwing up my hand and backing away from him. "You aren't going to get me down there. Why she's liable as not to give me a potion that'll kill me on the spot."

"Don't be silly, Gandhi," Tadd spoke soothingly. "She tolerates kids. And besides she wouldn't do a thing like that, leastwise in the broad daylight."

"Just the same, I ain't going," I said, but somehow I didn't sound too convincing, seeing as we were walking down the hill which would eventually lead us to the Squire's office.

"Tadd," I spoke in dead earnest, "you know it ain't safe to associate with that old witch. She's drunk too much chicken blood, and it's made her tetched in the head. She ain't right, you know that! Everybody in town is skeered of her 'cause she can put a spell on you if she's a mind to. How 'bout that time old Giz Barker went to her for his rheumatism? He got worst instead of better, and now he can't walk at all."

We took a few more steps. By this time, we were in front of the barbershop. I stopped solid in my tracks. "No, Tadd," I said with force, "I just ain't going to do it."

Tadd stared at me, and I could tell by the look in his eyes that he was primed for action. When he looked at me that way, I knew sooner or later I was a done goose. I took another look at the ugly warts on my hand. "Well," I drawled, "maybe it ain't such a bad idea after all. But mind you, I want you right at my side all the time."

"Don't worry," he assured me and threw his arm around my shoulder as we walked together toward the Squire's office. When we arrived in front of the office, it was my turn to spawn a bright idea. "Let's go in and speak to Squire Hazzard."

"Naw, we ain't got time for that," Tadd replied, tugging at my arm.

But I was persistent. "We got all the time in the world." I darted for the door. Before Tadd could stop me, I called out, "Howdy, Squire. Are you busy?"

Squire Hazzard was fat and short of breath through prosperity, since his father had died and left him a large sum of money. "Come in, boys, come in. You're always welcome. Sit a spell," he called out between breaths.

When we got inside and closed the door, all we could smell was the scent of strong urine. Everyone knew there wasn't any toilet in that office and whenever nature called, the Squire just went in the corner. After you were in there for a while, you got used to it.

"What are you boys up to today?" the Squire inquired.

"Well," I started, "we thought we'd go…"

Tadd interrupted me right in the middle of my sentence, "We ain't up to nothing, Squire. We're just out strolling. Thought we'd drop by to see you and pass the time of day."

I shot Tadd a glance that was supposed to say, "You're talking to the Squire now, and you had better not lie too strong." I guess he didn't catch the message. He rambled on, "How's Mrs. Hazzard?"

"Mighty fine, thank you."

For a minute, no one said anything, then Tadd suggested, "Guess we'd better shove off. Nice seeing you again, Squire."

I wanted to do something to delay our going but couldn't think of anything. Tadd had already opened the door and beckoned to me. I followed with heavy feet.

"Come again, boys, when you can stay longer." Squire Hazzard called out after us.

"Thank you. We will," Tadd replied.

When we got outside, Tadd turned to me and scolded, "What did you want to go in there for? He ain't as dumb as you think. He may smell a rat."

"Look here, Tadd Tobin," I always called him by his full name when I was in such a frame of mind. "I ain't exactly sold on that there idea of yours and besides them warts are mine. And I thought if we could casual-like drop a hint to the Squire where we was going he could keep his eye peeled for us. If'n we didn't turn up in a reasonable time, he could go for help."

"Well, ain't you the one," he spoke with admiration in his voice. "You do use your noodle once in a while, don't you? That's right smart thinking." He nodded his head and pressed his lips tight together.

"Let's go back in and tell him," I said starting toward the door. I realized that thoughts were beating about in Tadd's head searching for a way out through his mouth. He always was a quick thinker.

"I'll tell you what, Gandhi. Let's not bother the Squire. If'n the old witch acts too queer-like, I'll run out and get help."

"What about me?" It didn't take any thinking on my part to come up with that question, but Tadd seemed to have all the answers to any question. It was uncanny how his brain reacted so quickly.

His quick rejoinder was, "You run, too."

"I guess it's settled then," I sighed.

"Yeah. Come on."

We turned down the dirt road, which was shaded with weeping willow trees so thick you couldn't see through them. It wasn't long before we stood in front of the hut. We stood there for a minute as if waiting for someone to give us a little push toward it. Before we moved, the door of the hut creaked open and a dozen cats, all colors and sizes, ran out and there appeared the old witch, Chicken Johnson. Her long white tangled hair flowed to her waist, touching her rope belt that cinched her dirty feedbag dress to her wicked hypnotic body. She looked at us with her piercing eyes that could put a spell on a statue. We didn't move for we were immobilized.

She grinned and rubbed both her hands together as she spoke to us in a crackling voice, "Howdy, boys. What can I do for you?"

By that time, we had become so hair-triggered that we both almost shed our skin at the sound of her voice. I couldn't speak for the dryness in my throat, but Tadd was the brave one. "Afternoon, Miss Johnson. We have a problem and thought you could help us."

She smiled, revealing three dark-stained, sparse upper front teeth while her lower jaw was all gums. She stepped back into the hut and hissed the words, "Come in, boys. Let me get a good gander at you."

We didn't move. Our shoes seemed full of lead. "Come in, boys," she beckoned again to us with furious movements of her hands. Then she threw back her head, her tangled hair moved wild-like, and she cackled instead of laughed. I didn't know about Tadd, but right then and there I decided to run for all I was worth.

"Let's go home, Tadd. I don't mind them warts at all."

"Warts you say?" old Chicken Johnson rushed toward us like she was riding a flying broom. I turned tail and ran as fast as I could back the way we had come. I didn't look over my shoulder, but I knew Tadd was right behind me.

We didn't stop until we had gotten across Main Street and down the alley behind the hardware store, which bordered the creek.

"That there was a bad idea," Tadd admitted after he had caught his breath a bit.

"You're right there, buddy. I don't know what we were thinking. I sure have heard Rev. Thompson talk about miracles, but I don't think going to Chicken Johnson is any way to get one."

Deciding the best idea was to try and forget about Chicken Johnson, I said, "Come on, let's go see Capt'n Lacey."

We headed for the slip where the Marie Tomas was moored. She wasn't there. "Guess he ain't got back from fishing yet." Tadd observed.

"Let's sit and wait for him." I suggested.

We each grabbed a handful of stones as we had done many times before and threw them in the water one by one. We watched the ring-like waves they made, which fanned out to both sides of the creek.

"Gandhi," Tadd spoke after a bit, "I can hardly wait until school's out."

"Yeah, me neither," was my honest reply.

"I've been thinking."

"Sometimes," I said, "you think too much." But my curiosity nudged me. "What about?"

"I've been thinking how much fun it's going to be just you and me cruising down the crick and out into the bay."

"Yeah, can't wait, can you?"

"It'll take a heap of planning," he reminded me.

"We'll wait 'til summertime to do it," I assured him.

"You're right. But let's keep at it."

"All right. What's first?" I knew the wheels of his mind were rolling.

"Well, we'll have to get our lumber together."

"Yeah, that's right. What's wrong with using our skiff and rowing it down to our cave?"

"Okay. Sounds great."

"We could haul it by night so no one would know what we're doing."

"Good idea, Gandhi," Tadd replied, looking directly into the water, and I knew he was thinking deep thoughts. "Did you ever read about Huck Finn?" he asked after savoring his thoughts.

"Who's he?" I wondered out loud.

"You ain't never read the book about Huck Finn?"

I shook my head from the left shoulder to the right, wondering what he was getting at and getting tired of his asking all kinds of questions.

"Well, he was the most adventurous feller you ever heard of. In that there book, he and a runaway slave took a trip down the Mississippi River on a raft and they had a swell time."

"That's different," I said.

"What's different?" Tadd asked, jerking his head sideways to shoot me an inquiring look. "The Mississippi River. This here is just a crick, and we ain't got no runaway to take along."

Tadd didn't say anything for a minute and then he stumbled on another good idea. "We could kidnap somebody and take him with us. That would make it interesting, wouldn't it?"

Leave it to Tadd to come up with the most brilliant ideas that God could place in a body's mind.

I said, "That's a good one. Now, who'll we kidnap?"

"Ain't got that far yet," he replied honestly, "but I'll think of somebody."

While we were thinking, we heard a blast on a foghorn. We looked downstream, and it was Capt'n Lacey bringing in the Marie Tomas. She had clean lines and cut through the water like a sharp razor. The Captain waved to us and we waved back, standing up as we did so. The tide was running strong, as we could plainly see, but Capt'n Lacey cut the motor and called out, "What you boys been up to since I seen you last?"

"Nothing," I called back to him.

We went on board and leaned against the topsides. Tadd was bursting at the seams to tell the Captain about our encounter with Chicken Johnson. I didn't want to discuss it, but I didn't mind if the Captain knew for he would understand.

The gears of Tadd's imagination needed no oil, and he reeled off how the witch was fixin' to swoop down at us when we hightailed it out of there. He added some extra things that really didn't happen at all, but I got so interested that I could hardly wait to hear next what he had to tell. Whenever Tadd began to tell a lie, he really told a whopper. This was one of his whoppers.

Capt'n Lacey listened patiently as he slowed puffed his pipe. After Tadd had wound up his tale about Chicken Johnson, the Captain asked him to run an errand to Mr. Mason's store for a tin of tobacco. While Tadd was gone, Capt'n Lacey and I moved about his boat storing his working gear in its proper places all in Bristol fashion. After awhile I asked, "Capt'n Lacey, how is it that when Tadd tells about something, he always blows it up bigger than what it really was. That's lying, ain't it?"

"Guess you could call it that," the Captain reflected. He sat down on the engine cover. "If I was you, Gandhi, I wouldn't fret too much over Tadd's lying now and again." He drew hard to get the last bit of vanishing tobacco in his pipe. "Hand me that tackle box, will you, Gandhi?"

I jumped to and handed him the box, for he always told us that when a captain of a ship gives a command you were supposed to do exactly what he said immediately without any ifs, ands, or buts.

Tadd returned with a large tin of Prince Albert tobacco and observing the fast slipping westward sun said, "We'd better get going, Gandhi. It's about supper time."

I jumped onto the dock and called over my shoulder. "See you, Capt'n."

"See you, boys," he said as he busied himself about the boat.

As we walked up the hill toward home, I asked, "When are we going to start building that raft?"

"Tomorrow, right after school. Wait for me at the school gate."

We reached the top of the hill at the church corner. I turned to go home. "See you," I called out.

"See you," Tadd replied throwing his arm in a half circular motion.

I THOUGHT OUR LAST CLASS WOULD NEVER BE OVER. Finally, the bell rang and I made a beeline to the gate. Tadd ran toward me and the sight of him struck happy chords in my heart. God certainly smiled on me when he linked Tadd and me as friends.

"Let's go down by the sawmill," he suggested when he caught up with me.

"Okay," I replied beaming all over.

We kept on walking through the fields that led to the woods around the pond to the point where the sawmill was. We turned down the path in the woods that led us right to the sawmill. We had followed that path many a time. It was a very familiar to us. Mr. Ireland owned the mill. All the grownups called him Stoneface. They said he was just like Cal Coolidge. Tadd went up to him and asked, "Mr. Ireland, got any old pine slabs you could let us have?"

"Yep," was his reply.

"Which ones?"

"Them." Old Stoneface pointed to a pile of slab wood.

"Come on," Tadd said to me.

Tadd and I picked up three pine slabs about twelve feet long and began to tote them across the mill dam down to the pier. They were a bit heavy, but we didn't mind for they and a few more like them were going to be the deck of our raft. We put them in our skiff, and we rowed toward our secret cave.

I jumped out and secured our boat. The water had come up even more past the old tree stump. "This crick sure is rising," I called out to Tadd. "Look here. I'd say she's three feet past the stump now."

Tadd came toward me. "Sure is," he observed. "Ain't never seen it this high before. What do you suppose is causing it?"

"I don't know," I said. "Could be the crick is just filling up more, that's all. Come on. Let's get them slabs."

We stacked them high and dry back in the woods behind the cave. Tadd checked the cave. He said it was okay, and there wasn't any need to start a fire. He placed the branches back over the opening and said, "Let's go get some more slabs."

"Do you think old Stoneface will let us have 'em?"

"Sure. They ain't good for nothing 'cept firewood. Besides, he gives 'em to anybody who goes and totes 'em away."

"What're we waiting for?" I asked untying the boat.

I rowed back to the dock. We got three more pine slabs the same as before and Tadd was right. Old Stoneface didn't even say a word when we asked for them; he just pointed to the pile.

We toted the slabs back down to the dock. This was getting to be more like work than fun, but Tadd assured me it was pure fun and that made it easier. We rowed the pine slabs to the cave and placed them along with the others. "Well, that's enough for today," Tadd spoke after we had worked through silence.

"Yeah, we'd best be shuffling home," I suggested.

As I pulled on the oars with our bow headed for the pier, Tadd said, "Gandhi, we're starting on a real enterprise. Now, it ain't no use broadcasting it to everybody—not even to the Wandering Knights. What do you say?"

"You're right. Let's keep it a secret, if we can."

"What do you mean, *if we can?*"

"Well," I reasoned, "we're toting them boards right down the street in broad daylight, ain't we? If they got eyes, they can see us, can't they?"

Tadd nodded his head slowly. "Maybe," he began, "we'd better do this work at night 'cause nobody becomes upset about nothing that don't trouble 'em. It's settled then; we do our hauling of them slabs during the night.

Of course, I had dropped the seed of that idea before into his head and he believed it was his own. I didn't mind, though, because Tadd was my real buddy. Then I said, "Suppose somebody sees us? They might think that we're stealing."

"We'll ask old Stoneface if we can have more, and then it won't be stealing at all."

We secured our skiff and walked up the hill. At the church corner, Tadd left me with the words, "Now, 'member, Gandhi, mum's the word."

"I'll 'member," and I turned down the street toward home.

CHAPTER 3

When Tadd wanted his own way, he hit hard at the stacked up reasons in his mind and no one could cut short his answer to him. This day it was especially so. We Wandering Knights had been called together for a special meeting in our clubhouse. Tadd spoke softly, but his words snapped like a whip.

"Men," he began, "We Wandering Knights have been challenged by the Taylor gang. You know they're the dirtiest fighting bunch of boys in Lewiston. But no matter what, we're going to fight fair and square. We ain't going against our code of justice and fair play. Right?"

Every one of us answered as if in one voice, "Right!"

"Now, I have a surprise for you," Tadd said with a gleam in his eye.

Levin Mustard was as bad as me in not being able to wait out Tadd's long speech. He blurted out, "Come right out and tell us what it is, Tadd."

Tadd shot Levin a look that I'd seen many a time. "Keep your pants on, Levin. I'm coming to it."

Tadd reached down in the barrel desk and brought forth a contraption that we had never laid eyes on before.

Burrous Scull piped up, "What in tarnation is that thing?"

"This is our secret weapon," Tadd spoke with a certain amount of pride in his voice.

I was completely flabbergasted by Tadd's ingenuity. Our eyes feasted on a piece of pine board about twelve inches long, three inches wide, and about an inch thick. It was encircled with two pieces of inner tube cut into wide strips. At one end was a clothespin underneath the two strips of inner tube. A nail was pierced into the pine board about two inches from the clothespin, which served as a trigger. Tadd then took another one inch strip of inner tube, connected it around the far end of the pine board, stretched it to the other end, and made it fast by squeezing the clothespin open and then letting it shut tight on the stretched piece of inner tube. Then he aimed it toward the calendar on the wall. He squeezed the nail, which let open the clothespin from pressing against the pine board. This released the inner tube strip and it flew toward the calendar. We all sat there in amazement without murmuring a word. The look on Tadd's face reminded me of a peacock strutting about a castle's inner court.

"What do you think?" Tadd broke the silence.

"It's the most wonderful invention since the machine gun," I said in real admiration.

Levin asked the next question. "Is every member of the Wandering Knights going to have one?"

"Sure we are," assured Tadd. "This is how you do it," and he preceded to explain, step by step, how the rubber gun was made.

When he had finished his explanation, he said, "Now, I know every one of you has the material around home to make one of these. Is there anybody here who don't have an old inner tube laying in his garage?"

No one said anything, which meant that we had the stuff to build one of those newfangled guns.

"Good," replied Tadd. "Now, meeting's adjourned. Go home and get to work right away, 'cause this Saturday is the day we meet the Taylor Gang. And we're going to give 'em the surprise of their lives."

"Where's the battle going to take place, Tadd?" asked Burrous.

"The corncob pile behind the grist mill," was Tadd's crisp reply.

"Good enough," Burrous said, getting up with the rest of the boys as they began to move toward their homes.

When they had all gone, Tadd called to me and said, "Gandhi, you don't have to go home and make one."

"Why?" Disappointment was in my voice. "I want to be in on this here fight, too."

Tadd smiled and said, "You will." He reached down in the barrel and handed me a rubber gun all assembled. "It's yours. Go on. Take it."

That was twice I had been flabbergasted in the same day. When I finally got my tongue around some words, I said, "Tadd, you're the best buddy, ever. Thanks."

Tadd's offhand remark which went straight to my heart was, "What are buddies for, if it ain't to look out for one another?"

"Are we going to have enough ammunition?"

"You bet," he replied and he pulled out two old inner tubes from the barrel. "Let's get busy."

He gave me an inner tube and he took one. Then he passed me a pair of scissors and he kept a pair. We commenced to cut one-inch strips off the inner tube. The longer we cut, the more I realized that we would have plenty of ammunition, and I wasn't worried any longer.

After we finished cutting the inner tubes into strips for our guns, Tadd suggested, "We'd better start practicing. Our aiming has got to be just right." He stood up and looked around our clubhouse. He spied an old raincoat hanging on the wall. "Let's use that for our target. You go first."

I put the rubber gun close to my eye and aimed at the raincoat. Straight as a die, the rubber band flew into the middle of the coat.

"Nice shooting," Tadd complimented me.

"Your turn," I reminded him.

He held his gun hip level and squeezed the trigger. When the rubber band hit its mark, I yelled, "Bull's-eye!"

We smiled with satisfaction at each other. Then we practiced for many more satisfying moments.

"It's about time for supper," I finally blurted out.

"Okay," Tadd answered. "Suppose we leave our guns here, and that way no one will see our secret. By the way, Gandhi, you go see half of our members, and I'll see the other half. We'll tell 'em to keep the guns a special secret. And when we meet here early Saturday morning, the guns are to be carried under their clothes. You see Levin and Pete. I'll see Hunt and Burrous."

THAT APRIL SATURDAY WAS THE MOST BEAUTIFUL DAY I had ever seen on God's good earth. After we had all gathered in the clubhouse for final instructions from Tadd, we set out for the corncob pile. We didn't go down the street. Rather, we stole down to the mill from the woods behind the church. We raced up the corncob pile and with our hands, dug cavities in the corncobs big enough for us to hide ourselves in. We waited and waited some more. Still no Taylor Gang. We were 'bout to give up on them when Tadd whispered, "Here they come." His next command was, "Don't move. Don't say nothing 'til I give you the signal."

Granny Hobbs was the leader of the Taylor Gang. His name was really Granville but everyone called him Granny. He was a mean one.

Soon we heard Granny talking, "See, boys. I told you. They ain't going to show up. Them Knights are chicken with a yellow streak down the middle of their backs."

Bob Jones, one of the Taylor Gang asked Granny, "What are we gonna do? Go home?"

"Naw, we're here," said Granny. "Let's have some fun on the corncob pile. Last one to the top is a rotten egg."

With that, all six boys of the Taylor Gang began to scramble up the corncob pile. When they were 'bout six feet from us, Tadd shouted, "Now!"

We pelted those boys with inner tube bands just as fast as we could load and shoot. They were startled almost out of their skins as they tumbled and rolled back down the pile, covering as best they could their faces and eyes with their hands and arms. After they got out of shooting range, Granny called out, "Tadpole Tobin, we'll get you for this! Just wait and see!" He shook his fist in a belligerent manner.

Only Tadd's enemies called him Tadpole. It made Tadd fighting mad, but we all held our places to see what Tadd might do. Sure enough, he leaped from his cob hole and scampered down that pile.

We followed behind him. The Wandering Knights and Taylor Gang clashed right at the bottom of the corncob pile. If you've never had a fight on a pile of corncobs, then you won't understand what I'm about to say. Such rolling and slipping and wild fish throwing you never did see. Even the wind from a flying fist could easily upset you, especially if your feet weren't dug in deep. Our minds were made up to fight to the last man as anyone could plainly see. And I guess someone did see, for Mr. Higgins, the manager of the mill, came running toward us while two other men followed. They stopped us from fighting, but not before I got a bloody nose and Tadd a deep cut over his right eye. All the other boys were skinned up, too.

"Now, you boys break it up and get home," Mr. Higgins said in a stern voice. "I don't mind you playing on the pile, but none of this fighting. Do you hear? Now go home!"

His voice carried meaning in every word he said, and we skedaddled. We returned to our clubhouse by the same beaten path through the woods behind the church. After we were all inside, Tadd exhorted, "This fight ain't finished by a long shot, boys. No red-blooded American is gonna take an insult like Granny threw at me. Right, boys?"

"Right," we all chimed in.

"Maybe our guns ain't strong enough," Tadd mused. "Let's make 'em bigger. What do you say, let's make 'em twenty inches long. That'll stretch the rubber bands further and make 'em sting worser."

"Good idea," I concurred, blotting my bloody nose on my shirtsleeve.

"Turn in your guns, boys. Let's keep 'em here," Tadd ordered.

We each deposited our guns in the barrel, that is, all but Levin. "Where's yours?" asked Tadd.

"I guess I must of dropped it back there in the ruckus," bewailed Levin.

"Now, that was a smart thing to do," scolded Tadd. "Suppose one of them boys finds it? Then they'll have weapons just like ours."

"I'll go get it," groaned Levin as he scooted out of the clubhouse for the corncob pile.

We laid further plans of strategy while Levin was gone. By and by he returned, empty-handed. "Well?" Tadd asked.

"I couldn't find it."

"Then they've discovered it," Tadd reasoned. "Now, I know we'll have to make new guns, better and stronger."

We started to depart. "Before you go," Tadd said, "make sure you don't tell nobody about our secret, but make your guns twenty inches long this time. I don't believe them Taylor boys got sense enough to figure out the longer you make the guns, the stronger the shooting power. See you all right here next Saturday, bright and early."

They nodded their heads with dubious covered faces and filed out. When they were all gone, I asked Tadd, "What're we going to do for the rest of the day?"

"Let's go fishing."

"Good idea."

We set out for the pier. Our two fishing poles were hidden near our oars under the pier. I got the oars and fishing poles while Tadd untied the boat. We shoved off downstream.

The outgoing tide caused us to drift lazy-like. I asked Tadd when we would begin building our raft.

"How 'bout Monday night?" he asked.

"Suits me."

After an undetermined duration, Tadd hazarded a surmise, "I guess the fish ain't biting today. Have you had a nibble?"

"Nope, nary a one," I replied truthfully.

Just then Tadd bolted and whispered, "Hold on. I believe I've got something." He snatched his line and pulled in the boat a bunch of seaweed and his worm was gone.

"Well, I thought I had something," he confessed with a sheepish grin on his face.

"I'm for going back. How 'bout you?" I asked.

We took our bearings and realized we had drifted further than we thought. It didn't matter for we took turns rowing back to the pier. Tadd stashed the gear while I secured the skiff.

Instead of going straight up the hill, we meandered around the hardware store following the creek. We emerged on Main Street near the Red bridge. Over yonder was the squire's office. Squire Hazzard was sitting out front with his captain's chair leaning on the back two legs propped against the building. When he spied us, he called out, "Hey, boys, you're just the ones I'm looking for."

Crossing the street, Tadd called back, "What for, Squire? We ain't done nothing."

"Who said you had?" was his fast retort.

"Could we do something for you, Squire?" I offered.

"You sure can," was his amiable reply. "In just about an hour, a friend of mine is bringing his dog down here for me to get rid of. His wife says he can't keep it no longer. I was wondering if you boys might want him?"

Tadd looked at me and I stared right back at him. It seemed for the first time since I had known him, Tadd could find no effective reply.

Without giving it too much thought, I spoke up, "I'd be mighty pleased to have him, Squire Hazzard. I've always wanted a dog."

"Well, now, Marshall, that's right nice of you. He's a good dog, but John's wife says he barks too much, and he'll have to get rid of him."

Tadd spoke to me aside, "Gandhi, we don't want to be saddled with no dog to care for. Besides, what's your Mom and Pop gonna say 'bout it?"

"I just thought of that, too." I replied. "How's 'bout me keeping him in the clubhouse?"

Tadd nodded his head with a slow hesitancy, "Guess you could."

"What time will your friend be here, Squire Hazzard?" I asked.

"Well, he said in about an hour. But could be, he'll be here anytime now." He offered us a seat on the bench next to the office there under the shed roof, which jutted out over the sidewalk. "Why don't you sit a spell and wait for him?"

"We ain't got nothing else to do," I said to Tadd. "Let's wait."

So we sat on the bench, watched the people and cars go by and

The Good Ol' Days

waited. It wasn't too long before a car came to stop in front of the Squire's office.

"Here he is now," the Squire spoke, getting up to meet his friend. "I've got a good home for your dog," he said, speaking to the man in the car who was particularly slow in getting out.

"I sure do hope so," uttered the voice from inside the car, "for I hate to get rid of him. That's for certain." He got out and whistled to his dog. "Here, Harrison," he called and out leaped the most beautiful German Police dog I had ever seen.

"Who'd you find that'll take him, Eric?" the man asked the Squire.

Squire Hazzard turned toward me and said, "There he sits," pointing to me.

"A kid?" exclaimed the man.

"Could you think of a better one that would give Harrison the love and affection he'd like?" asked the Squire.

"Guess you're right," agreed the man, scratching his head like he had the seven-year itch. The man walked over to me. "You'll take good care of Harrison, won't you kid? You're sure your parents won't mind you having him?"

"I'm sure," I lied.

The man called the dog over to where I was standing and introduced him to me. The dog lifted his paw and we shook hands. He shook hands with Tadd, too.

"Maybe you boys better get the dog inside the office until after John has gone," Squire Hazzard reasoned. "He might not take to you right off and go back home."

"Good idea," the man affirmed. So Tadd, Harrison, and I went inside the smelly office.

We heard the man drive off and Squire Hazzard came in. "Now, you be good to that dog, Marshall. He's been used to proper handling. Treat him right, and he'll make a good companion for you."

"I sure will. Thank you, Squire." And then I got up to go. "Guess, we'd better be heading out. Here, Harrison," I called, opening the door for him to go out. He obeyed me like he had always been my dog. "See you, Squire."

We went back around the hardware store by the creek. I kept my eyes peeled on Harrison to see if he was scared of water because if he was, I had made an awful mistake. He never flinched at the sight of the restless creek.

Tadd broke his silence, "Gandhi, you ain't going to call him Harrison, are you?"

"Naw," I said, "that name ain't fitting for such a fine dog as him."

"What are you going to call him, then?"

I looked up and saw Capt'n Lacey waving to us. A bright idea flicked across my brain like a fresh piece of lightning. "I'm going to call him Skipper."

"That's a great name, Gandhi!" Tadd exclaimed. "I like it!"

"Hey, Capt'n Lacey," I hollered, "look what I got."

Capt'n Lacey stepped up on the pier. He petted the dog on the head. "What's his name?"

"Skipper," I said without hesitating.

"Apropos enough, knowing you boys," the Captain replied.

I didn't catch the meaning of the first word he used, but knowing Capt'n Lacey, I was satisfied that it had a good meaning.

We indulged in small talk with Capt'n Lacey for a while and then I reminded Tadd, "We'd better find Skipper something to eat. Come on, Tadd, let's go 'round to Mr. Mason's meat shop."

"See you, Capt'n," Tadd waved to Capt'n Lacey as we parted.

"Take good care of Skipper, boys," Capt'n Lacey called after us while he boarded the Marie Tomas.

I marched back to the meat block where Mr. Mason was cutting thick slices of T-bone steaks. "Mr. Mason," I said with pride in every word, "I've got a dog now."

Mr. Mason, a tall lean man with snow-cropped hair and kindly eyes remarked, "Good for you, Marshall. A dog, if he's treated well, is man's best friend." He continued to cut the meat. "And, sometimes, even if you mistreat him, he still showers love and faithfulness on his master. I love dogs. What kind do you have?"

"A German Police dog."

"They're usually a one-man dog. What's his name?"

The Good Ol' Days

"Skipper."

"A likely name, since you are such an old salt."

"Thank you, Mr. Mason," I hesitated to speak further. I don't know why for I had worked for Mr. Mason and knew him well.

"How about some meat scraps and bones for Skipper?" Mr. Mason asked.

"That would be swell," I answered, relieved and thankful for his thoughtfulness and generosity.

He stopped his work, gathered up some delicious looking meat scraps and a few bones, and wrapped them in orange colored paper. He retrieved the pencil from his ear and wrote on the package: No Charge.

"Thanks a million, Mr. Mason," I said and took my leave.

Skipper was a well-mannered dog. When I came out of the meat shop, he was sitting close to where Tadd was standing.

Tadd greeted me with, "Did you get the meat, Gandhi?"

"Yep, right here," I lifted the orange colored package for him to inspect.

With Skipper at my heels, we headed up the hill toward our clubhouse. Inside, I fed Skipper a part of the meat scraps and gave him a bone. "How about something to keep water in, Tadd?"

"I'll slip over home and get a bucket of water for him," Tadd volunteered. "But," he added, "you're gonna have to tell your Mom and Pop sometime 'bout Skipper. When are you going to do it?"

"Gimme time, Tadd. I'll tell 'em."

Tadd left and was back in a jiffy with a bucket of fresh drinking water for Skipper. We secured our clubhouse tight as a mink's skin stretched out to dry so Skipper couldn't escape on his first night away from his former home.

After church the next morning, I dashed to the clubhouse. I guess Skipper heard my footsteps for he began to whine even before I could get the door open. When I went in, he jumped up on me and gave my face a wet lick with his tongue. I didn't object. In fact, I liked his show of affection for me. "Come on, boy. Let's go for a stroll."

By the time we got outside, Tadd had joined us. "Where you going?" he asked.

"Let's walk down by the pond," I suggested.

"Okay."

Tadd and I strolled together down the back dirt hill toward the pond. Skipper trotted on ahead, his nose sniffing the strange air about him. His fluffy tail curled, almost touching his back.

"Ain't it nice to have a dog, Tadd?"

"Yeah, it's like having a bodyguard around you."

Tadd and I sat on the waste gates, and Skipper ran around inspecting every scent that struck his fancy. I threw a rather large stone in the pond. Immediately, Skipper leaped overboard, and he looked like he was searching for the stone I had just thrown.

Tadd seem excited, "I bet he retrieves!"

I ran to the corncob pile and grabbed two corncobs. While Skipper was still in the water, I threw a corncob about six feet past him. Within a matter of seconds, he had it in his mouth. I looked again and saw my wonderful, wet dog climbing out at the water's edge. Skipper came to me and dropped the corncob at my feet. I stroked his head with rapid movements but somehow that didn't seem enough, so I got down on my knees and kissed him.

I jumped back on my feet and exclaimed, "Tadd, I feel happy all inside—like I was agreeing with God!"

Tadd didn't answer, but the look he gave me silently bespoke his understanding. We started to walk again and our feet were headed in the direction of the old Camp Ground. Skipper leaped with joy. He was relishing our little jaunt.

Tadd observed Skipper dashing here and there, and then he remarked, "He sure moves with a fierce energy, don't he?"

"Sure does." I answered, brimming over with all the joy inside me.

As we crossed over the small wooden bridge leading to the Camp Ground, we caught sight of Mr. Jasper and his little daughter in a small dinghy. He was fishing. Mr. Jasper was the art teacher in school. Everybody said he was an atheist because he never went to church and wouldn't let his wife or daughter go either. We liked him, even if he didn't believe in God. I never did understand why he didn't believe in God for he was always drawing his landscapes.

"Hi, Mr. Jasper," Tadd hollered across the water to him.

"Hello, boys. Nice day." Mr. Jasper called back. He stood up to re-bait his line. All of a sudden the boat tipped and turned upside down. In a split second, he yelled to us. "Help, boys, help! I can't swim!"

In a flash we had our shoes and coats off and plunged in. Skipper beat us to it. Before we got to the boat where Mr. Jasper was clinging for dear life, Skipper was there. "My daughter! My daughter!" Mr. Jasper screamed. He was crying, "Oh, God, save her, boys."

We swam as fast as we could pull our arms through the still water. I looked and Skipper had the back of the little girl's dress between his teeth drawing her to shore. I swam toward him to give him a hand. Tadd was at the boat, trying to calm Mr. Jasper. "Just take it easy, Mr. Jasper. Hold onto the boat, and I'll have you to shore in no time. Gandhi will take care of your little girl."

After a few frantic minutes, which seemed like hours, we made shore. Mr. Jasper hugged his little daughter, crying, "Oh, my darling. I should have never taken you. I should have known better." She was crying, coughing, and spitting water, but, otherwise, all right. Still on his knees looking like a drowned rat, he said, "Tadd and Marshall, I'll never be able to repay you."

"Shucks, Mr. Jasper, we don't want no pay. We're glad we happened to be handy. Weren't we, Gandhi?" Tadd spoke real heroic-like.

"Yeah," I agreed.

We righted the boat and dragged her up on shore. Mr. Jasper got up and taking his little daughter's hand turned to us and said, "Boys, I'll never forget this. Oh, God, how I thank you."

"That's all right," I said, thinking how he referred to God a couple of times made me wonder if he didn't really believe in God but just hadn't said so or done anything about it. He was a nice man, and I just had to accept the fact that he was a God-fearing man anyhow. Mr. Jasper and his daughter went home.

We stood there dripping wet, looking at one another. I scratched

Skipper behind his ears. He seemed to like that. Just about that time, Mr. Budd, the town's newspaper editor, came by. He stopped his car. He called to us through the open window, "Kind of early for swimming, isn't it boys?"

"We didn't go swimming on purpose," Tadd answered.

He got out and came over to us. "What happened, then?"

I didn't answer for I knew that this was Tadd's department. He was always one for blowing up something bigger than it ever was.

Standing there dripping wet, Tadd began. "We was walking down this here road, minding our business, when all of a sudden we done saw Mr. Jasper and his daughter way out there in the middle of the pond, fishing."

"Yes, yes, go on," Mr. Budd began to get excited.

"Well," Tadd was relishing this moment to no end, "We paid 'em no mind. We was just walking out to the Camp Grounds." He pointed to the Camp Grounds.

"Yes, yes, I know the Camp Grounds. I'm on my way there now to get a picture of it. The Pilgrim Holiness Church is going to open camp meetings there next week. Go on, boy! Go on!" Mr. Budd exclaimed.

Tadd whirled toward Mr. Budd and said, "When all of a sudden, we heard these terrible screams for help. We looked and the boat had capsized, but we couldn't see nobody. They had all gone under. Probably for the second time."

Mr. Budd fastened his eyes on the middle of the pond. His face saddened. "You were too late, huh? Have you boys called the police?"

"I didn't say they were drowned," Tadd corrected him. "I said they went down for the second time. Then quick as a flash, Gandhi and Skipper and me..."

"Who's Skipper?" Mr. Budd interrupted.

"Gandhi's dog," Tadd said and pointed to Skipper lying peacefully at my feet.

"Like I said," Tadd began again, enjoying his moment of importance, "we seen 'em go down for the second time, and Gandhi and Skipper and me swam to 'em just as they were going down for the last time. We got there just in the nick of time. Skipper dragged the little girl to shore with Gandhi's help, and I dragged Mr. Jasper to shore. He clung to the boat with a death grip. Good thing he weren't holding onto me, 'cause being as big as he is, he sure would've drowned us both, and I wouldn't be here to tell you 'bout it."

"My, my," Mr. Budd said in a low breath. "Don't go away," he commanded us as he ran to his car. We weren't going anywhere in particular, but I guess he didn't know that.

He returned with a camera in his hand. "Here, boys," his voice rang with excitement as he began directing us, "stand at the water's edge. Marshall, get your dog in there with you. My, my, what a story!"

We did as he told us. We didn't care because we were wet anyhow and one more soaking wouldn't hurt anything.

He snapped our picture. "Just a minute. Hold it," he called. "I want to get one more. Just to make sure." I heard the camera click a couple of more times. Mr. Budd seemed beside himself getting himself all up in a lather. When he took our picture two times, we came back on the road.

"Now tell me," Mr. Budd continued, "where is Mr. Jasper and his daughter now?"

"Gone home, I guess," Tadd was truthful this time. "Leastwise, that was the direction they were headed when they left here."

Mr. Budd leaped into his car, slammed the door and started off causing a cloud of dust. "Thanks, boys," he called to us as he was speeding away.

"Well, what'll we do now?" I asked.

"Guess we'd better get home and get in some dry clothes."

"What're we going to tell our folks?"

"Tell 'em the truth."

"Yeah, guess that'd be the best," I answered and then I thought out loud, "Suppose they don't believe us?"

"Sure they'll believe us. 'Specially when they see our pictures in the paper and everything."

"That may be true," I agreed, "but the paper don't come out 'til next Friday. What'll they be believing in the meantime?"

"They'll just have to wait and see for themselves."

I was getting chilled from wearing those wet clothes because the wind had begun to blow and bite through to my skin.

We went home. As I entered the kitchen, Mother saw me and exclaimed, "Marshall! What happened to you?"

"Nothing much," was my feeble reply.

She made quick steps toward me and blocked my path. "You'll catch pneumonia. How did you get all wet? Fall overboard? You'd better stay away from that pond. Tell me! What happened?"

I told her of Jasper's mishap, explaining in the same breath that I had a dog that was a hero. She shook her head vigorously and commanded, "March right upstairs and get those wet clothes off. You stay in your room until I tell you to come down. Land-o-Goshen, I don't know what I'm going to do with you."

I went up to my bedroom by the back stairway, thinking to myself, "Wouldn't it be wonderful if parents could accept us kids just as we were without trying to force us to be something we weren't meant to be?"

AFTER SCHOOL THE NEXT DAY, Tadd and I walked down by the sawmill to see old Stoneface. Tadd asked him if we could have more pine slabs. By this time, I thought he would be curious enough to ask what we were doing with them, but he wasn't and only pointed to the pile.

We took our leave of the sawmill and Tadd said, "After supper tonight, we'll start toting them slabs to the cave. But we'll wait 'til dark. Ain't no use giving people something else to talk about when they got plenty to chew over as it is."

After supper with the sun gone noiselessly to bed, the stars twinkled like a million streetlights as Tadd and I met on the church corner. We went down the back hill to the sawmill.

All evening, we lugged six more pine slabs to the cave. It wasn't as hard as I thought it might be. And besides, you could see almost as

The Good Ol' Days

clear as day by the light of the full moon and stars. A light was burning in Capt'n Lacey's cabin, but we didn't bother him for he was probably reading, as was his nightly custom.

Skipper went everywhere with us. We didn't take him in our skiff, though, because those pine slabs were heavy enough and the rowing wasn't easy with them on board. He just waited for us on the pier.

As we were going up the hill to our homes, I asked, "Say, Tadd, when are we going to build that raft?"

"I told you, Gandhi. It takes a heap of planning and preparing. When we have everything together, then we'll start to build it." I said good night to Tadd and turned down my street at the church corner.

All that week, kids in school and people on the streets were stopping Tadd and me, asking us what happened down at the pond last Sunday. Tadd was always willing to oblige in telling them. It seemed the more he told it, the worse it got, until it was a wonder according to his embellished story that we ever saved them at all, especially since he had them out in the middle of the pond instead of closer to shore like it really was.

We couldn't wait until Friday morning when the *Lewiston Times* hit the newsstand. We didn't get downtown Friday morning when the papers arrived, but we almost flew to the newsstand after school was out. Mr. Linekin owned the newsstand and when he saw us he called out, "Here comes the heroes. You did a brave deed, boys. I'm going to give both of you a newspaper."

"Free?" I asked.

"Free!" he said.

"Gee, thanks, Mr. Linekin." Tadd and I both grabbed a paper, and sure enough, right there on the front page, bigger than life, was the picture of Tadd, Skipper and me, standing in the water looking like a couple of skinned jack rabbits.

Tadd read the headlines out loud, "Local heroes."

I had already scanned what Mr. Budd wrote under the picture and said, 'Read what it says, Tadd.'"

He continued to read aloud, "Without thought of personal safety, Tadd Tobin and Marshall Reed and Marshall's dog, Skipper, in the face of imminent danger, willingly sacrificed their very lives to save the lives of Mr. Harold Jasper and his daughter, Lindy. Their act of heroism personifies the qualities of action, courage, and honor, which all America loves. We commend them on their forthright call to duty."

Tadd looked again at our picture and beaming all over said, "Ain't that something, Gandhi? We're national heroes!"

Mr. Linekin put in, "We're all right proud of you boys. Our town needs more like you."

"I wish you'd tell that to my Mom and Pop," I said.

"I will when I see them," Mr. Linekin assured me.

Folding up the papers and clutching them under our arms, we went up the hill and made our silent journey to the clubhouse.

When we went inside the clubhouse, with Skipper right at our heels, we saw an awful sight. All over the walls of the clubhouse were large paintbrush stripes of yellow paint. Fire flew into our eyes. Tadd said what we both were thinking. "Granny and his boys have been here. We'll slaughter them for this. And after we've been heroes and everything."

"Yeah," I growled, "It's them all right. Nobody but them would do a dirty trick like this. What're we gonna do, Tadd?"

"We're gonna get some different paint and paint over it. That's what we're gonna do!" Tadd spoke emphatically.

We immediately forsook the clubhouse and marched right down to the hardware store. Mr. Mears was back in the storeroom when we went in by the path next to the creek.

"Mr. Mears, do have any paint you ain't using that we could have?" Tadd asked.

"Well," drawled Mr. Mears. "I believe I can find some paint to give to a couple of heroes." He brought us a gallon of paint that had already been opened, with spilled streaks of red dried fast on its side. "How about this?"

"That'll do fine, thank you," said Tadd. We retraced our steps to the clubhouse. For the remainder of the afternoon, Tadd and I painted the walls of our clubhouse a fire engine red.

CHAPTER 4

The month of May arrived with its continuous dribbles and the incessant rains that made everything khaki-colored. It had been raining for the past four days with no letup. We went down to see Capt'n Lacey, inwardly seeking freedom from our deep canyon of despair.

Inside the cabin, we removed our raincoats and hats, and Skipper shook himself three or four times to wring out his wet coat of hair. We sat down on the starboard bunk. Capt'n Lacey was most kind to let Skipper come on board, and I told him so.

"You might say he's our mascot, Gandhi. And, besides, a good dog like Skipper deserves to be inside out of the elements," Capt'n Lacey spoke kindly.

"I'm mighty obliged to you just the same," I said in words full of truth.

"What do you make of this weather, Capt'n?" Tadd tried speaking like an adult.

Capt'n Lacey took the coffee pot off the stove and poured us each a steaming cup. It quickly warmed the mug and felt like summer sunrays in our hands. "I don't know," he said, answering Tadd's question.

"So far I've measured seven inches of rain," Capt'n Lacey was picking his words careful like so he would not unduly alarm us. Even I could tell that.

"If it don't let up soon, do you think the crick will flood her banks?" Tadd was still in a questioning mood.

"Could be," Capt'n Lacey spoke reflectively. "You see, boys, that pond is like a watershed." He always talked to us like we were mature men.

"What's a watershed?" I asked, thinking it wasn't any use for him to go on if I didn't know what he was talking about in the first place.

"A watershed is just like a basin or bucket catching water from a rain spout during a storm. When it fills up, there ain't nothing for it do but spill over. Right?"

"Right," I answered, knowing now what he meant.

He continued, "That pond up there is just like a big washing tub. During rainstorms like this one, it collects all the drainage from the stream further up to its head. Lowlands and ditches drain into the stream, and the stream flows into the pond. That's why we have those waste gates there—you know the ones they lift up every so often to let the water fall into the crick."

Tadd and I nodded our heads. We knew exactly what he was talking about now.

"Well, with the crick rising like it's been, and this here rain, anything could happen if it don't let up."

"Like a flood, maybe?" Tadd threw him a calculated guess.

"Could be," the Captain mused and then reminded us, "Now mind you, I said 'could be.' At least all the signs are pointing to it."

"Don't you think you ought to warn somebody, just in case?" I queried.

"Ain't no use upsetting people about it," Capt'n Lacey said. And then he added, "Just yet awhile."

"By the way," he started the stream of conversation in a different direction, "what're you boys gonna do with them pine boards? Build a raft?"

"How'd you guess?" I piped up, letting the cat right out of the bag with my question.

"When I was about your age, I done the very same thing. Sailed this exact crick, I did. And it was fun, too."

I thought Tadd would be angry with me for disclosing our secret, but he didn't seem to be. He spoke up. "Did you sail her alone, Capt'n?"

The Good Ol' Days

"Naw, I had a buddy, just like you and Gandhi. But he's dead now. Lord rest his soul."

"How far did you go?" Tadd was still pumping him with questions.

"All the way to the inlet. She was fully equipped. Why, we even had a set of sails on her."

Tadd came right out with it, "Me and Gandhi are going to do that, come summer."

"And Skipper, too," I added pointing to Skipper who lay on the deck next to the stove. He pricked up his ears when I mentioned his name.

"Yeah, I guess Skipper, too," Tadd conceded.

"I've taught you boys most of the fundamentals of navigation: to know the tides and always check the wind direction and everything. Now's 'bout time to put 'em into practice. Experience will do the rest."

The Captain drew deep pulls on his pipe. "Don't leave nothing to chance. Study and plan and work out ahead of time what you're going to do before you do it. Liable as not, things will work out like you intended them to in the first place. Leaving things to chance or luck is like going into a field with a bucket and waiting for a cow to come to you and back up to be milked."

"Don't you believe in good luck?" I asked disillusioned.

The Captain reached for a book in the rack on the bulkhead and real aloud to us one verse from his favorite poem.

> Hoist up sail while gale doth last,
> Tide and wind stay no man's pleasure!
> Seek not time when time is past,
> Sober speed is wisdom's leisure;
> After-wits are dearly bought,
> Let thy fore-wit guide thy thought."

He closed the book, returned it to the rack, and said, "That's what I've been telling you boys. You've got to seize your own opportunities and bend even accidents to your purpose. That's the secret to success."

I remained mum, but I thought if Capt'n Lacey knew all this, and especially about success, why wasn't he successful? On the other hand, maybe he was successful in his own way, and I wasn't aware of it.

"Capt'n," Tadd was steering back into our first channel of conversation, "how long do you think it will have to rain before we might have a flood?"

"That depends on how hard it rains. If it continues like it is now, which is a real frog strangler, it won't take long."

"Don't you suppose the people in town know it might happen?" I blurted into the conversation. I was getting real concerned.

"We've never had a flood here before as I can recollect or ever heard tell of." Capt'n Lacey was expelling fast puffs from his pipe. "In fact, I know we ain't never had no flood before. It's no use getting people all riled up over something that might not happen."

I couldn't hold in from asking him, "But suppose it does happen, Capt'n Lacey. And if we thought it was going to happen and didn't tell nobody, wouldn't that be the same thing as sinning?"

Capt'n Lacey shot me a look I'd never seen before. "Gandhi, my boy, you're right. Come on. Get your coats on. Let's go tell the Squire."

Before you could say Mispillion Lighthouse, we had our coats on and were walking for the Squire's office. We went inside and the Squire was somewhat surprised to see us out in such a rainstorm.

"What in tarnation brings you out on a night like tonight, Capt'n? Howdy, boys. How's that dog of yours, Marshall? Oh, there he is. I didn't see him come in. He sure keeps you company, don't he?"

"Squire, I've been thinking about this downpour we're having." Capt'n Lacey began.

"What about it?" Squire Hazzard looked at the Captain over the aged rims of his black horned-rim glasses. He appeared formidable.

"It could spell a heap of trouble for us."

"What kind of trouble?"

"A flood."

"A flood!"

"Yep. I don't like the looks of it."

The Good Ol' Days

"We ain't never had no flood before, Capt'n. Ain't you being a bit over-anxious and fretting for nothing? We're just having the usual spring rain." The Squire seemed in a consoling mood. He had never seen a flood before and wasn't expecting one now. He wasn't a man to get excited very quickly. He was laid back and took things as they came, whatever they might be.

"It's never been like this before. Not in my memory," Capt'n Lacey assured him as complex worries creased wrinkles in his brow. Capt'n Lacey was a serious man who thought deep thoughts and was a far-looking man. I would trust his judgments more than any other man in town, well maybe, except the preacher's.

"Well, what do you propose for me to do? Tell the good Lord to turn off the spigots?" And Squire Hazzard laughed until his belly shook like it had the tremors.

Capt'n Lacey donned his slicker and hat and retorted, "Sorry to have bothered you, Squire. But if you have any feeling for this downtown, you'd better tell the Lord to turn off something!" He stalked out of the office with Tadd and me and Skipper at his heels. I knew the Captain was steamed at the indifference of Squire Hazzard; he was in a huff and we knew it. We also knew not to bother him with any questions. It seemed strange to me that a man like Squire Hazzard would not take Capt'n Lacey's warming more seriously. We knew him, trusted him, and believed in him. I was getting a little scared.

After we were back in the cabin of the Marie Tomas and all settled down once again, Tadd broke the silence, "He didn't believe you, did he, Capt'n?"

The Captain started talking as if he were holding a one-way conversation. "People are strange creatures. They see what they want to see and hear what they want to hear and believe what they want to believe, and no amount of talking will ever change 'em. There's a man who's supposed to be a leader of this town, but actually he wouldn't give a tinker's dam for what happens to it."

Tadd sensed the Captain was overwrought and so did I. We didn't want to leave him in that mood. I scratched my brain trying to figure out what to say. It was then that Tadd stumbled over a good question to ask him.

"Capt'n, what were you reading the other night when we went by here? Your light was on and I knowed you was reading something."

Capt'n Lacey smiled and appeared grateful for Tadd's question. "I was reading about Tom Edison. There was a great man, boys. You ought to read that book. He'd be a good pattern for you to set your sights on. We need more Tom Edison's and less..." He didn't finish the sentence, but I would have bet my wishbone to a nickel that he was going to say Squire Hazzard. He didn't though.

"Did you know that Tom Edison only went to school about two weeks out of his whole life?"

"Boy, I wish I was him!" Tadd chortled.

Capt'n Lacey continued as if he hadn't heard Tadd. "He was born in upper New York State in the early 1800s. His parents were very poor, and he himself said that he had to start out early and hustle. He sold newspapers on a railroad and later learned to operate the telegraph. But you know something? He had a keen sense of observation."

He seized his pipe out of his mouth and pointed it toward us. "Boys, that's what you've got to understand in this life. When you look you must see and learn."

Tadd nodded his head and answered, "Yes, sir."

"Well, Capt'n Lacey drawled, "That boy, Tom Edison, never spent an idle day in his life. He was always searching and learning. He read about mechanics and electricity. He got a heap of schooling on his own, mind you. He had a thirst for learning. And he had something else."

"What's that?" I asked.

"He had a way of learning from observing and weighing things out. That's important, boys."

"What'd he do with all that learning?" I was curious and interested in what Capt'n Lacey was saying.

"Why, Gandhi, don't tell me you ain't never heard of Tom Edison." Capt'n Lacey was astonished at my ignorance. "It was him that made the light bulb."

"Oh, yeah," I recalled sheepishly. "I'd forgot about that."

"Boys, it's coming on late. You'd best mosey on home. Your folks might be worried."

We slithered into our coats, bade good night to Capt'n Lacey and ambled home.

THE NEXT DAY, THE RAIN HAD SUBSIDED SOMEWHAT, and it seemed to be more like light showers. Tadd and I spent most of the day in the clubhouse fashioning plans for our sailing expedition.

"Are we going to have sails on our raft like the Captain's?"

Tadd looked at me with squinted eyes, and I could tell he was thinking. "We can't depend entirely on the tide," he began. "It appears to me we've got to have sails. Now where can we find some canvas? It's gotta be canvas. Suppose we sail into a gale? Nothing else will do. What about Capt'n Lacey? Suppose he'd have an old tarpaulin he'd let us have?"

"Let's go see," I suggested.

"Don't go off half-cocked," Tadd warned. "We'll have a sail all right, but what about stores?"

"What do you mean?" I wasn't with him when he changed his stream of thought so quickly.

"I mean food. Ain't you got no brains at all, Gandhi?"

"Yeah, I got some," I answered. My feelings were hurt. And then I threw him a curve, "Ain't I in the same grade at school as you?"

"Guess you are at that. Well, then you know that we gotta have food."

"What kind of food do you suggest, Tadd?"

"Mostly canned goods. Got any extra jars at your house?"

I thought a minute and then remembered, "Sure, Mom put up a mess of stuff last summer."

"Good," said Tadd, "let's go get some."

"Right now?"

"Right now!"

We donned our raincoats and hats and scampered to our separate homes. Within the hour, we both returned to the clubhouse with jars of peaches, applesauce, sausage, scrapple, tenderloin and cherries. Our mothers had preserved all of this the summer before.

"What'll we do now, Tadd?"

Tadd's mouth was always full of answers. "Take it to the cave."

"In this rain?"

"It's only a shower and, besides, we can't leave it here. What do you suppose the other boys would think if they saw all this food?"

"You're right," I agreed. "Let's shove off."

Down at the pier, Tadd and I busied ourselves putting our foodstuffs in our rowboat. It wasn't raining hard now at all, just lazy showers. Tadd noticed the corner piling as he called to me, "Must be high tide. See how far up the water is to the ring?"

We could always tell the tide by looking at the corner piling on the pier and seeing how far down or up the water was from the salty ring around it, which was the high water mark. As we rowed toward the cave, the old crick looked like an oil canal, yellowish and weak-like. My eyes made a loving survey of town. The chimneys of the houses appeared as if they were penciling the sky with smoke signals.

"Suppose somebody finds out what we're up to?" I asked.

Tadd drew himself in until he looked like a big fist. "Ain't nobody gonna find out." His word shot toward me like a crack from a rifle. Then he added, "Unless you tell."

"Tadd," I said, "You know me better than that. We've taken an oath on it, and I'd never break that." I was disappointed at his comment.

Tadd cast me a warm smile through the raindrops. "I know you wouldn't, Gandhi. I just said that to see what you'd say."

When we arrived at the cave, I leaped out and started removing the branches from the mouth of our secret hideout. Tadd tied up the boat and started bringing an armful of fruit jars. I ducked inside. The cave emitted a moldy breath; otherwise, it was dry.

"We'd better wrap these jars in that grass sack," Tadd directed.

The Good Ol' Days

"Take some of them pine needles and put them in there so these jars won't get broken."

"Right," I said, taking the jars from him and placing them gentle-like in the burlap bag. After we had stuffed all our canned food in the bag, I began to cover the cave's door with tree branches.

"Gandhi, we're gonna have a great time sailing down this here crick," Tadd spoke, with raindrops trickling down the end of his freckled nose. "I can just see us now. A gentle breeze blowing up from the south pushing us toward the bay as easy as a mother rocks a cradle. We'll have time to fish and talk and think. Nobody to be 'round to tell us to wash behind our ears or ever take a bath. Eat when we want to and sleep as long as we please. Boy, I can't wait 'til summer comes. Can you?"

"It'll be fun all right. That's for sure," I agreed. "But I guess we'll just have to wait 'til it does. We can't play hooky from school. Not yet awhile, anyways."

We piled in our boat and headed for the pier.

A question lodged in my mind, and it soon came unstuck. "Tadd, what about foul weather? What'll we do then?"

"What do you mean?"

"I mean, suppose a storm comes up?"

"We'll head for shore."

"I mean, where will we take cover?"

"Oh, you're referring to a cabin on the raft?"

"Yeah."

"Well, I've been thinking of that too. How's about us building a small lean-to on the raft? Just big enough for you and me?"

"What about Skipper?"

"We can squeeze him in there with us, too. He don't take up much room, and besides, he'll throw off enough heat to warm us in case it comes up cold, 'specially if it's raining."

"It all sounds good to me, Tadd. I sure wish summer would hurry up."

"Yeah," Tadd reflected.

By the time we had secured our boat, Capt'n Lacey met us. He seemed a bit riled up. He wore a serious face. He was flinging his arms about. "Where in tarnation have you boys been?"

"Up the crick," Tadd answered in an offhand manner. Skipper met us on the pier wagging his tail like he was happy to see us, as if we had been gone for days.

Capt'n Lacey spoke with concern. "You boys best skedaddle for home. Right now. Ain't fit out today for man nor beast. The wind is picking up, and it's commencing to rain harder. Them clouds are banking there in the northeast and the wind is shifting there, too. That's a bad sign." He turned to me. "Gandhi, give your boat plenty of line. I'd tie it above the high water mark. Better still, untie her and give me the line. I'll secure her to the stern of the Marie Tomas. I'll look after her. Things don't 'pear right. No sir, not one bit. You boys best move on home, now!"

"Right, Capt'n," Tadd replied, almost saluting Capt'n Lacey.

We had a pile of respect racked up inside of us for Capt'n Lacey. As far as we were concerned, he knew more about things than any six people in town put together. As we lumbered up the hill toward home, Tadd asked me, "Gandhi, have you ever seen the Captain in such a way?"

"Do you mean you think he's hitting the bottle?"

"Naw, I don't believe he's had a drop to drink. I mean, I ain't never seen him like this before. He's acting like there's something in the wind, and he don't know what to do about it."

"What do you mean?"

"I don't know what I mean. It's just that the Captain ain't acting like he usually does."

"Maybe he ain't feeling good," I suggested.

"Naw, it ain't that. Something more. I can't put my finger on it. He had a queer look in his eye."

"Aw, you're seeing things. I didn't see nothing different about the Captain except he appeared a little worried or concerned."

About the time those words dropped from my lips, the bottom fell out of the black, baggy clouds above. I'd never seen it rain so hard.

The rain seemed to cut right through our raincoats rather than roll off of them. We started to run, and we waved goodbye to each other at the church corner. By the time I reached home, I couldn't see six feet in front of me.

DURING THE NIGHT, THE FIRE SIREN STARTED TO WAIL like a choking, dying cow. It whined and groaned incessantly, alarming the whole town. Never had I heard it scream with such painful, prolonged wails. And then I heard the church bells ringing. This brought me from my bed, for I knew it wasn't New Year's Eve. I dressed quickly. By the time I reached downstairs, my parents were there in their nightclothes.

"What are you doing dressed?" Pop demanded.

"Something strange is happening, and I for one ain't staying in bed."

"You march right back to bed." And then Pop shook his bony finger at me. "Now, don't you have no fool notions about going out in this storm, or I'll tan your hide but good."

I stalked to my bedroom up the back stairway. My mind was entertaining all kinds of thoughts of what could be happening, but none of them stood still. They were just like waves, rolling in one after another. I hadn't even begun to undress when I heard several taps on my window like it was hailing. The siren and bells were still ringing. I went to the window and looked out. I couldn't see a thing. It was dark and appeared as if it were raining pitch forks and hoe handles. Then I spied a flashing light. I knew it had to be Tadd. He had thrown a handful of tiny stones on my window to get my attention. I reached in my pocket, found a match, lit it, held it to the window, and blew it out. Quiet as a mouse, I sneaked down the back stairway, put on my raincoat and hat and let myself out the side porch door, which was never locked because Pop had lost the key long ago and never bothered to get another one. Sure enough, there was Tadd.

He met me with a question, "Where's your Pop and Mom?"

"They were in the sitting room just a few minutes ago. Listen, Tadd, I'd best not go. Pop told me if I went out in this storm he'd thrash me good."

"Something terrible is happening, Gandhi. I just know it. If it weren't, why are they making all that racket? Something's mighty wrong. Maybe we can help. Come on."

Skipper slept in the side porch. (It was one of the benefits of his being a town hero. Ma said if he was good enough to be written up in the papers, he was good enough to sleep in our side porch.) He was by my side as soon as he heard us, and already his coat was soaking wet. He nuzzled his nose against my hand. I couldn't make him stay, not after his making up to me.

"Let's go," I said, buttoning the top button of my raincoat to keep out the drenching rain. We sloshed through the downpour straight toward the pier.

There on the church corner at the top of the hill were the town's two fire trucks parked in the street. Many men were piling furniture on Dr. Howell's lawn, and every piece of it became rain-drenched. I looked at Tadd, wondering, and he eyed me, too, but we said nothing. We hurried on down the hill. We had never seen so many people out in the rain before. About everyone in town was there. Some were carrying children on their backs up the hill, while others were burdened with furniture, and still others bore brand-new store goods in their arms. Everyone was busy, their lips unmoving. It was an awe-inspiring sight.

When we arrived downtown, there were at least six inches of water lying heavy on the street. The lights were burning in all the stores and many of the places of business had water covering the floor. All the men made deft movements without a word, grabbing what they thought was valuable and leaving the rest. Tadd and I saw Mr. Mason, and we asked him if we could help.

"Your sure can, boys." That's mighty nice of you to pitch in. Get my knives and books out of the back room and take them up to the church. Put them in the hall, will you?"

The Good Ol' Days

"Sure," we chimed in, speaking with one voice.

We lost no time gathering all the knives and books in the back room of Mr. Mason's store and carried them up the hill. We placed them in the church hall on a table. Once again, we descended the hill.

In that short time, the water had risen even higher. We spied Capt'n Lacey working, furiously giving orders like he was speaking to deck hands on a large vessel and everyone was obeying him. He saw us. "Tadd, Gandhi, get your boat, quick. Bring it to me right here."

We didn't stop to ask any questions, but raced to the Marie Tomas moored at the pier and untied our boat. "Grab the oars and oar locks, Gandhi. I'll get the line to the boat." Tadd shouted the orders now through millions of cold raindrops.

In a matter of minutes, Tadd and I had the boat at Capt'n Lacey's side.

"Thanks, boys."

And then, suddenly, someone shouted, "Look out! All hell's broke loose!"

Our eyes became riveted on the mill dam. We saw nothing but foaming water rushing over into the already swollen creek.

Capt'n Lacey shouted, "Everybody run to higher ground. Quick!"

We were standing knee deep in water near the Captain. The Squire's office was to our left, and the brick hardware store was on the other side of the street. Most every store in town had a wooden shed with a tin roof in front of it that served as an awning.

Without a word, Capt'n Lacey hoisted me in his arms and boosted me up the wooden pole supporting the shed of the hardware store. I climbed up on the rod. In a split second, Tadd was at my side. Capt'n Lacey threw us the line from the rowboat. Instantly, he was up there with us.

In all my life, I had never seen so much water at one time, and it was running so fast that before I caught my second breath, it was about ten feet deep, right on top of Main Street. I saw four parked automobiles fully submerged. You could see their shimmering forms underwater.

And then, we heard screams. "That's Mrs. Johnson and her two daughters," Capt'n Lacey replied briskly. "You boys will have to go fetch them. I'll stay here to see what I can do."

The water had ceased its roaring pace as if someone had poured barrels of oil on its surface. Downtown was flooded. The first floors of all the stores were submerged. What they hadn't salvaged was ruined.

We hadn't budged from the spot on the shed roof where we were anchored for neither of us yearned to rescue Chicken Johnson and her brood. Capt'n Lacey tugged us gently, all the while reeling in the boat to the shed roof, where she floated like a leaf in a light breeze. "Get going, boys. That woman and her girls need help. No telling how long that old house will hold out."

We made reluctant movements as we climbed into the boat. Both of us had to row with all our might for the current was still strong and we had to row against it. Finally, we reached the second story window of Chicken Johnson's house. All three of them were hollering to us and waving their handkerchiefs.

I held onto the window ledge while Tadd told one of the girls to step into the bow of the boat. "Mrs. Johnson, you and Abigail step into the stern and sit down and don't move."

When they were settled, I shoved off. It was easier rowing back to the hardware store's roof than it was going to the store. And it wasn't too great a distance.

Capt'n Lacey helped them get out of the boat. We were all standing on the roof of the shed when two other boats came by with people in them. One of the men who was rowing, called out to Capt'n Lacey, "Hey, Capt'n. Can you go look for Miss Stittum? We called for her when we came by her house, but there wasn't any answer. And, besides, we haven't got any room for her. We're taking this load up to the church."

"For God's sake! You don't suppose..." Capt'n Lacey left his sentence dangling, but we knew what he was thinking. Miss Stittum had a little hat shop in town, down from the hardware store. And she was an invalid. He must have thought she was drowned.

"Come on, Gandhi," he called to me. "You stay here with the Johnsons, Tadd. When another boat comes by, help put them on."

The Good Ol' Days

The Captain and I shoved off for Miss Stittum's house. "Capt'n, do you think, maybe…"

"I don't know, Gandhi. We'll soon see." He answered my question before I finished. I guess he and I were thinking the same thing.

I held onto the second story window casing while Capt'n Lacey forced the window up and crawled in. He was gone a long time, or so it seemed to me. And then he reappeared. In his arms was tiny Miss Stittum who probably didn't weigh over ninety pounds. She was alive and safe and sound.

"Howdy, Miss Stittum," I said as Capt'n Lacey let her down easy in the boat.

"Hello, Marshall," greeted Miss Stittum. "You are a fine, brave young man to help Capt'n Lacey in such times of peril. May the Lord bless you."

"Thank you, Ma'am," I said and shoved off and sat down in the bow while Capt'n Lacey rowed. I felt big and puffed up with generosity.

He rowed up to the hardware store roof. "Catch 'er, Tadd," he said as he threw the line from our boat. "Get in, Mrs. Johnson," he spoke with a commanding voice.

"What about the girls?" cackled Chicken Johnson.

"We'll come back and get them," answered Capt'n Lacey.

The Captain rowed toward the church. When we arrived there, it looked like the whole town had gathered. Women were carrying blankets and foodstuffs under their arms. Skipper was there, too. When he saw me, he wagged his tail like it would swing off.

I heard a familiar voice behind me as I was helping Chicken Johnson out of the boat while Capt'n Lacey carried Miss Stittum into the church. "Young man, you wait 'til I have you home. You'll get one like you never had before." I didn't have to turn around to know who owned that voice. It was my Pop's.

About that time, Capt'n Lacey came out of the church. "Mr. Reed," he spoke in a roaring voice, "don't you touch Marshall. (He called me Marshall when he spoke to other people around me.) If you do, you will have me to answer for it."

Capt'n Lacey was a huge man and carried a lot of weight in more ways than one. My Pop was short and skinny.

"I guess he's still my boy, Capt'n, and it's no business of yours what I do to him."

Capt'n Lacey walked over to him and looked him in the eye. "George Reed, if you had any guts at all, you would be doing the same thing your son is doing, helping people and saving lives and property. That's what he's been doing. He's giving a good turn where it's needed. What have you been doing all this time besides running your mouth?"

Pop didn't answer Capt'n Lacey, but I could tell by the glaze in his eyes that I was in for it when I got home. Mom made no reply; she just stood there and cried.

Daylight filled the air all around us, and it had stopped raining. Tempers were short and bodies were tired, that was for sure.

"Come on, Gandhi," Capt'n Lacey called out to me, climbing into the boat. "Let's go bring those girls back."

The Captain rowed toward the hardware roof and the two girls boarded the boat. I spoke up, "If it's all right with you, Capt'n Lacey, I'll stay here with Tadd."

"I understand," the Captain said and shoved off toward the church again.

I told Tadd all that had happened. His eyes lit up like hundred watt bulbs, and he shook his head and said, "Boy, you're in for it, ain't you?"

"Maybe."

"Maybe, nothing. You wait until you're home!"

"If I do, The Capt'n will whip my Pop," I said confidently, nodding my head. I believed what I just said because Capt'n Lacey was a man of his word. His word was his bond, and you could depend on it. I truly loved Capt'n Lacey and inwardly wished that he could have been my pop, but wishing don't change much of anything.

"I don't know about that," Tadd spoke in spurts of doubt, and his face showed his inner thoughts.

The Good Ol' Days

"Don't you trust the Capt'n's word?" I shot back to him, making him come to a conclusion about Capt'n Lacey's word as his bond.

"It ain't that," Tadd replied slowly and deliberately. "It's just that people don't go around whipping other people's pop 'cause he licks his own kids."

"I hadn't thought about it that way," I considered, running Tadd's words across my mind.

"Well," Tadd tried to be comforting. "Maybe you helping out in this flood and all that, your pop will let it go this time."

"My gosh, Tadd, what…"

"What's happened?"

"Our cave…and food…and raft boards…"

"Good grief," Tadd brooded. He screwed up his eyebrows, scratched the top of his head through his cap, and blurted out, "And all that work for nothing. It's all no good no more."

The edge of heavy silence was all around us. We didn't speak, but our thoughts were flying through our heads. I could see in my mind's eye our cave full of water, the food jars floating around, and the raft boards floating swiftly out to sea down the creek on the swift tide. I could have cried, but wouldn't dare 'cause all the people were around and they might see me. I sure didn't want that, so I kept the tears back and stifled them. I uttered words that I didn't want to say, but felt they should be expressed. "I guess our trip on the raft is all off. But it certainly would've been fun, wouldn't it?"

Tadd moved with a single forward thrust toward me. He always did that when he had something important to say, and I knew it was coming and I was prepared for it. He blurted out, "Don't say that, Gandhi, don't even think it. Nothing, not even a flood, is gonna keep us from building that raft and sailing her down the crick."

"You mean…"

"That's exactly what I mean. We'll collect more boards and more food and come summer, we'll be ready."

"You talk like you mean it, Tadd." My gloomy mood was changing for the better, and I was taking heart in what Tadd was predicting. I believed him and was pleased by it. He had a way of straightening things out in the best of ways. No wonder he was my best buddy. He was interesting to be around and could untangle things that seemed to get into knots. And somehow they got untied and straightened out again. Tadd was something and I held him in high esteem. He was my true friend, and I admired him.

"You just wait and see. We'll take that trip. Never you mind. We'll do it, just you wait and see." Tadd was forceful in his talk.

"I know we will, Tadd," and I threw my arm about his shoulders to prove to him how much I liked him, believed in him, trusted him. He just grinned.

"Here comes the Capt'n," Tadd was pointing in the direction of the land at the foot of the hill, which was covered with six feet of water.

"When do you think it'll go down, Capt'n?" Tadd greeted Capt'n Lacey as he threw us the line.

"It'll take a few days, that's certain," was his tired reply.

Just as he spoke, I spied a thin oblong box floating along with the water's current. It seemed I had seen a box like it before, but I sure hoped it wasn't what I thought it was. If it was, it would really be scary. "What is it?" I asked pointing at the floating box drifting along in the water.

"Well, I'll be damned," Capt'n Lacey said. He usually didn't swear in front of us, but, of course, this wasn't a usual time. He spoke through his smile as he said, "That's a casket from Atkins' Funeral Parlor. Hope nobody's in it."

It was black looking and hypnotic. I don't know why, but I had always been afraid of the dead. My heart flicked and twisted and then curled with fear. If the Capt'n was thinking of asking us to draw it in, I just couldn't because the further I was from the dead, the better. The hairs on my body just stood up when I was around or near the dead. Thankfully, he didn't say anything, just let it float on by, and I was happy about that.

"I guess the water got in old Harvey's funeral parlor. A few more of them floating in town will stir the people, won't it." And the Captain chuckled a dry laugh, which lacked the gusto of any mirth.

The Good Ol' Days

"What'll we do now?" asked Tadd.

"Let's head up to the church. I guess we've done all we can do here. We might be able to give a hand there," the Captain replied as he stepped into the boat and rowed us toward the church.

The women had brought jars of coffee and bags of sandwiches. They gave us some when we arrived like we were heroes or something. I felt deeply proud to be helping in any way I could in that disastrous time. My chest swelled as I took a sandwich and a mug of coffee.

Three stretched-out days passed before the water receded to high-tide level. The downtown stores were impoverished by the floodwaters. School was dismissed so the students could assist the town people in helping the merchants clean out their stores. The floors were mud covered, and much of the merchandise was damaged by the incoming water.

Strange, but I got the feeling like I have at Christmastime. Everybody oozed with friendliness and wanted to help everyone else. No one spoke any harsh words. We all worked together like we were one big family. Even the adults were extra friendly to us children who were helping.

But Capt'n Lacey was the man of the hour. He stuck out in the crowd like a red rose in the buttonhole of a white suit. He seemed to know just what to do and no one questioned his commands. During the flood, the women were milling about the church and hissing at one another like worried geese. Now they seemed more settled and helpful, especially since Capt'n Lacey was in command. There was a feeling of closeness in the air like God had put us all in a big bag and drawn the string. I liked that feeling, although I was sorry we had to have a flood to bring it about.

While we were carrying out ruined furniture from the stores and putting it on waiting trucks to be carried to the dump, I spoke to Tadd, "Don't you notice something different?"

"Sure do," he said, "This town is a wreck. Suppose we can salvage anything?"

"I don't mean about the damage. I mean about the people; they seem different. Better, I mean."

"Yeah, guess you're right. They seem more friendly or something, don't they?"

"Sure do," I answered, throwing a bolt of soaked cotton material on the truck.

"Wouldn't it be something if we could get along like this all the time?"

"I don't know whether I'd want it like this or not all the time. I suppose the Lord made us like He did so's we could appreciate the good after the bad." Then Tadd waxed philosophical and said, "Because if you didn't have the bad to put up with, how would you know what the good was like?"

"Guess you're right, Tadd. If you had the good all the time, you wouldn't know what the bad was like. So we have the bad sometimes to appreciate the good. Right?"

"That's about the size of it," echoed Tadd. "How's about giving me a hand here?"

The town folks worked shoulder to shoulder for five days, leaving their jobs and helping the merchants and the people who lived downtown. During that week, the school was closed, and this was the best part of all.

Finally, our town was returned to normal and the stores began to look like stores again, but it was said that the merchants lost a lot of money from the storm. And I guess they did, too, for many goods and furniture were completely ruined and could never be used again. The swollen water of Elk Creek had viciously ravaged Lewiston's downtown stores. The cars that reaped the unwanted salt-water bath downtown in the flood had to be hauled away to the junkyard. I never did get the licking my pop had promised. I guess he was too ashamed when everyone told him all that we did to help the town.

We had to return to school, and then we knew that things were back to normal. People didn't seem as friendly as they had before. I thought I would never understand why adults could be as nice as angels sometimes and mean as snakes other times. But I concluded that such was the adult world. I had an inward hope that I would never grow up to be like some of the adults I knew.

The Good Ol' Days

THE NEXT DAY, TADD AND I ROWED DOWN THE CREEK to visit our cave. A sad sight met our eyes. Only pieces of broken glass remained of our canned foods. Our pine and slab boards had washed away—every last one of them.

Tadd assured me, "Pay it no mind, Gandhi. We'll bring more boards here. You'll see. Nothing is going to stop us from our trip down this here crick."

"When?" I was quick to ask, wanting a solid answer.

Tadd let a drawn-out second slip by and, with a twinkle in his eye, threw his arm about my shoulder as we walked toward our boat. "Right now," he said. "Let's go and get with it!"

And we rowed back to the pier and walked up to the sawmill to start all over again, carrying pine slab boards back to our secret cave.

CHAPTER 5

That hoped-for day arrived when school was dismissed for the summer. Tadd and I tossed our notebooks and pencils in the wastepaper basket. "We'll not be needing the likes of them 'til next fall," he exclaimed eagerly as he thought about the fun we would have this summer.

Instead of walking down the street, we plodded back to the woods and cut across to the swimming hole. We were the first to arrive. Tadd started to unbutton his shirt. "Last one in is a rotten egg," he yelled.

Clothes flew and we hit the water, naked as the day we were born. The relentless sun blazed down on our wet bodies until we looked like moistened crystals. We felt all good inside, like we were harmonizing with God and His summer chorus of afternoon breezes.

Tadd was standing on New York. You see, each stump under water around the swimming hole had a name, according to its distance away from shore. I was on Philadelphia but swam on out to New York to be with Tadd. I was winded long before my toes found the protruding lumps on the stump of New York. As I sucked in fast gulps of air, Tadd sighed, "Ain't summer the best time of the whole year?"

"It sure is," I agreed completely between gasping breaths. Hope welled up in my heart with the desire to build the raft again. I pumped Tadd with questions. His answers were whimsical and had I not known him better, I would have sworn that somehow, somewhere, he had been sipping hard liquor. But we had come straight from school.

"Tadd, what is it? Don't you feel good?" I asked, baffled by his curious demeanor.

In the sunlight, his eyes appeared as glassy grapes and his cheeks looked like ripe pears. He replied, "No, I just feel wonderful. Everything is wonderful. Hear them trout a-jumping out there in the water? Listen to the bees a-humming. And look yonder at that butterfly. Ain't he beautiful? Listen, Gandhi, ain't that water musical running over the mill dam? Yes sir, summer must be God's favorite time of the year, 'cause He sure paints everything up real pretty like."

Tadd's sweeping words overwhelmed me. I could only stare and listen. He droned on and on. I had to restrain myself not to question his jumbled up statements.

"Gandhi, we're gonna have a swell time this summer. I just feel it in my bones. Don't you feel it, too?"

"Not yet," I answered, "but I'm hoping I will."

"Boy, she sure is pretty." Tadd commented, wagging his head slowly.

"Who's pretty?"

"Jeanne."

"Jeanne who?"

"Jeanne Adaire."

"Jeanne Adaire! Tadd, you must be sick! Talking about girls. You ain't never done that before. You know that they're soft, silly, and brilliant. And, we don't want no part of 'em."

"Just the same, Gandhi, she's the prettiest thing I've ever laid my eyes on." Tadd continued to talk, looking at me, but not seeing me. "And when she speaks, her words sound right musical, like her mouth was full of little bells instead of teeth."

I shot my arm out at Tadd and struck him on the left shoulder. "Come out of it, Tadd. You're talking like one who's got the tick fever. Are you sure that one of Skipper's ticks didn't jump on you and bite you real good?"

"Gandhi, ain't you never been in love?"

Tadd's question almost made me fall off New York. "In love! With a girl?" Such a terrible idea had never entered my brain.

"Well, I'm in love with Jeanne Adaire, and when I'm a man, I'm gonna marry her."

I was positively disgusted, and it showed on my face. "Does this mean our raft trip is off?" I asked Tadd.

"Naw, silly, it's just I feel good all inside. Now Gandhi," Tadd waxed real serious, "don't you go and tell anybody what I said. If you do, I ain't gonna speak to you no more. And besides, I might forget all about that raft trip." He eyed me suspicious-like.

"Tadd," I confessed, "I ain't never seen you like this before. I hope you don't stay in love too long 'cause I don't like it. You ain't nothing like the Tadd Tobin I know."

"Aw, Gandhi, what ails you? Just 'cause you ain't never been in love don't mean that there ain't such a thing. Jeanne is the nicest girl in the whole world." Tadd paused a minute, and then he reflected, "Wait 'til you fall in love."

I looked him square in the eye. "I ain't never gonna do a thing like that. Girls ain't like boys; that's why I don't like 'em. They're too soft and silly. They can't climb trees, play baseball, row a boat, and all those things."

"You're prejudiced, Gandhi."

"What's that mean?"

"It means you don't like girls."

"Guess you're right."

Many of the boys from school had gravitated to the swimming hole and were bewitched by the cooling tenor of the water on their nude bodies. Bathing suits weren't necessary; in fact, they weren't allowed.

Tadd spoke, "Let's shove off. It's too crowded now."

"Okay."

We swam in to shore and stood for a minute on the drying box, which was nailed to the old pine tree at the water's edge. When the sun had dried us enough, or so we thought, we donned our clothes and struck out for Main Street. Who did we meet but Jeanne Adaire and Louise Holden? I wanted to run. Tadd grabbed my shirttail and held me steady. He stammered, "Hel—lo, Jean—ne. Can—can I carry your books?"

Her long, black flowing curls danced about her shoulders as she dug the toe of her right shoe in the grass next to the sidewalk and without looking up said, "Yes, you may."

Tadd nudged me sharply in my right ribs. "What's that for?" I whispered.

"You dumb nitwit. Ask Louise if you can carry her books."

"I don't want to," I whispered back.

"Ask her, anyway," he demanded, all the while smiling at Jeanne.

"You don't want me to carry your books, do you, Louise?" I blurted out.

"No," was her staunch reply.

I was glad. Tadd gave me an awful glare, but I didn't mind 'cause I knew that if you carried a girl's books it meant you like her. And I didn't like girls. I was very uncomfortable around them.

Tadd and I walked on ahead. The girls followed. I felt foolish for fear someone might see us walking with the girls.

The town library and yard was girdled with an iron pipe rail fence. When we approached it, Tadd leaped on the rail, balanced himself, and proceeded to walk it. I thought any minute he would fall, and secretly I wanted him to so he would stop fraternizing with girls. He didn't.

When we arrived in front of Jeanne's house, Tadd gave her the books, she thanked him, and the two girls went inside. I was glad.

When the girls were out of earshot, Tadd snapped at me. "Gandhi, ain't you never going to grow up?"

"Nope," I said honestly, which ended that conversation. There was a silent understanding between Tadd and me that caused us to be aware of our inner feelings. Words didn't have to be spoken for us to understand each other. Many times it could be conveyed just by eye contact.

"What'll we do this afternoon?" I cracked the silence barrier between us.

Tadd's eyes lit up, "Let's go horseback riding."

"Sounds like fun. Suppose your Uncle Scank will let us ride Niter?"

"If he ain't using him, he will."

"Let's go ask him."

"All right, let's."

We set out for Tadd's Uncle Scank's house on the other side of town near the end of the land, as everybody called it. He wasn't home when we got there, but Tadd's Aunt Abigail said we could take a ride on Niter since Uncle Scank had gone fishing and wouldn't be back 'til tomorrow.

Down at the barn behind Uncle Scank's house, we went to the stable and put the bridle on Niter. He was black as charcoal all over, even his eyes were black as night. We left the saddle in the stable since it isn't any fun riding with a saddle when two are on board.

We followed the back road to the Camp Ground. It was a dirt road, and we thought it would be better for Niter who was unshod. The day was hot and sticky, so we walked Niter. Later, we would take turns galloping him for he loved to run. He was always full of ginger. As we crossed the little wooden bridge leading over in front of the Camp Ground, we looked across the pond to the swimming hole. The boys were jumping up and down like leaping frogs. And they were waving their hands at us, too. We waved back.

I slid off the rear end of Niter and gave him a good slap on the rump. He leaped into a fast canter. Tadd's shirttail sailed in the breeze. He rode him as far as the railroad tracks and galloped back. In just that short distance, Niter had worked up a lather on his neck. Tadd slid off and gave me the reins in his descent. I grabbed them and jumped aboard.

"Not too fast, Gandhi," Tadd advised, "it's kinda hot and we don't want to get him overheated."

"Okay."

Niter and I flew down that dirt road, nevertheless. There wasn't any holding him. I gave him a little rein, and he was off like greased lightning. As we returned, I held back on him and he trotted, which makes your backside sore when you're riding bareback.

Tadd took the reins and suggested, "Maybe we'd better walk him for a while to cool off. Then we'll ride some more."

We cut off into the wood's road. It was cooler in there and the pine needles covering the road made it feel like we were walking on an expensive carpet. It felt pleasant to our bare feet, since we had taken off our tennis shoes, tied the strings of each shoe together, and slung them over our shoulders.

Tadd looked up at the treetops where the sun was striving to shimmer though the thick canopy of leaves and said, "Wouldn't it be swell if God decided to make summer all the time?"

"It sure would," I agreed, looking up at the branches and leaves, which were a riot of color with clouded green patterns.

"It's nice in here, ain't it Gandhi?"

"Yeah."

Tadd continued speaking, "It's so much cooler and refreshing—gives you the feeling that heaven's blowing fresh air just for us."

We walked on without saying anything. Even Niter was quiet and gentle as if he sensed something special, too. We drank in all the goodness of God's good earth about us. There's something about a forest with its green finery, its tall stately guards that gives you a feeling of strength and comfort and envelopes you with a desire to stay there the rest of your life with no outside interference to your secret communion. We were brushing against summer's enchanted moments and had tremors of delight all afternoon.

"Where do you suppose God spends His nights?" Tadd shot the question to me right out of the hush about us.

"I would imagine in some thick woods with the birds and animals to keep Him company and no people to disturb His rest."

"Sounds reasonable to me." Tadd almost whispered his answer.

"Tadd, do you suppose it's all right to board Niter now and ride? I'm growing tired."

"Me, too, I guess it's all right."

I made a stirrup with my cupped hands for Tadd to climb on first. He gave me his hand, and with one leap I was right behind him.

"Let's follow the railroad tracks back to town," I suggested.

"Okay." Tadd reined Niter to the left and on out to the tracks. In the distance, we heard the moaning sound of a train whistle. We had been with Niter before when the train approached the town, and Niter was not afraid of the train's noise.

"Must be the four-ten freight."

"Must be," I replied. "Guess we ought to be taking Niter back, don't you think? Don't want your aunt to worry."

"Yeah," Tadd agreed and then added, "How about after supper you and me tote some pine slabs from the sawmill and start on our raft?"

"Now, that's a swell idea. Suppose old Stoneface will let us have 'em?"

"Sure he will," Tadd assured me. "He ain't a bad sort."

Back in the barn, I found a grass sack and wiped Niter dry. Tadd pumped a bucket full of fresh cool water. Niter pushed his velvety noise in the water until his nostrils were almost covered. He drained every drop from the bucket. As we walked up to the house to thank Aunt Abigail, we heard excited voices. Three or four women were gathered there in the yard. The town gossip, Miss Bloomery, was doing all the talking. Rev. Thompson said that she was a very "garrulous" and "loquacious" woman. But Tadd and I thought that since she was always talking so much, she must have been vaccinated with a phonograph needle.

"Oh, it's a crying shame," Miss Bloomery brooded over her clasped hands. "What will his poor mother and father do? I've always said that if I ever got married and had children, I would know where they were or else. But you know Lizzie; she always thought her little Sammy could do no wrong. No, sir, not her Sammy."

"Now, now, Sara," Aunt Abigail was trying to slow down Miss Bloomery. "We mustn't judge. The Good Book says, 'Judge not that ye be judged.'"

"Just the same," Miss Bloomery's speech gained force. "She should have kept him home after lunch. Don't the doctors always say to wait at least an hour after you eat before you go in swimming?"

"Excuse me, ma'am," Tadd interrupted the talking machine, "What'd you say about Sammy? Oh, Aunt Abigail, thanks a lot for letting me and Gandhi ride Niter."

The Good Ol' Days

"You're welcome, son," Aunt Abigail replied in despondent sorrow.

The other women were gathered with closed mouths as if their lips had been sewn with strong, silk thread, but not Miss Bloomery. She blurted out, "Sammy's dead."

The other women standing around began to cry, including Aunt Abigail, but Miss Bloomery was dry eyed.

Aunt Abigail addressed her remarks to Tadd and me, "Boys, wasn't Sammy in your grade at school?"

"Yes, ma'am," Tadd replied. "Sammy's dead? Why? How? When? Gosh!"

"Yes, the poor dear," Aunt Abigail spoke through sobs. "And this being the last day of school and the summer all before him, and he was so young."

Miss Bloomery got in her two cents worth to us, "Now, maybe you boys will be a mite more careful, or you'll be winding up dead, too."

As hot as it was, I felt a chill ripple my spine from my neck all the way down to my heels. Tadd and I got real scared.

"We'd better mosey on, Tadd."

"Yeah, guess so. Thanks again, Aunt Abigail."

"You're welcome, boys, and please be careful."

"We will," Tadd assured her and we pressed on toward the church corner.

"Ain't that awful about Sammy Weir?" I asked Tadd as we walked on downtown still barefooted.

"Yeah, it's real awful!"

"Do you suppose they'll have a funeral?"

Tadd surveyed me sideways. "Sure they'll have a funeral, stupid. Everyone that dies has a funeral."

"Do you suppose we'll have to go?" I pried, knowing full well my fear of the dead, especially of someone I had known well.

"I suppose it's only fit and proper for us to go. He was our classmate, weren't he? And besides, if it was you who was dead, wouldn't you want me to come to your funeral?"

"Don't talk like that, Tadd."

"Well, wouldn't you?"

I squirmed a bit and answered reluctantly. "Yeah, I guess so."

As we ambled by the Squire's office, he spied us and called out, "You boys hear about little Sammy Weir drowning?"

"Yeah," Tadd replied.

"Well, let that be a lesson to you," he called back.

We walked on toward the church corner up at the top of the hill. Not one word spilled from our lips for our minds were host to sad thoughts, which were like sharp arrows to us.

A little change of pace in our thinking, I decided, was just what we needed. "What time will we meet tonight to go fetch our boards?"

"How about eight o'clock?" Tadd suggested. "It'll be coming on dusk about then, and after what's happened today, nobody will pay us any mind."

"See you then," I called out as I turned down the street at the church corner.

That evening Tadd and I hauled eight pine slabs to the wharf and rowed them down the creek in our boat to the place where our cave used to be. The flood took care of that, but the high bank still remained. We worked on into the night, laying out the boards and arranging them like we wanted for our work awakened our heart's expectations. We rowed back to the pier, which was easy to see since there was a full moon.

The funeral was Wednesday afternoon at two o'clock in the church. Tadd and I went. We sat in the back pew because we didn't want to get too close to the coffin. Tadd was almost as horrified about being near dead people as I was. Mr. Harvey, the undertaker, came over to us and whispered in his husky voice that sounded like he was speaking from the bottom of a barrel, "Boys, would you like to go up and view the body and pay your last respects before the service begins?"

"Thank you just the same, Mr. Harvey," Tadd responded, "but we'll pay our respects from right back here."

"Many of the other children from his class have gone up and paid their respects. Don't you think you ought to? I'll go with you." Mr. Harvey sounded insistent.

He took Tadd by the arm, and Tadd clamped my arm with a vice-like grip, which hoisted me to my feet as Mr. Harvey dragged us up to the coffin. Everything I owned inside my skin was shaking as if it was strung up on a line during a gale wind.

We stood a minute before the coffin. Sammy had on his Sunday suit with a rosebud in his lapel. His face and hands were all purplish. He looked cold and ghastly still and stiff. Mr. Harvey stooped over and whispered to us, "Would you boys like to touch him? Some folks believe that if you touch a dead person, you will never be frightened again."

"No, thank you," Tadd replied, and we were compelled to move quickly to our seats in the back pew.

Rev. Thompson appeared and mounted his pulpit. He spoke heartfelt words over Sammy. I wondered if he would have said the same about me, but knowing Rev. Thompson, I was sure that he would.

After the funeral service, Rev. Thompson said something at the grave about ashes-to-ashes and dust-to-dust, and then Tadd and I went home and changed out of our Sunday clothes.

On our way downtown, we met some boys from our gang. Our thoughts were still riveted on Sammy. "How'd it happen?" Tadd directed his question to Levin Mustard. "Sammy was one of the best swimmers in town."

Levin answered, "Well, it seems that Sammy had just ate and went straight down to the swimming hole and jumped in. You know how he liked to swim?"

"Yeah, we know," I said.

Levin wet his lips with his tongue like a dog licks his chops, "Well, all of a sudden we heard him yell. We were all skeered, but Pete swam out to him. By the time he got there, Sammy had gone down and never came up."

"What'd you do then?" asked Tadd.

"Hunt ran to the mill to tell Sammy's Grandpop," Levin responded. "You know he's over six and a half feet tall."

We all stopped walking and just waited for Levin to go on with his narration of the drowning.

Levin seemed to enjoy being the center of attention, for after all, he was there and saw everything with his own eyes.

"Well, sir, Mr. Wagner waded right out into the water, clothes and all, right up to his chin he was, before we saw him go under and bring up Sammy. It was a sorrowful sight. Mr. Wagner carried him just like a baby as he waded in with him. He carried him in his arms down to the mill, and they took him to the doctor. But, it weren't no use. He was already dead."

No one said anything after Levin had finished his verbal picture. We just shuffled our feet slow-like toward downtown.

We took our leave of the boys at the post office for Tadd had to post a letter for his mom and get the mail. We took the mail back home to her and went to the clubhouse—just Tadd and me and Skipper, who was always our constant companion.

"Now, we got to lay our plans," Tadd began. "Remember how Capt'n Lacey said it was important to plan your adventures before you start?"

"Yeah, I remember."

"Should we make the lean-to out of wood or canvas?" Tadd was asking the question more of himself than he was of me; I could tell by the inflection in his voice. I heard him before talking to himself and he sounded just like that.

"Better be out of canvas," he continued, "since we don't want too much dead weight. I bet the Capt'n will give us all the canvas we need. Don't you think?"

"Yeah, I'm sure he's got more than he needs right there on the Marie Tomas." And then I thought of another question, "When are we going to start nailing the raft together?"

"Let's work on her all day tomorrow," Tadd suggested.

"That's fine with me," I assured him. I felt tickly and happy all over since we were going to get our raft built. I could just imagine us sailing down the river under a cold breeze, relaxing, and enjoying the scenery.

The Good Ol' Days

Tadd struck me with a real question: "How much money have you got on you?"

I reached in my pocket and pulled out six pennies. "There's every cent of it," I answered pointing to the pennies on the barrelhead.

Tadd emptied his pocket. "Eight cents," he said with a forlorn voice after he counted them three times.

"Let's go buy that much worth of nails," I said.

We pocketed our pennies and strolled down to the hardware store. Skipper was right at our heels. If he could help it, he would never let us out of his sight. He was our constant companion, and I looked on him like he was almost my brother. He had more sense than some people I knew. He was a smart dog and dependable.

With the nails secure in the brown paper bag that Tadd held, we made our way behind the stores along the crick's edge toward the pier.

Tadd was the first on board the Marie Tomas. "Capt'n Lacey!" he called out.

The Captain poked his head out of the companionway. "Well, boys, it's good to see you. What do you have in that bag, Tadd?"

By that time Skipper and I were on board. Tadd answered, "Nails."

"Gonna start building her, are you?" Capt'n Lacey knew immediately what we were up to.

"Yep, tomorrow morning we start putting her together," Tadd spoke up proudly.

"Capt'n Lacey," I began, "we need some canvas for our raft, a piece for the sail, and another piece for our lean-to. Do you have any old canvas about that you ain't using?" Our hope hinged on his answer.

"Hmm," Capt'n Lacey mused as he thought. "I believe I can fix you boys up. You got to have canvas for your sail, that's for sure." He went below to look around while we stayed topside.

It wasn't long before the Captain returned with an armful of canvas. It was quite dirty and peppered with oil stains, but it was a beautiful sight to our yearning eyes.

"This ought to do you. You can have this and cut it up to suit yourselves. I'll stash it here in the stern, and you can pick it up tomorrow morning. All right?" the Captain asked.

"Gee, Capt'n Lacey," Tadd said, straight from his heart, "it's good to have a friend such as you. We're mighty obliged to you for your kindness and generosity to us."

"That's for sure, Capt'n, you're the best friend we've got in this whole town," I assured him sincerely and honestly.

"Thank you, boys, for them kind words. And I might say, that you both are the best friends that I've got in this town."

"We're even then," I said.

Capt'n Lacey gave us one of his broad smiles, rumpled our hair, and said, "We're even Steven."

We bade goodbye to Capt'n Lacey and shuffled home for supper.

The next morning, bright and early, Tadd and I and Skipper met on the church corner. Tadd was carrying an old hammer that had seen better days, and I gripped a handsaw whose teeth wouldn't chew through a wet dumpling, but it was all we had. How great was the sum of our expectations that day! We were so happy and bubbling with enthusiasm as we looked forward to our accomplishments. Nothing stirs the soul like high expectations and longing hope. It was something that had been stirring in our hearts and minds for a long time—to sail down the river at our own leisure, doing what we wanted to do when we wanted to do it. Talk about freedom! Just the thought of such an adventure can cause one to explode with joy.

"Let's go," Tadd said grinning from ear to ear.

He began to whistle the tune, "We're off to see the wizard, the wonderful wizard of Oz." I like to hear Tadd whistle. It produced a good feeling inside of me, and I wanted to jump up and whistle myself. But my mouth never seemed to pucker just right for whistling, so I only listened to Tadd and kept my mouth shut.

Tadd's mom had fixed us lunch of four yeast rolls spread thick with peanut butter and jelly. I had my pop's World War I canteen strapped to my belt. It was gurgling with sounds of fresh cool water.

The Good Ol' Days

We gathered the canvas from the stern of the Marie Tomas, put it in our skiff, and made off down the crick toward our secret place. The sun resembled a ball of fire. The tree leaves along the bank of the creek were as still as a dead motor. The tide was going out as we could see, real quiet like with hardly a ripple on the water. I was beginning to swelter, and I hadn't done anything but cast the canvas in our boat. Skipper was panting like a small, struggling locomotive, and it was four hours before high noon. Tadd pulled long strokes on the oars, and beads of sweat on his face made him look like he had the measles.

"It's gonna be a scorcher today," Tadd commented between pulls on the oars, wiping his brow with his right forearm. It was an unusually hot day, real unusual.

"Sure is," I agreed, scraping my forehead with my fingers and snapping them together over the side of the boat to flick off the salty droplets of perspiration.

Tadd turned around to see if our secret place was near. He appeared to be standing on the tiptoe of expectation, although he was still sitting down. There's something about anticipation that stirs a fellow, and Tadd and I were no exception.

He continued to row with steady strokes. I was the first to spy it. "There she is," I declared, pointing with my right index finger like I had discovered new territory. But, of course, we hadn't because we had been there hundreds of times.

Tadd beached our skiff with the skill of a seasoned sailor. All three of us piled out. The first thing we did was to strip our clothes down to our undershorts. Skipper swam along the shore to cool off and then found the nearest tree to relieve himself.

We hammered and sawed and nailed for a long time. Our raft began to take shape, manifesting some semblance of a sailing vessel—at least to us. Our bodies were a moistened mass of flesh covered completely with spent sweat, but we remained in the highest of spirits. We were doing something that we desperately wanted to do.

Tadd wiped his forehead with his arm and observed, "Boy, if that sun keeps blazing down like that much longer, it's gonna burn up everything it touches."

"It might do that," I agreed. I scanned the big oak tree behind us and pondered aloud, "Look at them leaves, Tadd. They're turned up like parched lips craving a drink."

We had stopped working and were sitting there talking. Tadd smiled at me and said, "Gandhi, you sure do dress your thoughts in flowery words sometimes. You ought to be a poet."

"Aw, shucks, Tadd. Poets are sissies, ain't they?"

"Some of 'em are and some of 'em ain't. If you'd be a poet, you'd be among the ones that ain't."

I just looked at Tadd and smiled, approving him all over. And he knew it. *That Tadd is some fellow,* I thought to myself. *Why, he had charm that would melt a statue.*

"Let's take a swim," urged Tadd, and we dropped our drawers and hit the water, which was almost as hot as dish water. Skipper joined us. He was a good swimmer and loved the water about as much as Tadd and I.

We didn't do much swimming. We stayed under the water to cool off, floated around awhile and came up on shore. Tadd decided to swim out into the middle of the creek. Finally, he swam back to the high bank and climbed it like a wet dog climbing out of the water's edge, and I told him so and laughed. He laughed with me because we were sworn and confirmed friends forever. After we put our drawers back on, my stomach started growling.

"I'm starved." I said.

"So am I," Tadd responded as he fetched the brown sack with the rolls in it. He gave me two and he kept two. We ate in silence. I passed him the canteen. And we took a drink of the tepid water.

After we had finished eating, I spoke, "I'm still hungry, Tadd."

He eyed me from neck to ankles and replied, "What do you want, Gandhi? To get fat or to get nourished?"

"I just want to get filled up," I answered truthfully.

"Well, that's all we got, so it's no use wanting more."

"But I'm still hungry."

"So am I, but we'll have to wait 'til we go home. Now, let's get back to work."

We set to work on our raft, and Skipper showed good sense by seeking the shade of the oak tree for his afternoon's repose.

"Let's join Skipper for awhile," I suggested.

Tadd put down his hammer and said, "That ain't a bad idea."

As we laid on our backs on the soft earth, hands behind our heads, in the cool of the shade, Tadd asked me, "Gandhi, did you ever read that book about the Captain who stuffed the ears of his sailors and tied them to the spars of the ship so they couldn't hear the sirens singing?"

"How in tarnation could they hear the fire whistle out at sea?" I asked, realizing how incredible that would be. In fact, I knew that it was impossible and thought Tadd should have enough sense to realize that, too.

"It weren't no fire whistle, silly." Tadd laughed. "They were beautiful women singing and playing harps on a lonely island."

"There you go again, talking about girls," I retorted in disgust. But to keep the conversation going, I inquired, "What's the name of the book?"

"I don't know; it don't matter about the name, but it happened. That was right smart thinking on the part of the Captain, don't you think?"

"What's so smart about that?"

"You dumb bunny." Tadd called me by silly names sometimes.

"Don't you see? If he didn't do that, the sailors would head the ship toward the women and run her aground, and the cargo would be lost."

"Yeah," I said, but I didn't see.

We just lay there thinking and saying nothing. A wide range of thought was not closed to us. Then Tadd spoke up. "I wonder what song them sirens sang to woo the sailors to their island? If you knew, you could have it published and become a millionaire."

"Who wants to be a millionaire?" I asked. "All they do is get fat and lazy and skeered they'll lose their money. I bet they never have any fun like you and me."

"Aw, Gandhi," was Tadd's retort to me.

"Shall we start building again?" I asked.

"Yeah," Tadd agreed, getting up, grabbing the hammer and stuffing his mouth full of nails.

"What'll we use for our masthead?" I wondered.

Tadd spit the nails out of his mouth, dropped his hammer, and said, "Let's go look for a strong sapling."

"Right," I said, jumping in stride with him.

"Okay. Let's do it."

The sun was moving westward in the vaulted, cloudless sky. Even the birds had stopped their flying, it was so hot. I looked out over the creek, and on the opposite bank, I saw a crane standing silently on one leg as if it were too hot to put his other foot down on the scorched sand. It must have been too hot for him to fly.

We eyed each sapling as we passed them by. Suddenly, Tadd called out, "This is it. Look how straight it is. Not a crook in it. Give me your saw, Gandhi."

I handed Tadd the saw, and he sliced the oak sapling right off even with the ground. We trimmed the scattered sprouts from the bark with our fingers and carried it back to the raft. I would have guessed it was fourteen or fifteen feet long—just right for the spar on our raft.

Our raft was almost complete. She measured about eight feet by twelve feet. She would float on four pine logs that we had soaked in water beforehand. We righted the sapling near the bow, or what we thought was the bow, and in front of that we planned to make our lean-to. The raft was bluntly built as anyone could plainly see, but in our eyes she was like a spanking new cruiser.

We donned the rest of our clothes and stood further back to get a better look at our masterpiece. She was a beauty and floated like a small schooner on a mirrored lake. Pride puffed up our chest. We could feel it all inside us. If pride came before the fall, we were about to have a catastrophe.

"What say we frame the lean-to?"

"Yeah," said Tadd, "we got some scrap pieces of lumber here. Let's frame it up."

"Okay."

Without speaking another word, we began to construct the frame as if each of us were following a blueprint. But, of course, there were no such plans except the grandiose thoughts in our head.

"Finished at last," I exhorted when the last nail was driven. "I can't wait to try her out. Can you, Tadd?"

"We'll have to give her a trial run."

"When?"

"Maybe tomorrow," Tadd answered.

The sun was slipping down below the treetops in the west. We didn't say anything but began putting things away, gathering up our tools, and untied the boat. Skipper was the first aboard. I got in and sat down in the stern with the tools in my lap and Tadd shoved off and took command of the oars.

"What about our stores?"

Tadd smiled at me because he must have been thinking the same thoughts. "Yeah, we got to have plenty of stores. But we won't make the same mistake as last time."

"What do you mean?"

"Last time they got washed away. This time we'll keep 'em in the clubhouse. When we're ready to go, we'll take 'em with us."

"That makes sense. We can't keep gathering stores and losing 'em, can we?"

When we reached the dock, Skipper was the first one ashore. Tadd secured the boat while I climbed out with the tools.

A familiar voice called out, "How'd you make out, boys?" It belonged to Capt'n Lacey.

"Just fine. She's launched and raring to go," I answered.

"What about the sail?" he asked.

"We ain't got to that yet," Tadd spoke in a tone that rang with importance.

"Give 'er plenty of sail. The more the sail, the more power and control you'll have," the Captain advised. And then he asked, "How tall is your spar?"

"About sixteen feet," Tadd guessed the answer.

"She could stand more," the Captain mused, "but I guess that'll do. Good luck, boys." He turned and seemed to be swallowed up in the shadows of the cabin on the Marie Tomas.

"Did you notice anything?" I asked Tadd.

"Yeah," Tadd answered in a sad voice. "He's starting to hit the bottle again. That'll mean he'll be in his cups for a week or two."

"It's a shame that a man as good and smart as the Captain lets that stuff get the best of him, ain't it?" I pondered.

"Yep, I don't quite understand it. But then, I ain't grown up like he is and don't know all he does that might make him do it." Tadd answered in words wiser than his years. "Let's go eat." Tadd started off toward the hill and the church corner.

"Gosh, there for a minute I almost forgot how hungry I was," I confessed as I fell in step with him. Skipper was way out in front of us, leading the way home.

"Tomorrow we cut the sail," Tadd stated as if giving a command.

"Good," I said, "meet you after breakfast."

"See you," Tadd called over his shoulder as we parted company at the church corner.

"See you" was my promise more than an answer.

But cutting a sail was not what we would do the next day. We had forgotten that the summer's main attraction was coming to town. So our sail would have to wait for another day.

CHAPTER 6

From the dressed-up appearance of the barns and vacant buildings around Lewiston, everybody knew what was going to happen the next Friday—the circus would be in town. What a day! It wasn't a big circus like Barnum and Bailey with three rings and all that. But it was a circus just the same with a big top and one ring.

Late Thursday night, Tadd and I were waiting at the big vacant lot opposite the old school grounds. We weren't disappointed. The roar of big truck motors could be heard grinding and groaning as they made the hill and turned in the dirt road that led to the lot.

We climbed a tree to command a better view and to be out of the way. There was a full moon just as if God had turned on His lesser sun for us to see. Todd and I marveled how the circus people moved about. Each person seemed to know exactly what to do. And before you knew it, the big top began to rise heavenward like a huge umbrella going up at half speed against a strong wind.

There were three elephants, a dozen or more horses and ponies, and cages full of roaring lions that sounded like they could tear anyone to shreds who dared to come near.

After the tent was securely anchored down, we couldn't see much, so we jumped down from the tree and went home. The circus was in town for only one day. There would be two shows: one in the afternoon and one in the evening.

Early Friday morning, Tadd and I were the first to arrive at the lot.

A sweaty man in dirty clothes called out to us, "You boys want to earn free tickets to the circus?"

"You bet," called out Tadd. We sped over to him.

"Grab them buckets and tote the elephants some water from the school pump, will ya?"

We ran to our task. But before those elephants got their fill of water, we were dragging our feet and thinking our backs would break from carrying so much water. The elephants' insides must have been all empty cisterns. When we finished, that same man came over to us and said, "Let's go inside, boys. Those chairs in the reserve section have to be put up."

We followed him inside the tent but not as quickly as when we ran to fetch the buckets. The reserve section had folding chairs that had to be taken from the flat bodies of trucks which were backed up under the tent flaps. And then we secured boards that slanted down to the ground from the truck bodies that made stairways for people to walk up on.

After the chairs were all in place, the man in dirty, wet clothes came over to us. He shoved two pink tickets in our hands and said, "See ya at two o'clock, boys."

At two o'clock sharp, the circus band struck up the music and the man we had previously seen in dirty clothes, all sweaty and everything, walked into the center of the ring. He was dressed in black, shiny boots, white pants, and a beautiful red coat with gold braids interlaced over his shoulders and around his sleeves. He wore a tall, black silk hat, and he looked handsome.

We had to look a second time to be sure that it was the same man who had spoken to us that morning. He announced all the acts that took place: the woman on the high trapeze; the man in long, silk-looking underwear that walked across the loose high wire; and the man who went into the cage with the wild lions. And then the clowns were jumping all over the place, doing all kinds of crazy stunts.

All at once, the drums began to roll. A hush settled over the spectators like a descending cloud, sealing their lips. The man with the tall, silk hat walked into the center of the ring.

The Good Ol' Days

"Ladies and gentlemen," he began in a loud but stirring voice, "It gives me great pleasure to introduce to you the daring Lola!"

From the far end of the tent a beautiful girl with golden hair and wearing only two pieces of small clothing with peacock feathers hanging down from her bottom piece of tight pants, walked to the center of the ring. I heard some of the older men whistle. Following her were two men carrying a ladder about six feet tall that had sharp swords for steps up one side and down the other.

The man in the center of the ring continued, "This daring young lady will walk the ladder of swords barefoot without harm or injury. She comes straight to you from Austria and has charmed thousands the world over with her daring feat."

There was loud applause. I overhead a man behind me remark, "I bet she's from Austria—probably straight out of Brooklyn!"

I didn't pay any attention to him for I was hanging onto every word the man said about Lola.

The drum continued to roll and with her arms stretched high, the beautiful lady stepped slowly upon one sword, then another until she had walked up the ladder of sharp instruments and down the other side. The crowd went wild, clapping their hands and whistling.

Then, suddenly, the small circus band struck up a lively march, and some performers rode horses while others walked in all their finery, and they paraded by for everybody to see this grand finale. It was all wonderful.

As we left the tent, Tadd wondered out loud, "Why don't we put on a circus, Gandhi?"

"How in the world can we put on a circus? We ain't got no tent, no animals, no nothings. And besides, where are you going to get anybody to do all the stunts?"

"There's a kid in town here that can do lots of things," Tadd stated.

"Like who?"

"Like a lot of kids," Tadd spoke from behind a serious face.

"Are you crazy, Tadd Tobin?"

"Nope, I ain't. Besides we could charge admission, divide the money among us, and you and me can take our part and buy stores for our raft trip."

"Now you're talking. I guess maybe we could put on a circus."

"Gandhi, you sure are slow in catching ideas. But once you do, you're all right. Let's head for the clubhouse and make plans."

On our way up the hill, we spied Levin, Hunt, and Pete. Tadd motioned for them to join us. He explained to the boys what we were scheming. Every one of them thought it would be a good idea.

In the clubhouse, Tadd presided. And then he offered a terrible proposal. "What about asking some girls to be in our circus?"

"There you go again, thinking about girls," I said with words full of disgust.

"Now, Gandhi," Tadd talked straight at me in a stern voice like he was my pop bawling me out for something I had done wrong. "You just come from that circus, didn't you?"

"Yeah, we all did."

"Well, did you see any girls there? What about the lady that walked them swords?"

"There ain't no girls in town that can do that!" I assured him strongly.

"Maybe not," he conceded, "but there are some girls that can do stunts that would add to our circus."

I didn't believe him, but I remained tight lipped. When Tadd got an idea in his head and it got set in there real good, it was like concrete, hard to break loose.

He began shooting orders at us. "Levin, you go fetch Louise and come right back here. Hunt, how about asking your sister if she will come?" He directed each boy to contact a certain girl and bring her back to the yard in front of our clubhouse, which no girl had ever seen. When his eyes fell on me, he shook his head and said nothing. He knew how I felt about girls.

Within a few minutes, the boys returned with the giggling girls. I had never seen Tadd in better form. He was a born speaker before people. And the more people, the better he was. He was explaining to the girls all his ideas about us staging a circus. He spoke to them in clear sentences. He smothered them with wordiness, and they jumped right up in the air, clapping their hands with glee. They joined in, exchanging their own ideas with Tadd's.

Without delay, we began making preparations for our circus. Pete went home and found some clothesline wire. We stretched it between the barn and the old woodshed about three feet from the ground. That dumb Betty Waffles said she would try to walk the wire. I was hoping she would fall down and crack her head open and cause the rest of the girls to go home and leave us alone.

Tadd had asked Jeanne Adaire to come. She brought her two-wheel bike to show off more than anything else, I guess. Tadd jumped on that bike backwards and tried to ride it. He did! He jumped off after he had ridden it a short ways and pronounced that he would be the clown of the circus. Then Louise piped up for everybody to hear and said, "Oh, no, Tadd. You shouldn't be the clown. Let Gandhi be the clown. Look how sad his face is. Everybody knows that clowns are sad."

The sea of faces in front of me stared me down. I felt the blood rushing to my eyeballs. They were the most words I had ever heard Louise speak. And she sure did spit them out that time.

My first thought was to run and hide, but I knew right off that wouldn't look manly. So I just stood there like a wooden Indian with my bare face all colored up.

Tadd dashed over to me. "That sounds great, Louise." He put his arm around my shoulder, "You'll do that for us, won't you Gandhi?"

How could I refuse my best friend, especially since he put it to me the way he did? I just shook my head in the affirmative. Tadd slapped my back and said, "Good."

Hunt's sister had been taking some sort of dancing lessons. So right off, she began doing cartwheels and handstands and then she came down to the ground with a thud, doing a split all the while. Everybody applauded. I did, too.

"You all stay here and practice, Tadd commanded. "Come on, Gandhi."

"Where to?"

"Just come on." Tadd waved his arm for me to follow him. I did.

"I'm going to get Niter. At least, we'll have one horse in our circus."

"Good idea, Tadd." I fell in step with him as we headed toward the end of the lane and the home of his Uncle Scank.

Aunt Abigail said it would be okay for us to ride Niter. We bounded straight through town riding Niter and on up the hill to the clubhouse.

When we arrived at the lot where all the gang was, screams of delight gushed from the girls. The boys just grinned like they were actually enjoying themselves. I was wondering what had happened to them all of a sudden.

Tadd slipped over to his house and secured a rope clothesline. He tied it to Niter's bridle and clucked to get him trotting. I'm afraid Niter wasn't much of a show horse. Finally, Tadd said, "Grab his head, Gandhi, and walk him around in circles. I want to teach him that first. Then maybe we can teach him to jump over a washing tub or something."

"Oh, that's a wonderful idea." said Jeanne.

I was positively disgusted, but I did as Tadd asked.

We worked and practiced until suppertime. When the kids started to go home, Tadd reminded them to come back the next morning, and they all agreed.

He turned to me and asked a favor, "Gandhi, will you take Niter home?"

"Sure," I said and climbed aboard. I didn't ride through town but went down the back hill over the mill dam. I enjoyed the sights better that way. Niter wanted his head. After we crossed the mill dam, I let him have it and we sailed like a breeze over the road on out to the end of the lane. I had a vicious determination to do what I pleased, namely, to let Niter run as fast as he could. And he did!

I rubbed him down with a grass sack, gave him a bucket of water, put him in the stall, thanked Aunt Abigail, and walked home.

Next morning, there wasn't a boy or girl missing who was going to be in the circus. Everyone had gathered on the backyard next to

The Good Ol' Days

Tadd's house. We waited anxiously and hopefully. We were spiced with the joy of life and our spirits were honed to a keen edge.

Tadd suggested I go get Niter so we could put him through his paces.

"Don't you reckon I ought to tell your Aunt Abigail what we're up to?"

"Sure I do," Tadd agreed with me. "Tell her we're practicing for a big circus we're gonna put on after we whip it together. And she and Uncle Scank can have free passes."

I jumped on a convenient two-wheel bike nearby and peddled it fast toward the end of the lane. I explained to Aunt Abigail what we were doing. She said it was a splendid idea and to come get Niter anytime we wanted him. I thanked her, bridled Niter, and took off for our circus grounds.

That day was more of the same as the day before: training Niter to go around in circles; watching Hunt's sister cutting the air with her cartwheels, backflips, and then jumping high and coming down in a split on the ground. Betty was willfully stubborn for she was still trying to walk the clothesline we stretched for her about three feet from the ground. Jeanne was the costume designer and scenery manager. She had some pretty good ideas, but I still didn't like having girls in on this big operation. And besides, it kept us from working on our raft, cutting the sail and everything.

We worked hard all through the day, only taking time off to eat lunch and then continuing to shape up our circus.

Tadd came running over to me as I held the line on Niter's bridle while he nibbled some grass. I had seen Jeanne whisper something in Tadd's ear so I knew that whatever he was going to tell me was her idea first.

"Gandhi," Tadd eyes were lit up like a Christmas tree, "What about Skipper riding on Niter's back as he goes round in circles? That would be just like the big circus wouldn't it?"

I had to admit it sounded good, if only it hadn't come from a girl. It was a sad thought, but I had begun to believe that nobody, but nobody, could ever truly escape girls in this life.

"Yeah, that sounds okay," I said with a sigh.

"Let's try it," Tadd said, lifting Skipper right off the ground while he was enjoying a sound sleep. Skipper pricked up his ears and looked at Tadd and then at Niter.

Niter paid no attention to what we were doing. But when Tadd put Skipper on his back, he reared up on his hind feet, and Skipper slid to the ground. Then Niter kicked his hind feet two or three times, just missing Skipper's head. Quickly, Skipper put plenty of distance between the horse's hind feet and his body.

"That ain't such a good idea, after all," I said in a I-thought-so voice.

"Naw, we'll think of something else," Tadd commented.

"Why don't you let the clown stand on Niter's back as he gallops around in the ring?" Louise put her two-cents worth in, and by what she said I knew she was figuring a way to get me quickly killed.

"What do you say, Gandhi?" Tadd whirled around and fired the question at me. I could tell by his overtones that he wanted me to do it.

I made up my mind right then and there that I'd show Louise. "All right, I'll try." And Tadd gave me a boost onto Niter's back.

I kicked off my sneakers and cautiously stood up. Niter didn't seem to mind, but I soon learned that balancing myself on a horse's back isn't the same as walking a rail fence. When Tadd began to lead Niter around in a circle and urged him to trot, the next thing I knew I had made a hard clean fall to the ground. I was embarrassed and hurt. Niter grazed my hair with his long, rough, wet tongue. I just lay there and looked up and admired the trim way his legs were fastened to his body.

Tadd helped me up on my wobbly feet. Niter ate grass with placid contentment like nothing had ever happened.

"Maybe you'd only better ride him bareback. What do you say, Gandhi?"

"Guess you're right, Tadd," was my painful answer as my fingers probed my head for any swollen lumps.

Some of the girls giggled at my discomfort, but the boys had more sense and they launched understanding glances to me.

Our acts were shaping up, and Tadd said that tomorrow would be dress rehearsal. That meant that Jeanne had to get all our costumes together and the other boys would have to help her make backdrop scenery.

Jeanne had a pair of pants for me that were baggy enough for five boys to get into. She had dyed them yellow. They stayed up on me by being fastened to a pair of red suspenders that looped over my shoulders. You had to give it to that Jeanne. She had ideas galore.

Tadd wore Hunt's riding boots and riding breeches, his pop's old band coat, and a beat up tall, silk hat that belonged to Jeanne's pop.

The girls wore long dresses and hats that fell down to their ears. And streaming from the hats were the longest feathers and plumes that I had ever seen.

Jeanne had thought of everything. Why, she even had a costume for Skipper. And when she dressed him, he didn't flinch a muscle, but stood unruffled and let her fuss over him like a cat licking her kitten clean.

The boys and I strung two ropes over the hanging limb of the big maple tree that stretched out over the yard, and we tied a sawed-off broom handle to each end of the dangling ropes. This was the trapeze that Levin would climb on and swing back and forth, suspended by his legs.

Everything was moving with a roaring rhythm. Then Jeanne made a horrible suggestion.

"We'll have to use your clubhouse, Tadd, for a dressing room the day of the circus."

The eye of every boy riveted on Tadd. That clubhouse was our secret place, and we had vowed that a girl would never enter there.

Tadd looked each of us point-blank in the eye. And then he asked, "Do we want to have this circus or not?"

Levin hazed at Hunt and Pete squinted at me. We wanted to have the circus all right, but girls in our clubhouse? We peered at each other in mute astonishment.

"Either we use the clubhouse for a dressing room or the circus is off. What'll it be, boys?" Tadd put it straight on the line for us.

"Well, maybe this one time," Hunt ventured.

Tadd glared at Pete. Pete slowly nodded his head yes. Then he looked at Levin. Levin's stare met mine, and he glanced quickly down at his feet. Without raising his eyes, he nodded his head in the affirmative.

Tadd didn't even look at me. I guess he knew what my answer would be. "All right," he said, "The majority rules. We'll use the clubhouse for our dressing room this one time."

I stood there wondering what girls possessed that made boys do what they wanted. It seemed that girls always got their way without throwing one fist, and I was baffled by their constant victories. Then and there, I vowed to myself never to try again to understand girls for it was too tiring and perplexing a task.

As the girls rushed into our clubhouse, they began shrieking. We boys trailed them inside like whipped dogs.

"Why, this is lovely!" exclaimed Jeanne. "An ideal dressing room. But why did you paint it this gaudy red color?"

Now, if Tadd had told her the real reason, I had made up my mind that I was going to quit the circus right then. He answered in a matter-of-fact tone, "That's the only color we could buy at the time we painted it."

His answer satisfied me, and I stayed with the circus.

Levin and Hunt strung up a rope between the two clothesline poles, and they clipped the three old bedspreads with safety pins to the rope. This was our curtain, and it would prohibit the people from seeing what was coming next until the proper time.

Louise and Betty made posters describing our circus, the date, place, time, and admission charge. We boys delivered the color posters to the storekeepers and got their permission to put them in their windows.

THE BIG DAY ARRIVED. We were all dressed in our costumes.

Jeanne brought her mother's red lipstick and painted my nose and a big ring around my mouth. We burned the end of a cork and rubbed it on the rest of my face. She had even made a big red plume to attach to Niter's bridle.

All of us, including Skipper, were arrayed in gaudy costumes. We trudged out to the end of the lane. Peter pulled a wagon that Betty and Louise had decorated. Betty sat in it, attired in her tightrope walking costume. Also, in the wagon was a Victrola with one worn band record on the spindle.

As were about to start our parade, a state trooper drove up to us and stopped his car.

"What's going on here?" he asked politely.

Tadd spoke up, "We're gonna put on a circus, but first we gotta have a parade."

"Well, well, that's fine. Maybe I'd better lead you through town. Would you like that?"

"That would be great," Jeanne acknowledged.

Tadd reached in his band coat pocket and pulled out a ticket and gave it to the state trooper. "It's yours, for free," he spoke generously.

The trooper tipped his hat, thanked Tadd, and hopped into his patrol car. He turned on the revolving lights that were perched on the top of his car and we were off.

Behind the car, Tadd rode Niter in all his splendor. We had the saddle on Niter for this occasion. I walked behind Tadd. Following me, Pete pulled the wagon in which Betty sat cross-legged. She quickly cranked up the Victrola and started the lone record of scratchy band music. The other kids straggled next after the wagon. As we marched along Main Street downtown, some of the people stopped and looked and smiled. Some laughed. Hunt carried a big poster nailed to a beanpole on which was imprinted:

LEWISTON'S GREATEST SHOW ON EARTH, COME SEE IT. FOLLOW US. ADMISSION 5 CENTS.

When we arrived at the backyard where the circus was to be held, there were seven people already gathered there. We had borrowed a dozen chairs from Mr. Harvey's funeral parlor with a promise that we would accord them special care and return them promptly.

Louise was the ticket seller and money taker. More people came and we began. Aside from a few falls from the tight rope and trapeze, everything went well. Betty kept cranking the old Victrola again and again, and played the same worn band record over and over. Everyone seemed solicitous. Skipper performed no tricks, but he sniffed the circus mood. He barked, trotted around with that silly little cone-shaped hat fastened to his head, and visited the people in the audience to receive pats and scratches around his ears and on his back.

After we had finished all our tricks, we had a grand parade around in a circle for everybody to see us. Everyone applauded like they were viewing the Barnum and Bailey Circus. We quickened our pace and marched round and round in jubilant gratitude.

When the people finally filed out of the circus grounds, it was just a vacant backyard again. That is, everyone except those of us who were in the circus. We remained, still basking in our exhausted splendor.

Once again, we all streamed into the clubhouse. Louise began counting the money. "Two dollars and ten cents," she said after she had counted it four times.

"How much is that apiece?" I asked thinking about our raft voyage.

"That's about a quarter for each of us," she explained.

"Better than nothing," chimed in Pete.

Tadd was as silent as a mummy, and I could tell that he was disappointed at the small return for all our efforts.

We all took our share of the money and then began gathering up the stuff we had borrowed and returned it. I dashed into Tadd's house and washed my face at the kitchen sink.

When Mrs. Tobin came into the kitchen she laughed and said, "Marshall, you made a very funny clown. You children will have to do that again sometime."

"Yes, ma'am," I said, scrubbing my face with Old Dutch Cleanser. Most of the make-up came off.

When I returned to the backyard, Tadd said, "You look like your old self again, Gandhi. Let's take Niter home."

"What do you say we go by the swimming hole first and take a swim?"

"Good idea, Gandhi."

Tadd stretched his arm toward me and with one pull and a jump, I was right behind him on Niter's back.

We cantered straight for the swimming hole. Shadbelly Greeves and Sol Goldstein were the only two boys there. Tadd and I untied the girth and slid off the saddle from Niter's sweaty back. We shed our clothes and started to lead him into the water.

Shadbelly (which wasn't his real name but everybody called him that) walked over to Tadd and demanded, "What do you think you're going to do?"

"We three is gonna take a swim," Tadd answered him unperturbed like. "Any objections?"

"You're darn right there is." Shadbelly was becoming angry. "I ain't gonna swim in no water a dirty horse is messing around in."

The next thing I knew, Tadd had struck Shadbelly right in the jaw and then I saw Shadbelly's nose bleeding like a garden hose turned on full force.

Shadbelly turned and warned, "I'll get you for this, Tadd 'Pole' Tobin," all the while shaking his fist at Tadd, while mopping his nose with a handkerchief in his other hand.

Tadd started to run after them, but they had a head start and scooted away.

"Come on, Gandhi, let's take a swim," Tadd said as if nothing had happened.

He climbed aboard Niter and all three of us went out into the water, and we had the swimming hole all to ourselves. Niter seemed to enjoy the swim, especially after his ordeal at the circus.

Tadd took him up on shore, tied him to a tree and ran back into the water hollering to me, "Race you to New York!" New York was one of the boulders that stuck up out of the water.

I was standing in knee-keep water. But quick as a flash, I dove underwater and breast stroked as far as I could, holding my breath. You can go faster underwater so I beat Tadd to New York.

When we were both standing on New York, Tadd looked at me and said, "How'd you like the circus, pal?"

"It was just great," I answered. "Only the next time, let's not have so many girls."

"Aw, Gandhi, you'll change your mind someday. Girls ain't so bad."

"Tadd Tobin," I said, "if I didn't know you better, I'd swear you was grown up already."

Tadd grabbed the helm of our conversation and steered it in another direction. "We didn't make much, did we?"

"Nope, we didn't. But at least we got about fifty cents between us to buy some stores with."

"You're right. Let's buy some stores this afternoon and stash them in the clubhouse. If we don't, we might spend it for something else."

"No sir, we won't," I admonished him. "That there money is to be used for stores."

"Well, we best be walking Niter home. Come on." And with that, Tadd shoved off, swimming for shore. We stood on the drying box, and the blazing glare of the sun soon dried the water bubbles right off our bodies. We saddled Niter and rode him home.

"Let's go by and see Capt'n Lacey," I suggested when we had crossed over the town bridge.

"Okay," said Tadd swinging in behind the hardware store to make our way along the crick's wall to the wharf.

"Uh oh," I said.

"What's the matter?"

"Look," I said pointing to the flagstaff on the forward deck. The blue ensign was flying upside down. To the general passerby he might look at the ensign upside down and conclude that the eccentric Capt'n Lacey, who hit the bottle too much, did not know the difference between right side up and up side down. But Tadd and I knew. It was a signal between Capt'n Lacey and us. When he flew the ensign that way, we weren't to draw near. He never wanted us to see him when he was on the toot.

We backtracked and walked through town. Up by the post office, Rev. Thompson stopped us and commented, "Boys, that was a delightful circus you put on. Almost like the real thing. Who knows? Someday you might own a circus all your very own."

"Thank you, Rev. Thompson," Tadd said. "Glad you could come." He started off walking up the hill.

I hesitated. Rev. Thompson sensed my unspoken desire to speak with him.

"Is there anything wrong, Marshall?" Rev. Thompson asked in true concern.

Tadd saw me pause and waved to me with his hand to join him. I waved back to him to go on.

"I was wondering, Reverend, if you could do anything to help Capt'n Lacey?"

"Do you mean you would like me to go visit him?" inquired Rev. Thompson.

"Yes, sir," I answered, "only I wouldn't want the Captain to know that I asked you."

"Don't you worry about that, Marshall. I won't tell him you asked me. I promise you, I will go see the Captain today. He has a grave problem, but he can be helped. Anyone can receive help if he has a sincere desire and really wants to be helped."

"Thank you, Rev. Thompson," I said, feeling as if a big load had been lifted from my shoulders, and I ran up the hill.

TWO DAYS LATER, TADD AND I WERE DOWN AT THE WHARF. We untied our boat to row out and take a look at our raft.

Tadd saw it first. "Look," he cried. He pointed to the ensign. It was flying right side up.

"Let's go," I said.

We boarded the Marie Tomas. "Hey, Captain!" Tadd yelled.

Capt'n Lacey poked his head out of the companionway. His hair was all disheveled and his face was sprouted with an unshaven, extra heavy growth of beard. He didn't look himself. His profile was lean looking and his eyes bloodshot.

"Hello, boys. Come on in." His voice wore a shroud of loneliness.

Tadd shot an anxious look at me. I was apprehensive.

Skipper, Tadd, and I stepped down into the cabin. The Captain snatched the coffee pot off the stove and poured each of us a cup of coffee.

"I haven't been well, boys. That's why you ain't seen me about," the captain broke the icy silence with a sheepish grin on his bearded face.

"Feeling better now, Captain?" Tadd asked.

"Not much," he answered.

"We had a circus, Captain. Sorry you couldn't make it," I said.

"I'm sorry, too, Gandhi," he apologized. "Maybe the next time."

We just sat there drinking coffee without a word passing between us. Then Capt'n Lacey spoke.

"You know, boys, that Rev. Thompson is a mighty nice feller."

"Yeah, he sure is," I agreed.

The Captain spoke again, but he didn't seem to aim his words at us. "He has a shepherd's heart. And he knows the affliction of his sheep, too."

The Captain seemed to be struggling under the burden of something. His hand was shaking as he lifted the cup of coffee to his lips.

"You know what a preacher is, boys?"

We didn't say anything because we felt that the Captain itched to do the talking. He continued, "He's a high voltage transformer changing God's message into jets of light that make things clearer for us."

"And he marries and buries people, too," Tadd put in.

Capt'n Lacey went on talking as if Tadd hadn't said anything. "That man, Rev. Thompson, don't say his prayers, he prays." Capt'n

Lacey drew a couple of long puffs on his pipe and continued, "He sure lives his life open on the God-ward side."

"I take it you like the Reverend," I said.

"I sure do," he answered.

"How come, Capt'n Lacey, that you never go to church?" My question was an innocent one.

Tadd shot me a look like I shouldn't have asked that question.

Capt'n Lacey took the pipe out of his mouth, set his coffee mug down, and looked me in the eye. "Gandhi, I guess it's because a long time ago my religion had been short-circuited by the pious hypocrites in the church."

"But we ain't supposed to pattern our lives after the people in the church. Leastwise, that's what Rev. Thompson said. He said we are supposed to be more like Jesus. He said that Jesus is supposed to be our example, not people."

There was another long stretch of silence. Skipper began to scratch the irritating fleas behind his ears. The Captain poured himself another mug of hot, black coffee. For the first time, I saw a glimmer of light in his eyes. He asked, "Boys, how's the raft coming? Have you got her all rigged?"

"We sure have, Capt'n," Tadd seemed glad the way the stream of conversation was heading. He was always quick to pick up on asked questions, and he seemed to always have the answers.

"When do you plan to shove off?"

"I guess we ought to wait 'til after the carnival." Tadd turned to me. "What do you think, Gandhi?"

"Well, I ain't one for waiting. Summer is slipping right on," I reminded him. And then I had another thought. "It'll soon be the Fourth of July. Time and tide waits for nobody. Ain't that right Capt'n?" He had said that to us many times over, and I was just repeating what he had said for it was true. That was for certain.

"You're right, Gandhi," Capt'n Lacey said to me with a wink.

"Just the same," Tadd spoke slowly, like he was measuring each word, "I'd like to stay for the carnival. Besides, we might win a basket of food to take with us on our raft."

I knew he threw out that last sentence to bait me and hook me fast to his suggestion. I guess I must have nibbled, for I said, "Well, I guess it would be fun at that." I look at Tadd and gave him a broad smile.

"Then it's settled?" Tadd asked.

"As far as I'm concerned, I said.

"You boys will have plenty of time after the carnival," the Captain assured us. Turning to Tadd, he said, "And you might be right. It won't hurt to have plenty of vittles along with you."

There was another gap of silence. The Captain got up and went to his chart rack. He unrolled a chart on the table. He took the pipe out of his mouth and used the stem to point with. "Now this is the way you'll be taking. I'd leave on the outgoing tide. Down to here," he pointed to a spot on the chart that had a buoy on it, "is Bloody Point Light. That's about sixteen miles from Lewiston."

Tadd puckered up his lips and whistled. "Think we'll make it that far, Capt'n?"

"Easy. And more," the Captain assured us. "You taking a fishing pole with you?"

"Sure," said Tadd. "We ain't going to get off without that. We both got a fishing line. And we both know how to clean and fry fish." His words were punched through and through with pride.

"That's good," the Captain said. "Now, if I were you, I'd tie up at Bloody Point Light and try my luck at fishing. There's usually a school of fish that feeds in and around there."

"Now, see this?" the Captain pointed to a finger of land sticking out into the water. "That's Hell's Point. Under no circumstances do you go past that point for you'll be in open sea there. That's the inlet and the tide flows strong. The undercurrent is wicked and could swallow you up like an eel swallows a toad."

I gasped a big gulp of air that made a funny noise. When I sucked it down, I said, "We sure don't want to venture out that far. We'd better try to stay in the crick. Don't you think, Tadd?

"Yeah, we ain't equipped for much more than that."

The Good Ol' Days

"You going to tow your skiff?" the Captain inquired.

"Ain't thought about that, either," I said.

"I think it's best you keep your skiff to tow," the Captain suggested. And then he added, "Just in case. What's the draught of the raft, Tadd?"

"I'd say no more than a foot," Tadd answered right haughtily.

"Just the same, I'd keep her mid-stream. This here crick is clogged in certain places with silt and underbrush that could give you a heap o' trouble."

"Yes, sir" was Tadd's answer as if he were the only one going.

"What'll you be using for holding your drinking water?"

"How about two one-gallon jugs?"

"That'll be fine but keep plenty of water on hand." The Captain rubbed his whiskered chin. Then he fired another question. "What about your cooking gear?"

It seemed to me he was holding a conversation with Tadd only and I wanted in on it too, so I piped up and said, "One saucepan, a skillet and a sterno burner."

"That's good, Gandhi, that's good." The Captain seemed to be caught up in the excitement of it all.

"We're taking a flashlight, two blankets, and canned goods enough to last for at least a month." Tadd told him and it was the first I ever heard of what we were taking or how long we would be gone. I wasn't in favor of staying that long.

"That's a long time, Tadd. I don't believe we should take that long." I was getting a bit squeamish.

"Well, maybe we won't stay that long, but we'll have enough grub, just in case. Right Capt'n?"

"Sounds like good planning to me," he confided.

Tadd stood up and said, "Well, we'll be checking with you again before we shove off, Capt'n. Guess we'd better be moving on home."

"All right, boys. Thanks for stopping by. So long, and you too, Skipper," the Captain said as he leaned over and patted Skipper's head. Skipper wagged his tail for he enjoyed a true canine fondness for the Captain.

We untied our boat and towed out to check on our raft. She was floating like the Queen Mary, moored, secure to the old big oak tree. We jumped on board and walked about on her deck.

"She's okay" said Tadd. "Let's head on back."

"Okay," I said as I turned the boat around by giving a strong pull on each oar and then going in the opposite direction. We secured our boat and went home.

CHAPTER 7

It was raining. Tadd and I decided to spend the dreary morning of gloom in the tower, another one of our secret rendezvous places. It was located in Tadd's house over his parents' bedroom. Tadd declared that his home was just like an ancient castle on the Rhine River. He had shown me pictures of castles in Germany, and I believed him for his house sure did look like one. It was painted a dark gray and was wooden up to the second floor. From the second floor to the roof, it was protected with dark gray slate, including the roof.

In front of the house, protruding up from the heavy roof, was a tower-looking thing with small circular windows in it facing north and south, east and west. Dull shadows sneaked down from the peak of the house into slow curves. I said it looked more like a lighthouse, but Tadd insisted that it was a lookout tower of a castle. This was our favorite hideaway when we wanted to brood over our troubles or lay real secret plans. The tower could only be reached by entering his mom and pop's closet in the bedroom. We had to climb a rickety ladder and lift a trap door in a certain way. His mom and pop had never scaled the ladder the entire time they had lived there. Or so Tadd said.

A huge front porch hugged the front of his house with fancy pillars and rungs all around it. The entrance was two large, wooden, windowless doors that came to a point at the top just like the doors standing sentinel duty in a castle before a mote. The key had long been lost, so the door was bolted at night with a heavy, oaken bar.

The long, dark hall separating the parlor from the living room contained a lone hat rack with a full-length mirror in it. A threadbare rug with an oriental design covered the wide unpainted floorboards.

We had to go through the living room to enter the hall that housed a winding staircase. There in the middle of the living room was a huge, potbellied coal stove that lay dormant for the summer. A davenport, with loose cushions that held in springs that had long ago been sprung, was pushed against the far sidewall. Two large, overstuffed chairs were placed strategically around the rug with a wooden rocker near the Atwater-Kent radio. An old upright piano was situated catty-cornered in the front, near the bay windows where dark mahogany shutters were anchored and always closed. At least, the bottom ones were. I always felt spooky when visiting Tadd's house.

"Come on," Tadd beckoned to me. We opened the tall, black-looking living room door that led into the musty-smelling hall. At the far end of the hall, the crooked stairway wound up to the second floor.

Upstairs in the hall was a little nightstand with a coal oil lamp on it. They didn't have electricity upstairs. We went into his mom and pop's bedroom through the clothes closet and up the ladder. I was glad when we reached the tower. We were all alone there 'cause Tadd's parents both worked until five o'clock.

After we had replaced the trap door, I asked, "What's that smell, Tadd?"

"Don't you know?"

I guess I was supposed to, but I shook my head back and forth.

"It's moth balls," Tadd said. "Mom is nuts on moth balls. Puts 'em in every closet of the house."

"Oh," I said. Then another thought flicked over the screen of my mind, "What'll we do now?"

"Lay plans for the carnival, silly."

"What kind of plans? I thought our only plans were for our raft trip."

Tadd stuck to the subject at hand and started talking fast. He always talked fast when a brand new idea was whirling in his head. "You know that greasy pole the firemen always have at the carnival?" He didn't wait for me to answer. "Well, I got an idea." There's a five dollar bill tacked at the top of it, ain't there?"

I nodded.

"We're gonna win it this year."

"We ain't never got it before," I reminded him.

"No matter. We will this year."

"What makes you so sure?"

"My idea. That's what."

"Well, what is your idea?"

"Look," Tadd began to slow down his chatter. "A mess of kids always try to climb it. Right? Okay, let 'em try. And in their trying, they'll wipe off a lot of that grease. Right?"

I just looked at him with my mouth open, but saying nothing for I didn't rightly know where he was steering his idea.

"Now, after them kids try for a spell, I'll try and shimmy right up to the top."

"How?"

"I'm gonna put thumbtacks or something through my pant legs. That'll hold me fast until I get to the top. It's simple, ain't it?"

"Sounds simple enough. But can you do it?"

"I don't see why not," Tadd assured me.

"May not be as simple as it sounds," I warned him.

Tadd leaned back to take a running jump at me with a tongue lashing of harsh words, "Gandhi Reed, ain't you got no faith in me? Have you been 'round me all these years and still don't know what I can do and what I can't do? What ails you, anyway?"

"I don't mean no harm, Tadd. It's just that there'll be lots of other boys there trying for that five dollars like they usually do. What about Martin Short? He's tall and skinny. And he got it last year."

"Martin Short!" Tadd snorted. "Why, he was just lucky last year. And besides, he's so anemic that he couldn't get up enough steam to toot his whistle if he had to, let alone climb a greasy pole."

"Just the same," I said with no conviction in my voice, "you ain't ever done it yet. And I ain't so sure you can do it now."

I looked straight at Tadd, and it seemed that my words had

shunted him into the blackness of despair. I was sorry I'd opened my mouth.

"I got it, Tadd." He looked at me with question marks all over his face for by now doubts were puncturing his mind about me. "Well?" he asked in a growling, sour tone.

"Why not practice for it? Right now."

"Are you out of your head, Gandhi? We ain't got no greasy pole."

"What about that old barber pole down there in the barn?" I asked.

Tadd's eyes lit up and then the light faded out as quickly as it had flashed on.

"What about it?" he asked.

"Let's grease it up and you can practice."

"What with?"

Tadd didn't seem to be taking to any idea too well.

I was warming up to my subject nevertheless. "Lard," I said with pestering persistence.

The light appeared in his eyes again. "That's a great idea, Gandhi. Now you're using your head for something besides a hat rack. Come on."

We lifted the trap door, replaced it, and then slid down the ladder. Tadd ushered me out into the kitchen where a round table and three chairs were in place with the knives, forks, spoons, and glasses all set. The plates were facing down on the tablecloth. An American Store calendar hung over the table beneath the mantle piece. In front of the table was a kitchen range. Behind the stove and a little to the left of it was the pantry where Tadd entered.

"Here it is," Tadd cried with glee. And he brought forth a quart preserve jar full of country lard.

"Now for the tacks."

In a matter of seconds, he returned with a fistful of thumbtacks. He proceeded at once to push them through his pant legs since he already had his pants off and was fast at work.

"Gandhi," he said from his sitting position on the floor, "take the jar of lard and go grease that pole in the barn."

I put on my raincoat and ran out to the barn with the jar of lard under my coat.

Before I was halfway through greasing the pole, Tadd was beside me, coaxing me to hurry up. When I had finished, he said, "Let me at 'er."

"Wait a minute," I cautioned. "You climb up there on that ledge and hold the pole for me."

"Why?"

"That's the way it's gonna be at the carnival. You ain't gonna be the first to try, are you?"

"You sure have got the cobwebs out today, Gandhi. Go ahead. I'll hold 'er."

I sat down on the ground and wrapped my legs around the greasy pole. I tried to climb it by squeezing my arms tight around the slippery pole and pulling myself up, but I didn't budge from my sitting position. After many futile efforts that produced profuse beads of sweat on my upper lip, I said, "Okay, Tadd. She's all yours."

I climbed up on one of the barn's underpinnings and held the top of the barber pole. Tadd sat down on the earthen floor of the barn and began to climb. He didn't make any more headway than I had.

"Maybe I ain't got enough tacks in my pants." Discouragement dripped from each of his words.

He put on his raincoat and dashed back into the house. Before you could say Mispillion Lighthouse, he returned to the barn. I hadn't moved from my position holding the pole, and my whole body ached from the strain.

Off came his pants and he pressed more thumbtacks through the inner seams. "There. Let's try that." He pulled his pants back on and sat down once again with his legs round the pole, hugging it tight with his strong arms.

He hugged and squeezed and grunted and then, "Gandhi," he called up to me, laughing with glee, "I'm moving. Look. My bottom's off the ground about a foot."

When I leaned over to get a better look, I lost my balance and we all three, greasy pole, Tadd and me, fell to the ground with a thud.

"Gandhi, you dumb ox. Look what you've done. The pole's all covered with dirt."

I was ashamed for my bungling clumsiness.

Tadd looked at me and then consoled, "Never mind, ole pal. We done it. It worked. We'll grab that five dollars. You wait and see."

THE DAY BROKE SUNNY AND HOT. It was the day of the big parade, a ballgame in the park, and the Firemen's Carnival at night. It was the kind of day the whole town waited for. Stores were closed. Flags were flying from every flagpole and from the porch of every home. Anyone that didn't fly Old Glory that day was considered a true furriner. The cars that whizzed by had a set of five or more little flags flying from their shiny radiator caps. Kids paraded up and down the street, waving flags in their hands. Sweet smells of baked goods wafted out from every open kitchen door. Everybody seemed in a festive mood. And no wonder—it was the Fourth of July!

Tadd and I were at the end of the lane long before one o'clock, the time the parade was to begin. And when one o'clock approached, the parade assemblage resembled a forsaken head of uncombed hair. Some of the band members hadn't arrived. The first truck wasn't there, and three floats were missing from their assigned places.

At a quarter of two, Squire Hazzard, who was riding in the rumble seat of a convertible Model A Ford, waved his hand. At last, the parade was underway.

Rev. Thompson had asked Tadd and me to be in the church's float. It had something to do with the fight against the demon Rum. Old women from the church were sitting in chairs on the truck body, which was one of the floats. It was decorated with crepe paper. There was a small table in the middle of the truck body, and Tadd and I had little hammers that we were supposed to use to drive down the nails on a cigar box that contained an empty whiskey bottle. But, we had instructions that we weren't to actually hammer the nails until we got in front of the judge's stand that was located downtown. Along the way, we were just to pretend that we were hammering the dead soldier tight in the box.

The Good Ol' Days

When we arrived in front of the judge's stand, the band blared forth a lively march, and Tadd and I hammered solidly the lid of the cigar box that entombed the empty whiskey bottle. We beat and hammered for the rest of the parade until we reached the ballpark.

The old women and Rev. Thompson thanked us time and again for being in their float. They said we played our part very well.

Sitting on the bleachers before the ballgame started, Tadd leaned over to me and whispered, "Where do you suppose Rev. Thompson got that empty whiskey bottle? Suppose it was one of his?"

I gazed at Tadd and was about to tell him of my astonishment of his ever thinking such a thing when all of a sudden somebody set off a loud firecracker that rocketed in the air and exploded right over our heads. Then the band began playing "The Star Spangled Banner."

We all stood and removed our caps and put our right hand over our hearts. When the band finished, the umpire behind the pitcher hollered out, "Play ball!"

Squire Hazzard had the honor of throwing out the ball to the catcher, and the ballgame was on. We were playing the neighboring town of Houston.

"Who do you think will win?" I asked Tadd.

"We will!" was his cocksure answer.

The sun throbbed down on us until I thought we would melt right there on those bleacher seats. Between innings, Tadd and I went to the soft drink stand and each bought a bottle of Whistle, our favorite soda pop. It was really cold, right out of a washing tub full of ice. It was deliciously good with a tangy, orange taste.

The game was finally over and we had won seven to three. Our town team was good and could lick most other town teams except Middletown. Somehow, we never could win over them.

Tadd and I walked home by the way of the swimming hole. "Let's take a swim," Tadd suggested. "And that way, we won't have to take a bath before we go to the carnival tonight."

"Good idea," I concluded, pulling off my sweaty shirt and dropping my pants.

Before we came out of the water to dry off at the box on the pine tree, it seemed as if every boy in Lewiston had the same idea as we did. In fact, the traffic was so heavy we had to stand in line to get on the drying box.

That night, Tadd and I met at the church corner about 7:00. The carnival didn't open until 7:30, but Tadd thought we ought to get there early. We wanted to see what was going on and take a real good gander at that greasy pole.

Lewiston's Firemen's Carnival was renowned throughout Sussex County. Summer time was the happiest time of the year or at least that's what we thought. It was the time of no school, sweet smells, pleasant sounds, easy living, swimming, and cruises down the creek. And if that wasn't enough, we had ballgames, parades, and now the Firemen's Carnival.

We arrived early, but most of the firemen were there already, preparing the booths that were constructed from two by four pine boards and open at the top. Just the bare skeleton framing, that's all they were. But around the tops of the four poles of each booth was strung a two foot wide piece of bunting with red and white stripes and blue stars, which looked almost like our flag.

I glanced at Tadd and was surprised to see him walking bow-legged. "What in the tarnation ails you, Tadd? Are you chafed?"

"Naw, I ain't chafed. I just gotta be careful about these here thumbtacks in my pant legs that I just put in. If I walk with my legs too close together, them tacks might rip one of my pants legs and there goes our five dollars."

"Maybe we ought to sit down?" I pondered.

"Are you crazy, Gandhi? Then they would suspect something is wrong with us. Nope, we'll keep moseying around, slow like. And all the while let's edge over to the greasy pole."

Because of our finagling, my conscience took a bite of me for a short minute. We walked past the penny booth with its jars of cherries, cans of applesauce, two-pound bags of sugar, boxes of corn flakes and shredded wheat, and other stuff on its shelves.

Next was the candy booth and Mr. Green was stacking up the beautifully wrapped candies on the shelves. "Evening, boys. How's about trying your luck?"

The Good Ol' Days

"Not now," Tadd replied. "Thank you, Mr. Green. We may be back."

Mr. Green beamed a big smile and called after us, "All right, boys. Have fun. But I'll be looking for you to come back and play at my booth. Remember, this is the sweet tooth booth." And he chuckled.

The booths were anchored around the big Bingo stand, which was located in the center of the carnival grounds. There was plenty of space between the booths and the Bingo stand so that as many people as possible could walk around and spend their money.

There was the blanket booth that looked like some Indian display. The booth that seemed to be the most crowded was the Big Wheel booth, the only one where you could win cold cash. Billy Trice usually ran that one. And all during the night, you could hear him singing out, "Right over here, folks. Play the little game of chuck-a-luck. For the more you lay down, the more you pick up." Everybody knew he was lying, but they went over there just the same hoping they'd get lucky and win some money.

At the far end of the carnival grounds, the firemen had rented all kinds of rides. There was the Ferris wheel, and it was our sport to see who could swing the most and who would get scared first or throw up first. And then, there were the swings that flung you out over the crowd and gave you the feeling of flying low in an open airplane. And of course, the merry-go-round with its ring of beautifully painted wooden horses going round and round to the carousel music. We would always try to catch the gold ring as we went round.

We finally spied it.

"Look at that!" Tadd spoke out of the side of his mouth to me for my ears only. "They've made 'er taller this year. It wasn't half that tall last year. No wonder Martin Short climbed it."

"Do you think you can do it, Tadd?"

"Think it! I know it! You wait and see." But somehow Tadd's voice wasn't as strong as it usually is when he is certain of something. I thought I detected a tone of doubt and maybe fear. But, of course, I had to be wrong because Tadd Tobin wasn't afraid of anything. At least, most things.

"Let's stay close by so's we don't miss nothing." Tadd directed.

"Okay," I agreed, looking at all the people swelling the carnival ground like a flood tide moving inland.

Charlie Lockerman was about to speak over the public address system that always squeaked and squawked when anybody used the mike.

"Hello, folks. Welcome to Lewiston's Firemen's Carnival. We've got a lot of nice gifts and prizes for you to win. Visit all of our booths and try your luck. And don't forget our Women's Auxiliary booth." Then he laughed right into the mike, and it squeaked to high heaven. He continued, "I see you haven't forgotten that booth. Yes, sir, them ladies cook the best hotdogs and hamburgers there is. And have you tried the oyster sandwiches? Yum! They'll melt in your mouth."

I scanned the sea of faces looking up at Charlie Lockerman and most every mouth was stuffed with either a hotdog, hamburger, oyster sandwich or popcorn, and they were sloshing it all down with their favorite soda pop.

"Listen, folks." It was Charlie Lockerman's voice again over that squawking mike. "We've got big goings on here. Every night before we close the carnival, we will give away a grand prize. So don't dare go home before the drawing. Somebody tonight is going home twenty-five dollars richer than when he came here. You can sign up at the car booth. It's free. Just walk yourself over there to the car booth and sign up for the grand prize.

And, folks, while you're there, take some chances on that beautiful, new, sleek 1939 Chevrolet sedan. Isn't she a beauty? Some lucky person is going to own her in just six short days. And listen, you may win her for a dollar. That's what I said, just one dollar. Go ahead, folks, try your luck. Six chances for one measly dollar. You might be the lucky winner of that brand new car."

Charlie Lockerman, speaking through a mike or standing before a group of people, never lacked for words nor did he seem to take a breath. Everybody in town said that Charlie sure did have the gift of gab.

"And listen, folks, that ain't all. Tonight, we'll have the greasy pole climb at nine o'clock."

Tadd jabbed his elbow in my ribs. "That's us, Gandhi. It's as good as in our pockets."

"I hope you're right," I whispered back into his ear.

Charlie Lockerman sure was wound up tight, and by the way he was talking, he was going to take a long time to unwind. "Folks," he still gripped the mike and his lips were poised as if he would chew the microphone, wire and all, right out of his hand. "Tomorrow night is the pie-eating contest. Every youngster here will want to try out for that. Nobody loses. Everybody is a winner there. The boy or girl who eats the most pies the fastest wins two dollars."

Without taking a breath, Charlie droned on, "And Wednesday night, folks, will be the Firemen's Parade. Prizes will be awarded to the fireman coming the longest distance to participate in the parade. And, of course, there will be a prize for the best band. Thursday night will be the greasy pig scramble. Some lucky person is gonna go home with meat for the table. And I mean, ham what am!" Everybody laughed. Tadd and I didn't see anything funny, so we just sat there waiting for him to shut up. And besides, we didn't want a pig anyhow.

"And listen to this, folks," Charlie Lockerman was continually throwing out words that appeared to be swallowed and digested by everybody on the carnival grounds, "Friday night, we'll have a long trough of money hidden in a meal. There'll be fifty-cent pieces, quarters, dimes, nickels, and pennies in the meal. Anybody can enter this contest, and you can keep all you can find."

This was something new and Tadd looked at me with eyes that had dollar signs instead of pupils. "Now he's talking sense again. We'll get into that, Gandhi."

I nodded my head, "You bet. Ain't gonna miss that free money."

Charlie was coming to the end of his spiel now. "And the last night, folks, that beautiful car over there. That brand new 1939 Chevrolet sedan will become yours. But you can't win if you don't have a ticket, so go over there right now and buy yourself one. Don't be sorry Saturday night that you didn't buy your tickets tonight! I'm going over there right now and buy my tickets. Let's support our firemen who protect us and our property all year round. Come on, now!"

He jumped down from the stake body of the truck and marched over to the car booth. A crowd followed him. The public address system filled the air with music from the record, "A Tisket, A Tasket, I Lost My Yellow Basket," and the carnival was in full swing.

"Ain't we gonna take any chances, Tadd?"

"Naw, leastways, not yet. I ain't moving from here until I have that five dollars pinned up there at the top of that there pole."

"Well, I've got three cents. I'm going over to the penny booth and see what I can do."

"Go ahead," Tadd said, "but I'm staying put until after this here greasy pole climb."

I made my way over to the penny booth. I put my first penny on number seven because I read somewhere that number seven was an ancient, lucky number. The man behind the booth spun the wheel after four or five of us laid down our money. The wheel stopped on number fourteen. Nobody was home on that number. I stuck with my number seven. The lady next to me put her penny on number fourteen. I guess she thought if it stopped there once, it could stop there again. This time the wheel halted on number two. No winner again. I was determined. I placed my last penny on number seven. He gave the wheel a good hard spin. I thought to myself there couldn't be anything crooked about that since I couldn't see any wires or brakes to stop the wheel. The women next to me played number six and sure enough it stopped on six. She let out a squeal that would have put any pig to shame. She selected as her prize a can of applesauce. I wandered back to where Tadd was waiting.

"Win anything?" he greeted me.

"Naw," I said and added quickly, "but I didn't really try."

"You played your pennies, didn't you?"

"Yeah, all three of 'em."

"Well, that's trying, ain't it?"

"In a way, I guess it is," I answered and let it go at that.

The Good Ol' Days

Charlie Lockerman was back on the truck body. He had that funny-looking mike in his hand and was blowing in it to see if it was on. "Well, folks, it's time for the greasy pole climb. Some lucky person is going to scale this pole smothered with grease and take home a crisp, new five dollar bill."

"And that's gonna be me," Tadd whispered in my ear, taking his right index finger and poking himself square in his belly.

"Gather round, folks," Charlie Lockerman said, not even taking time to catch his breath. "Let's watch and see who can scale this pole and get that greenback with old Abe Lincoln's picture on it. Now, who'll be the first to try?"

Tadd and I went right down in front of the truck body looking up at Charlie. "Now, here are two likely prospects. How about you Tadd?" Charlie's voice just boomed Tadd's name.

Tadd shook his head, but pointed to me.

"I ain't gonna try to climb that pole, Tadd. You are." I whispered to Tadd.

"Come on, now, Marshall, give it a try." Charlie's voice echoing all over the carnival ground.

"Come on, give it a try, Gandhi," Tadd said, "I'll give you a boost."

We walked over to the pole. All eyes followed us as if they were located in the sockets of one big head. Tadd stooped down real cautiously and I got on his shoulders. He boosted me up. I wrapped my arms around the pole. As I squeezed tight, I could feel that axle grease seeping clean through to my bare skin. I hugged and tugged, but to no avail. Some laughed. Others called out my name. Still others whistled. Tadd backed away from the pole, and I slid smack to the ground.

Two or three other boys tried. We didn't know them. They must have been strangers from another town. They had the same luck as I did.

All the while we were trying to climb the pole, Charlie Lockerman was making small talk through the mike he held in his hand as if it were his magic wand that wafted him to prominence.

"All right, boys," he boomed, "who's next? Just think, now.

There's a new five dollar bill waiting for you up there." He pointed to the top of the pole that appeared like it was as tall as the Empire State Building.

Tadd looked at me and I looked right back at him as Martin Short stalked up. He had a tantalizing grin on his face as if to say, "Let me at it. I can do it. I've done it before."

Tadd and I held our breath. Martin made slow movements. His lean body inched up the pole. Even the people watching stopped feeding their mouths for a second. Up he climbed. It looked as if he were going to the top. Then he began to slip, but he gripped the pole tighter and held fast. Slowly, he moved toward the top. He was about four feet from the five dollar bill.

"Think he'll make it, Tadd?"

"I'm praying he won't," Tadd spoke back to me without bothering to take his eyes off of Martin.

Then Martin reached out to see if he could grasp the money and when he did he lost his grip and came sliding to the ground.

Tadd was right there to make his try.

"All right, folks," Charlie prattled through the mike, "let's see if Tadd can make it. This isn't easy, you know. We used over five pounds of axle grease on that pole. It's greased really good."

Tadd moved even slower than Martin had. He gripped that pole like he would squeeze the juice right out of it. Now, he was over halfway up. It might have been my imagination, but it seemed to me that everybody standing around had stopped breathing. Even the merry-go-round music had ceased. All eyes focused on Tadd. He didn't reach out like Martin had for he was determined not to lose his grip. Like a cat on electric pole wires, he made his way up the greased, stripped tree pole, slowly and lingeringly. Another foot or so to go and he would make it. I had my fingers crossed hoping against hope that those thumbtacks would hold out. I threw my conscience to the wind. Just a little longer, anyway. I watched him grip the pole in a bear hug with his right arm; and with a slow deft outreach of his left arm, he lifted it toward the top of the pole. We all gasped as if in one breath. The bystanders roared a loud cheer. He made it. The five-dollar bill was lodged safely in his hand. And he made his oily descent to the ground. There was applause. I was real proud. I knew he could do it.

"He made it folks. Tadd Tobin wins the greasy pole climb. Make way for the winner, folks. Come up here, Tadd. Tell us what you are going to do with the five dollars you just won." Charlie Lockerman shoved the mike against Tadd's lips.

Tadd scratched his head with his greasy fingers and looked out across the sea of faces and said through the mike, "I'm gonna spend it."

Everybody laughed and broke up once again into little groups, loitering about the booths of blankets, candies, groceries, and money.

Charlie boomed through the mike again, "Now, folks, don't forget the Bingo stand. There you can win some real fine gifts. Lamps, stuffed animals, yes, even money. Over to the Bingo stand, folks, for the next game is free. That's right. Free. Come on now and win yourself a mighty nice prize."

There was a mad scramble for the Bingo stand. Everybody's mother, uncle, brother, and sister were seated at the Bingo stand waiting for their free card and a handful of corn.

"Let's head on home, Gandhi, before we might take a notion to spend some of this here five dollars."

"Okay, Tadd," I said. "I'm too greasy to stay around here anyway. I feel like I've been rubbed down with a dozen jars of Vaseline."

"What do you say we take another swim to get all cleaned up?" Tadd suggested.

"Good idea. I feel squishy all over."

We cut across the field behind the school and made our way to the swimming hole. We shed our clothes faster than a butterfly does its cocoon and were soon splashing around in the refreshing pond water.

"You said you'd do it, Tadd. And by gum, you did."

"Gandhi, I don't believe you thought I could do it. Now did you?"

"Well, I guess I did have a little sliver of doubt. But that don't matter now. You done got it. And that's what's important. What're you gonna do with it?"

"You know what I'm gonna do with it," Tadd shot back to me through the night. "I'm gonna buy grub for our cruise, that's what."

"I feel pretty clean now. How about you?" I asked.

"Sure do," Tadd agreed. "Nothing beats the swimming hole for a bath."

We wiped off our bodies the best we could with our hands to dry ourselves. There wasn't any sun to do the job for us. As we parted for home at the church corner, Tadd called out, "Don't forget, I'll meet you right here at the break of dawn."

"I won't forget," I promised. Ever since there had been a carnival and ever since I could remember, Tadd and I made it our ritual to go out to the carnival grounds the next morning after every carnival night to scavenger around. We found all sorts of things. One time we reaped a dollar bill, but usually we picked up a comb with all its teeth intact or a Canadian penny or a tie clasp. Once we found a pair of women's blue garters. I wanted to hang them up in our clubhouse, but Tadd decided it wouldn't be right. He said he wouldn't want somebody else to find our mother's garters and hang them up in their clubhouse. This made sense, so we threw them away.

FRIDAY NIGHT, TADD AND I WERE ON HAND AT THE CARNIVAL. We hadn't missed a night, and we never failed to search the grounds early every morning. The trough of money hidden in pounds of meal was something new, and we were anxious to try our luck. At that moment, we were as happy as a dog finding a new fire hydrant.

Charlie Lockerman was at his usual stand, there on the truck body with a mike in his hand. But that night, he had his handkerchief wrapped around the mike. He explained to us that his handkerchief around it helped keep down the squeaking, but it didn't. "Listen, folks, tonight we'll try something new. Anyone can enter this contest. As you can see," he made a grand gesture with his hand, sweeping it toward the trough there on the truck body, "this trough is full of good old hog meal. But in that hog meal is over twenty dollars in coins. Now, who'll be the first to try? Oh, oh, here's the winner of the greasy pole climb. How about you, Tadd? And Marshall? That's right boys, jump right up here beside me. Now, don't start until I give the signal. Who else will try their luck? Keep your hands out of the trough, boys. That isn't the way it's done. All right, step right up here. That's it, Martin. Take it easy now. Save your strength to get yourself some money. Is there a lady here who would like to try for the money? Don't be bashful now, ladies. Are you going to let the boys and men outshine you? How about you, Mabel? Come on. There's nothing in there that's going to bite you. Here, give me your hand. That's it. Upsy daisy."

Charlie talked on and on through his handkerchief covered mike, never stopping for his second breath. And the way he could talk on, I wondered where he ever got his first breath.

"Are we all here? Let's see." Charlie was busy arranging us around the trough. We were all lined up side by side. He never ceased to talk, although he was busy getting us situated on each side of the trough. "Now, we can take three more. Who will it be? Come on, Jim. You can use some spending money, can't you? Hoist him up here, boys. Now, you contestants do not start until I give you the signal. Otherwise, you will be disqualified. Do you hear? Hey, Harry, come here and give me a hand with this contest, will you? You know what to do, don't you? Did they tell you? Here, you start on this side. Hey, Joe, we need your help here. I can't do everything. All right now, one more. Who will it be? Franklin, you look like a man who can find money easy enough. Come on, hop up here. That will just make it.

"Harry, have you started yet? Now listen, folks, gather around. You know that it would be too easy to just stand up here and reach in there with your hands and take the money. Now, wouldn't it?" The tight-packed faces about the truck body nodded their heads. "So," Charlie drawled out the word with a twisted grin from ear to ear, "each contestant will have his hands tied behind him, and he will root out the money from the meal with his mouth. He will not be able to use his hands at all. All the money he gets will have to be hoarded in his mouth. Now this is a fine looking bunch of hogs up here, don't you think, folks?" There was applause.

"No, you don't, Mabel. Get right back there. That's a good sport. This is all in fun, you know. Come on, Harry, start tying their hands behind them with that binder's twine there. Joe, you go on that side. That's it. How are we doing now? Remember, if anyone uses his hands, he's disqualified. Folks, don't go 'way. You're going to see the sight of your lives. Do you have them all tied, boys? All right, now to make this just as interesting as we can, I'm going to ask Harry and Joe to each take a box of lard and rub it on your faces. Now, be good sports. This is all in fun. We're here to have a good time. No, Mabel, lard won't hurt your complexion. Hold still everybody while Harry and Joe gets your faces good and covered with the lard. Stand still, Marshall, I'm sure you've had worse than lard on your face."

By the time my face and ears and even my hair were all greased up with that lard, I was wishing I hadn't volunteered. But we needed money for our cruise, so I stood still while Mr. Harry smeared me with a thick coating of lard, which seemed to go right up my nose.

"All ready now?" Charlie gloated at the bound victims. "When I say 'go' I want you all to root in that meal like you've never rooted before and get your mouths as full of money as can hold. Ready? One. Two. Three. Go!"

Those standing round about screamed, whopped, whistled, and cheered their favorite contestant, like we were racehorses or something. My eyes got so full of meal that I could barely see them wide open. I thought to myself that the firemen had certainly spread out the coins because they were few and far between. Every one of us wore faces covered with meal. Such coughing and spitting. And it was difficult to do, too, because you had to keep the coins in your mouth. Tadd and I steeled our minds with determination to hold in our mouths every coin we rooted out of the meal. Nothing, but nothing, would make us cough or spit out a solitary coin.

The music from the merry-go-round and the record player blared forth an awful racket, but we continued to root for money with our greasy mouths in the trough of meal. I didn't have time to look at Tadd to see how he was making out since I was busy thrashing about myself.

Finally, Charlie Lockerman shouted through his mike, "Time. All right, Harry, you untie that row. Joe, you untie this row. How are you doing, folks? Quite a game, wasn't it? Now, let's see what you've done. Mabel, you're first. Show us how much you've got And let's go right around the trough. Each contestant shout out the amount of money they rooted out of the trough."

Miss Mabel counted her money and in a disappointed voiced called out, "Eleven cents." All around each contestant divulged his remunerative reward. Between Tadd and me, we chewed out the trough of meal eighty-seven cents.

The crowd gave us a round of applause and went about their business of trying to win things for themselves.

Mr. Charlie Lockerman gave paper napkins to each of us to wipe our faces clean. They crumpled up and tore into tiny bits, but he gave us all the napkins we needed to get the worst of the lard off our faces and out of our hair.

"You were all fine sports," he said to us and this time not speaking through the mike, which he laid on the top of the trucks' cab. "Now, go and spend your money and win yourself some fine prizes."

I looked at Tadd. "Are you gonna try the money wheel?"

"Maybe we could try a quarter's worth. What do you say?

"It's ten cents a chance, ain't it?" I asked. "Maybe we ought to try thirty cents worth."

"Okay."

We shifted from the money trough to the money wheel, lorded over by Billy Trice.

"Who's gonna play the money?" I asked.

"I'll do it, if you want," Tadd said, not waiting to find out whether I wanted him to or not. Three spins of the big wheels and we had lost thirty cents of our eighty-seven cents. We had only fifty-seven cents left. We decided it best to go home.

CHAPTER 8

We yearned to smell the salt air and breathe in the scent of marshland. Lewiston was close enough to the bay that when the wind blew in from the east, the sea breezes would roll over us with a delicious tang of freshness. We were gripped with an anxious expectancy and longed to taste the sweetness of anticipated adventures.

On each side of Main Street, the leaves on the trees were aflame with sunlight as Tadd, Skipper, and I walked downtown with five dollars and fifty-seven cents in Tadd's pocket. An old lop-eared hound was drooping along on the other side of the street. Skipper barked at him. There was something uppermost in our minds and that was the thought of a sea voyage. At least, our idea of a sea voyage, since we would only sail on the crick and just pretend it was the sea. The low branches of the trees shrouded the houses in protective shadows and strangely intermingled with streaks of sunlight. Our whole being drank in the beauty of the fresh newborn day. And for the past three weeks there had not been enough rain to slake the thirst of the dry ground. The gears of our imagination needed the oil from the tales of Capt'n Lacey.

As we made our way down the hill toward the wharf, we spied Miss Bloomery who always bore an air-conditioned conscience punched through and through with a capital "I." To evade her inquisitive tongue, we walked to the other side of the street and quickened our pace. We did not want our morning spoiled by her asking a mountain high pile of questions from us.

The Good Ol' Days

She called out, "Good morning, boys. Where are you going? I was wondering...."

Tadd interrupted, "Morning, Miss Bloomery. We're going downtown."

And we started to run. Skipper was close at our heels.

Soon our feet were on the thick, weather-beaten boards of the wharf. Tadd boomed in a loud voice through his cupped hands about his mouth, "Hello, Capt'n Lacey!"

Capt'n Lacey poked his head out of the hatchway and his silvery hair was all combed with not a strand out of place. "Come around, boys. The coffee pot is on." The Captain was in a blustering, expansive mood. I could tell by the ring in his voice.

We leaped first on the rail of the boat and then on the deck for the tide was out and the Marie Tomas was floating about four feet below the level of the dock. Skipper made his way on board by jumping on the bow first, walking the rail, and then dropping down into the cockpit by us.

Inside the cabin, Capt'n Lacey greeted us. "Well, boys, when is the big day?"

Tadd, as usual, was quick on response, "Tomorrow, maybe, if we can round up all our stores. Right, Gandhi?"

I nodded my head and scratched behind Skipper's ears all at the same time. Capt'n Lacey stretched for two more mugs in the rack on the port side bulkhead and poured our coffee. Taking wee sips of coffee, we looked at Capt'n Lacey. He had shaved that morning as we could plainly see and was cleanly groomed. Capt'n Lacey was a pert man for his age and always admonished us that cleanliness was next to godliness, although he didn't bother to worship God, that is, in church. But somehow this morning, he didn't appear well. And he hadn't been in his cups for a week or more. Maybe he just looked that way from the effects of his last drinking spree. Anyway, he seemed his old self and a twinkle filled his eyes as he surveyed us, all the while knowing what we were going to do come tomorrow.

"Boys, I was figuring to draw you a course on the chart and let you take it with you. But then I got to thinking that if I did chart your course, it would take the adventure out of your cruise. So I decided against it. You'd best learn on your own. That way you're not liable to forget so easy. That all right with you?"

"You bet!" was Tadd's lightning reply. "But if you got any advice, Capt'n, we're willing to listen." That was Tadd's way of getting any information or help or advice he could from Capt'n Lacey for he respected him as I did. We both hoped he would give us some direction or information that would prove helpful on our anticipated cruise.

The Captain smiled, stroked his chin, and said over a silvery cloud of smoke from his pipe, "Tadd, my boy, advice is the cheapest thing in the world. It don't cost a cent and is worth just as much. No, I ain't gonna hand you no advice. We've had many talks together, and I believe that you boys are sensible enough to take this trip. You know that on the water you never take chances or leave anything to luck. I've done told you that many times over. The captain of an ocean vessel or a raft has the full responsibility for the safety of his ship and passengers. By the way, who is to be the captain?"

Tadd looked at me and waited for my answer. I said what he expected. "Tadd will be the captain. I'll be the first mate. And Skipper can be the deck hand."

Capt'n Lacey laughed. "That's all right. But for any kind of craft on water there must be someone in command. There ain't no room for two bosses on board ship." His words were hard as bullets.

"Capt'n Lacey," I asked, "what kind of stores do you think we ought to take?"

"Mostly canned goods, Gandhi. Fresh goods spoil mighty fast in salt air. Now, I'd take some apples and peaches and grapes and eat 'em first off. But your canned goods will be your staples on board."

"How's about making a list for our stores right now, Capt'n?" Tadd asked.

"Good idea, Tadd," I chimed in for Capt'n Lacey knew more about food stuff you should take on a cruise than we did since he had years of experience of living on the water. Capt'n Lacey fetched a pencil and paper and gave it to Tadd.

"First off," Tadd began, "we'll be needing plenty of drinking water."

"I wouldn't overstock yourself with water," Capt'n Lacey advised. "If you run short, you could put into shore and go up to any of the farm houses along the way. They'll be glad to let you fill your jugs.

"How many jugs then?" I asked.

"I'd say two one-gallon jugs ought to be enough," Capt'n Lacey suggested.

Tadd wrote down at the head of the list: Two one-gallon jugs.

"How long will you be gone?" asked the Captain.

"About a month," Tadd said right off.

"Ain't that kinda long?" I wondered out loud with much concern.

"Do your folks know you're going?" asked the Captain.

"Yeah, we told 'em we were going on a camping trip, being we won all that money at the carnival," answered Tadd.

"How long did you tell them you'd be gone?" inquired the Captain.

"We didn't rightly say, did we, Gandhi?"

"Nope, we just said we was going camping. I reckon they'll be glad to be shed of us from underfoot for a spell."

"Don't you think they'd worry if you were gone a whole month?" Capt'n Lacey posed a question that we hadn't considered or paid much mind to. We just wanted to get going without too much fuss.

"Guess you're right," Tadd agreed. "Maybe two weeks would be long enough. Okay, Gandhi?"

"That sounds all right with me," I said with relief.

"It's settled then. Two weeks. Okay. How much grub will that take?" Tadd wet the lead of the pencil with his tongue like he had seen the Captain do many times over.

"Fourteen days," I said. "Let's see. How about fifteen cans of potted meat? One extra can, just in case."

"Yeah, that sounds good," commented Tadd, writing down on paper. Fifteen cases of potted meat.

"Do you boys like baked beans?" Capt'n Lacey asked.

"Love 'em" was my reply.

"Fifteen cans of baked beans?" Tadd scratched his head as if he thought that fifteen cans of beans was too many.

Capt'n Lacey threw in the remark, "Won't hurt to have 'em on hand."

Tadd added fifteen cans of baked beans to his list, although I thought I saw doubt dancing in his eyes. I had seen his eyes like that before when we were considering a huge undertaking, but he included the beans.

"You like applesauce, Gandhi?" Tadd asked.

"Yeah."

"Six cans of applesauce," Tadd spoke aloud as he wrote it down under the list of baked beans.

"How about some cans of Spam?" I was thinking it would be good to have enough meat and even some left over for Skipper. He had to eat, too.

"Spam," Tadd jotted down under the applesauce.

"Boys, it might be good to have a few boxes of raisins along," the Captain always had helpful suggestions. I guess he had done some things like this when he was a kid. The expression on his face showed glee, and I knew he was happy for us and our plans.

"Raisins," Tadd uttered aloud as he wet his pencil again with his tongue and wrote "raisins" under Spam.

"Don't forget toilet paper. That's a handy item." Capt'n Lacey chuckled.

Our list grew as we shared our ideas with one another. We even listed the few essentials for a small medicine kit like Raleigh's ointment, band aids, iodine, tweezers and scissors, and some safety pins, just in case.

After we had almost filled the piece of paper with the names of stores we thought we would need, Tadd said, "Now, we'd better go to Mr. Mason to add up all this. We might not have enough money. If we don't, then we'll cut out what we think ain't important."

"Tadd and Gandhi, I wish I was going with you. Just sitting here with you boys and going over this list of stores brings back some mighty fond memories for me," the Captain spoke reflectively.

The Good Ol' Days

"Why not? Come on and go, Capt'n. Be glad to have you aboard," Tadd spoke from his heart and mine, too.

"No, that wouldn't be right, boys. And besides I'm too old for that sort of thing now. I've had my fun. You have yours, and you store up summer memories for your old age."

"What is memory, anyhow?" I asked.

Capt'n Lacey drew long puffs on his pipe and smoke clouds spiraled overhead. "Mostly," he said, "it's our mental pocket where we carry important collateral."

"Like something you can spend?"

He nodded his head, clenching his pipe between his teeth and speaking all at the same time, "Yes, like something you can spend, over and over again."

"That's good," I said, "then I hope Tadd and me have a lot of memories so's we'll have plenty to spend."

Capt'n Lacey had a blissful smile on his face; his eyes were afire. He grasped his pipe and poked it upward as he looked upward and said reflectively, "If memories were truly money, I'd be a multimillionaire."

He blinked his eyes, shook his head as if coming out of a sleep, and said, "Well, boys, you'd best scuttle over to Mr. Mason's and check up on your stores." He didn't get up and follow us out on deck like he usually did, but I guess he was tired. He just sat there on the bunk and smiled to us as we took our leave.

Mr. Mason was a kind man and seemed very understanding. He always had a deep regard for Tadd and me, especially since the flood. "What can I do for you this morning, boys?" Mr. Mason smiled as he greeted us.

"We'd like you to do some figuring for us, if you ain't too busy," Tadd asked him.

"Come right on into the back room," Mr. Mason said, ushering us up to his big roll top desk in the back room behind the meat counter.

Tadd pulled the list of our stores from his shirt pocket and handed it to Mr. Mason. "How much do you think all this will cost?"

Mr. Mason put on his glasses that slid down his nose and rested at the very top of his nostrils. "Let's see." He took a pencil from his desk and began to figure each item. He mumbled to himself all the while he was figuring. At last he had it. "Six dollars and ninety cents."

I spoke up. "Mr. Mason, can you trim it down to five dollars and fifty-seven cents?"

Mr. Mason smiled and said, "That shouldn't be too much trouble. Yes, I think I can do that. May I ask, boys, if you are going on a camping trip?"

"Yes, sir, that's right," Tadd put in quickly before I could answer.

Mr. Mason looked over the rim of his glasses at the figures on our store list. I wondered why he did that while still wearing his glasses, but I didn't say anything. Finally, he turned and looked at us, still peeping over the rim of his glasses.

"Boys, it appears that I've made a mistake in my figuring. The amount is only five dollars and fifty cents. Let's just make it five dollars even. Okay?"

"Okay!" we both cried with glee.

"Do you have a wooden box we could put our stores in, Mr. Mason?" Tadd asked.

"I think I have just the thing," Mr. Mason replied, walking back behind the meat counter and through the door to the storeroom. He emerged with a large, empty, wooden apple box. "How's this?" he asked, holding it up for us to see.

"That's the ticket!" I exclaimed. "Just the very thing."

We pitched in and helped Mr. Mason pack our stores in the wooden box. I noticed six cans of dog food that we hadn't ordered, and I was going to say something but on second thought, I kept quiet wondering if Mr. Mason just gave them to us for Skipper. He loved Skipper, too, and he always had bones for him whenever I asked for them. Mr. Mason was a good, generous man, and we loved him. He always treated us fair and square, and we would do anything for him that we could. I blurted out from the very depth of my heart, "Thanks a million, Mr. Mason. We're obliged to you." I was bubbling over with thanksgiving.

We toted the box between us as we made our way down to the wharf. It was heavy, and we grunted noises like a goose flying in a winter against a strong, biting wind. Capt'n Lacey was on board the Marie Tomas as if he were waiting just for us. The old boat seemed to be wearing a new shine in the still heat of the sun, although she was aged and had to be caulked and painted every year.

"Ship ahoy, boys. Here let me help you. We'll just set this here box on the motor cover while you best go home and pack your duds."

"We got 'em on," I said to jog the Captain's memory.

"You mean you ain't going to take any extra clothes?" The Captain asked as if he didn't understand. And that wasn't like him.

"We don't need no more," Tadd put in. And that made sense to me.

"Well, boys, far be it from me to tell you what to take and to do, but it 'pears to me you oughta take an extra pair of pants and a shirt just in case you get washed overboard, accidentally like."

I looked at Tadd, hoping he would come up with an answer because I had none.

"Guess that ain't such a bad idea, after all. What do you think, Gandhi?" Tadd's voice was filled with doubt, and it sent some distress in me. I didn't want to be washed overboard and maybe out to sea.

I didn't see any sense in burdening ourselves with a mess of clothes, but one pair of pants and a shirt weren't too much so I said, "Guess not, if you say so."

"Then let's carry an extra pair of pants and a shirt. Just in case," Tadd suggested.

I shrugged my shoulders and followed Tadd. Skipper was at our heels. "See you in a minute, Capt'n," I called back over my shoulder. "We gotta go home and get our duds."

"I'll be right here, boys," Capt'n Lacey answered as he waved his hand toward us.

We wasted no time in walking up the hill. I turned at the church corner for home, and Tadd moved faster toward his house. It wasn't more than two minutes before Tadd and I met at the church corner again with the front of our shirts bulging. You see, we both had the same idea, unbeknownst to each of us. We had stuffed a pair of pants and a shirt underneath the shirt we were wearing so nobody could see what we were up to. We didn't want to tell the whole town what we were going to do 'cause we didn't think it was any of their business.

Skipper was panting, as we made our way as quickly as possible back down the hill. It wasn't going down the hill that made him pant. It was the hot, sticky day that was pressing in against us from all sides making us feel like we had been shoved into a hot oven.

I turned to Tadd and remarked, "I can't wait to get on that raft, Tadd. Can you?"

"Nope. But it won't be long now."

When we arrived at the wharf, Capt'n Lacey was sitting on the stern of the Marie Tomas, and I could have sworn that I saw lines of pain scratched all over his face. But then again, maybe it was just my imagination trying to play tricks on me. The Captain was a robust man, full of vim and vigor. Now he was a man you could love and respect for what he was. Tadd and I had a very high regard for him. In fact, we looked on him as our second father.

It seemed we all three jumped on board at one time like a trumpet player pushing down the three valves of his horn with the palm of his hand.

"Boys, I think you ought to have something to eat before you shove off. Come on below. Let me see what I can rustle up." The Captain motioned for us to follow him. He moved slower than I had ever seen him move before. Somehow, I sensed that things were not right for the Captain. *Could he have a deadly disease? God forbid!* My thoughts jumped from thought-pole to thought-pole, fast and furious. I was in a quandary. My imagination drew weird pictures of the Captain's state of being. Or was I just conjuring up false images? I prayed that was what I was doing.

"Capt'n," I began, "let Tadd and me take care of the grub. You sit down and take it easy. Tadd, grab them mugs and the coffee pot. I'll check in the ice chest. Okay, Capt'n?"

"Don't mind if I do, boys. To tell the truth, I ain't been feeling up to par lately." The Captain spoke with a sigh.

I had a funny feeling in my stomach. I couldn't help myself from speaking, and I turned to the Captain and said, "Capt'n Lacey, I've been noticing that you ain't your old self lately. And I've been wondering what might ail you. Have you been to the doctor?"

"Naw, it ain't nothing serious. I guess I'm just getting old and can't take it anymore," Capt'n Lacey said with a grin. But somehow his grin didn't seem real to me. It lacked its sturdy strength.

Tadd turned and gave me a dirty look. "Gandhi, there must be something ailing you. Why, I don't see nothing the matter with the Captain. He looks fit as a fiddle to me. Ain't that right, Capt'n?"

"Right you are, Tadd. I guess I'm just a little tired. Been trying to do too much lately. Now, don't you boys go worrying over me, 'cause I'm old enough to take care of myself. Hurry up with that grub, Gandhi. You sure are a slow poke."

I knew I was right in my thinking, and that Tadd and the Captain were trying to cover up something. Well, maybe Tadd didn't know or didn't see the Captain as I did, but the Captain understood my concern. And yet, he gave off the strange scent of the sea, which was a luxury to our nostrils.

We sat down and ate and drank our coffee. It sure was good. After we had eaten, the Captain asked Tadd to get his tobacco tin. He filled his pipe, and we were all enveloped by a tender coziness in the cabin of the Marie Tomas.

We didn't rush for there was no need to, we had all the time in the world. It was a grand feeling. Expelling my breath, I swept away all my doubts.

Finally, Tadd suggested, "What do you say, Gandhi, shall we shove off?"

"That's what I've been waiting to hear. Up and at 'em." I put a smile on my face.

"Thanks, Capt'n, for the grub and everything." Tadd spoke for us since we both possessed keen appetites and empty hands.

"You're welcome, boys. This is my home, and you're welcome on board anytime. And remember, gratitude is the fragrance of noble souls. Use it often," replied the Captain with sincerity. I read a warning gleam in his eye when he said, "God speed, boys. Don't take any chances. And have fun!"

"Thank you, Capt'n," I answered. "We aim to have a swell time."

Capt'n Lacey came out on deck and watched us as we loaded the rowboat with our box of food. Skipper jumped into the boat. I stashed our fishing gear on the starboard side while Tadd put the oars in the oar locks. I untied the line, waved to Capt'n Lacey, and shoved off. He seemed to have moist eyes, but I wasn't sure. Maybe he got some kind of particles in his eyes that could have made them run. I had an inner concern for Capt'n Lacey, but I didn't know what it was.

"So long, Capt'n. See you in a couple of weeks," my voice carried my inner feelings, which rang with a vibrant urgency.

"So long, boys. Good luck." Capt'n Lacey saluted us as Tadd pulled deep, long strokes on the oars. All too soon we were around the bend and the trees blocked our view of Capt'n Lacey and the Marie Tomas. Somehow, I was in no hurry to lose sight of the Captain.

"Tadd," I said. "didn't you see some difference in Capt'n Lacey? I mean, he ain't acting like he used to. Didn't you notice nothing?"

"Yeah," Tadd answered. "I seen it. But, you dumb bunny, it ain't polite to tell people they don't look good or they look sick. That's why I lied and said that he looked fine."

We didn't say anything for a while. We had our own inside thoughts to ponder on, and we prevailed on the silence to think about them. Then Tad spoke, "Don't you go worrying now about Capt'n Lacey. As he said, he can take care of himself. He's been doing it all these years, ain't he?"

"Yep, guess you're right." I sat for a few minutes more on the stern just thinking. Then I said, "Let's take a vow, Tadd, that we're just going to have fun on this trip and that's all."

"Right," Tadd said, holding the oars with his left hand while he stuck out his right hand, and we shook hands with our secret grip.

We backed in toward the high land, and there floated our raft riding softly at anchor. It was a beautiful sight for sore eyes. We were proud of her for she was the work of our hands and that made our chests swell somewhat.

We tied our skiff to the raft and quickly began transferring our gear from the boat to the raft. We didn't talk. We knew what had to be done and we did it.

Aboard the raft, Tadd called out in an Admiral-like voice, "Cast off!"

"Aye, aye, sir," I felt the nautical jive in my bones. I was tingling all over with excitement and anticipation.

I untied the raft from the big oak tree, put one foot on board, and shoved off with the other foot from shore, leaping on the raft as she moved out like a lazy crocodile. Tadd manned the rudder at the stern of the raft. Skipper took his station at the bow as if he were a lookout scout in a crow's nest. I busied myself lashing down the gear to keep it from being lost overboard.

"Grab that pole, Gandhi, and push us out into the crick. The tide'll take us from there." That was Tadd talking now, and his voice sounded more like himself.

I didn't answer but squeezed our long pole and began pushing with all my might toward the mainstream of the creek. Once I almost lost our pole because it stuck deep in the slimy mud below. We moved silently and slowly past the green edges of the pine trees and finally made it midstream of the creek. A light gentle breeze stirred. The puffy clouds were the color of glistening slate. The warm scent of the sea caressed our faces with its soft brilliance. We were exhilarated to be on our way at last. It made us feel good all over.

"Hoist sail!" Tadd commanded in his Admiral voice.

An eddy of soft, sudden wind drummed over the sheltered waters and spun us forward. I hoisted sail. I tied the halyards to the spar and turned to Tadd at the rudder, "Tadd this ain't no luxury liner or pirate ship. Now, fun is fun, but too much is none.

"What on earth are you talking about, Gandhi?"

"You know what I'm talking about, Tadd Tobin."

"Didn't Capt'n Lacey say there must be one in command aboard any vessel at sea?" His talent for seamanship appeared raw and undisciplined to me. In fact, I was bristling with anger.

I threw him a rejoinder. "Tadd Tobin, we ain't at sea. We're just floating down this dirty, smelly, slimy-coated crick. Now, hop off your high horse and let's be buddies like we really are."

Tadd chuckled, "Gandhi, buddy, take it easy. Don't get your dander up. Remember we took a pledge and sealed it with our secret grip to have fun on this here trip." He let go of the rudder and came towards me, hugging me and messing up my hair at the same time. His face was wreathed in smiles. I smiled, gave him a gentle shove and messed up his hair, too. That was our way of making up with each other. As Skipper barked, we looked around. We were heading straight for a bunch of unripe Ned cattails. Tadd lost no time in moving the rudder full to the starboard to keep us from getting bogged down this early in the journey. The blazing glare of the hot sun reflecting back at us caused us to remove our shirts and pants. We donned our lone pair of shorts and felt much more comfortable and at ease. We were underway, and joy and happiness filled our hearts.

Our sail began to flutter for the wind had died down considerably. We would have to depend on the current alone. I lowered the sail, and tied it and the boom to the mast. I sat down to relax.

"Gandhi, how's about taking over the helm for a minute?" Tadd asked me that question in his own voice again, not that Admiral tone. I preferred his own voice because then I knew he was his old self and not some put-on other person. He could get that way now and then, and I didn't like it when he put on airs. No sir, not one minute, did I like it.

"Just a minute," I said, "and I'll be right with you." I had a warm feeling toward Tadd like he could have been my blood brother.

The silence of the vast sky pressed us into the shadowy land of communication. Mind you, we didn't say anything that you could sink your teeth in. We just talked about things that struck our fancy at the time. Sometimes when we talked like that, Tadd would say things that I didn't understand. He'd just let out a fragrance, and I'd have to smell his meaning for myself. Once in a while he would say things to me that were annoying and useless as fleas, but I didn't care. We drifted downstream until about high noon, or so it seemed, for the sun was almost directly overhead.

The Good Ol' Days

My stomach felt like it was gnawing on my backbone so I asked, "Tadd, are we going to stop to eat or keep moving?"

With a hard right rudder and pushing with all my might on the long pole, we made it to the port bank. Skipper was the first to alight and seek the closest tree. I jumped ashore with a towline in my hand and secured our raft to an aged stump. Tadd searched through our box of stores and brought out two cans of potted meat and some crackers to share for our lunch.

"Ain't this the life?" I greeted him, as I lie stretched out on the pine needle bed with my head cradled in my cupped hands while my body drank in the secrets of the woods and sky.

"It sure is," Tadd agreed. "Likely as not, we'll take to this life so well that we'll keep right on going and not ever come back to Lewiston. We'll head south in the winter taking the inland waterway to Florida. At night, we'll travel, so's no truant officer or some such monster can see us, and we'll sleep and eat during the day. Ain't no use going back to school. I know all I want to know. How about you?"

"You're absolutely right," I assured him. "We ain't in no need of any school. That's for educating people to go to college, and I'm as close to college right now as I want to be. I can read and write and do a little figuring. That's all you need to know, ain't it?"

"Sure it is. Look at all the great men of history. They weren't for digging education. Jesus didn't go to college. Neither did George Washington or Abraham Lincoln or any of the presidents. They was too busy learning things. That's why they didn't go to school. I hate school! Don't you Gandhi? Let's take an oath that we'll never go to school no more and then we can learn like the other great men. Maybe one of us might even make president of the United States."

We indulged right then and there in the time honored custom of shaking hands with our secret grip. We lay back down on the pine boards and basked in the reflected glory we thought we'd have when each of us would become president of the United States. Finally after we had dreamed awhile about being president, we sat up and ate our lunch.

While we were eating, a boat skimmed by. It was Mr. Carey

Pennevil. I guess he had been fishing in the bay since early morning and was heading back to port. He waved a silent greeting to us, and we waved back. There's an unwritten code on the water that makes you want to be friendly. It could be the salty air, the fresh, crisp breeze or the feeling of need for one another or a common fear of the water that's bigger and stronger than any of us. Anyway, it gives you a good feeling to wave to people even if you don't know them.

"Where do you 'spect we'll spend the night?"

Tadd put his hands behind his head as he lie back down and spoke, "Don't know. Don't care. How 'bout you?"

"Same feeling," I said.

After a few moments of silence, I popped Tadd a question, "Tadd, what kinda man do you really suppose ole Squire Hazzard is?"

"Why are you asking?" He didn't bother to turn his head toward me when he spoke, but just rested his head in his clasped hands and his eyes drank in the treetops and sky above.

"No reason," I replied, "Just want to talk 'bout something."

Tadd turned to me and said, "I think ole Squire has a God complex or something 'cause he thinks the world can't move on without him. Remember the flood? That should of taught him a lesson, but it didn't."

"I don't follow you, Tadd," I said looking him straight in the eye as I always do when we talked seriously.

"Well," Tadd drawled, "I mean that he's the kind of man who thinks that every bright idea he has was put in his skull by God Almighty."

"Has he ever had any bright ideas, Tadd?"

"None that I know of."

We sat quietly and contentedly for a while. Since we were talking about people, I thought of another one. I broke the silence. "How's about old Darby Baynum? Ain't he a skinflint? And him working in the bank, handling all that money. You'd think it would make him more generous, wouldn't you? I've heard tell that he always walks on the shady side of the street and never on the sunny side for fear his shadow might pop up and ask him for a match. Why, he's so tight, he squeaks."

Tadd shook his head, "He sure is. I've heard tell he possesses a strong insulation against the cry of the poor."

I pushed the conversation further because I was actually enjoying tearing old skinflint Baynum apart with words. "He can't even speak one sentence without referring to himself. Didn't Capt'n Lacey say that old Baynum's disease was 'meism,' and it was eating his innards right out of him?"

"Yep, that's what he said all right. Boy, that Capt'n is a noble man, ain't he?"

"He sure is," I agreed and began thinking to myself how Capt'n Lacey was getting on with his health. I was really concerned about him 'cause when we left he didn't look none too good.

Skipper got up from his sleeping place and walked over to us, sniffing around like if he could talk he would say, "Let's go."

I reached out and scratched behind his ears. "Tadd," I said, "supposing we'll make Parrott's Point tonight?"

"Don't know," he answered. "That's pretty far downstream. May make Hayes Landing, though. For sure we don't want to stay where there might be people who'll come snooping around."

I silently agreed with him by shaking my head and wondering where we would really land for the night.

"Ready to shove off?" he asked.

"Anytime." I let him know my feelings.

"Let's get underway."

Maybe Skipper couldn't talk, but he sure could understand what we were saying because he was the first one on board. I checked the knot on the line that secured our skill to the raft. It was okay. Then I untied the line that held our raft, used the pole to navigate us in midstream, and slowly we began to drift along with the outgoing tide.

"Shall I put up the sail, Tadd?"

"No use. There ain't a breath of air about. Look at that water. Not a ripple, just like a mirror. See them water bugs swimming around making little do-dads? Ain't that living?"

"Yeah," I said, "but they're just swimming around in circles like. But look at us, we're going somewhere. Right?"

"Right with Eversharp," Tadd agreed.

After a spell, Tadd said, "We sure ain't making no progress, but we're having a lot of fun."

"I know what, Tadd. Let's go swimming. Maybe after we have had a swim the wind might pick up. Okay?"

Before you could say Mispillion Lighthouse, Tadd dropped his shorts and drawers and plopped overboard. I threw out the anchor, dropped my pants and drawers, and joined him. The water smelled from the tomato factory in Lewiston which emptied its waste in the creek, but aside from that, the water felt cool to our hot bodies. The softness of summer flooded our hearts and we swam dizzily in the ecstasy of it all. Skipper couldn't resist jumping overboard with us and swimming around, all the while lapping that stinking water. I'm sure he wasn't drinking it 'cause it would have made him sick. Nonetheless, I got a tickle at the bottom of my stomach just by watching him.

Tadd crawled back on the raft and I did likewise and then helped Skipper on board. He shook three or four times right in our faces, but we didn't mind because we were wet anyhow. We just laid there and let the sun dry us. It was a delicious feeling, the kind you can't rightly put down in words. There are some indescribable feelings, and this was one of them. I was filled with a mysterious exhilaration. There was quietness and peace all about, and we savored the echoes of the happy hours.

Reluctantly, we donned our drawers and shorts and hauled up anchor. We had hoped for a breeze, but there wasn't one, and we had to be satisfied to drift with the tide which was moving at a snail's pace. That was for sure. We floated like a green leaf in a still pond and made no headway at all. But then again, we didn't really care because we were in no hurry with no particular place to go. Just living, real living.

"What'll we have for supper, Tadd?"

"If you ain't the beatingest one. Ain't been so long since we had our lunch. Now you're starting to worry 'bout supper. Boy, you must have a straight gut." Tadd spoke all in fun, but I knew it and didn't mind his joking one bit. In fact, I enjoyed his ribbing me, most of the time, that is.

"Aw, Tadd, I ain't really hungry. Leastwise, not at this very minute. I only wanted to make conversation, but if you don't feel like talking, then we'll just sit here and ponder."

"Let's ponder for a spell then," Tadd suggested, and I agreed.

We drifted slowlike with the tide providing weak energy to move our raft. It was a lazy time in the afternoon. We relished every minute of it, not caring whether we moved fast or slow. The important thing was just being where we were. Solid shadows lurked among the trees along the shoreline, and there was a lonely beauty about it all. Almost suddenlike we were surrounded by what appeared to be acres of fragrant thickets of blue and white flowers that shot up through the green finery of growing cattails. The huge quietness hugged us tight and it was too much for me. Why, there wasn't even a sea gull squawking or a crane flying under the naked sunlight. We had an easiness of desire that amounted to nothing really.

"Tadd, let's talk," I broke into our silence.

"What do you want to talk about?" Tadd still manned the tiller with his toes while he lay flat on his back.

"I don't know," was my honest reply, "but let's talk about something."

"You name it."

"Well," I began, "How about tonight? Are we gonna sleep on board or go ashore?"

"All depends," Tadd sure was short on words. He appeared to me like he had thinned out his thinking until he lost his main thought.

"Depends on what?" I was determined to keep the conversation rolling.

"Mosquitoes."

"Skeeters? They ain't that bad down here, are they? Did we bring any citronella?"

"Naw," Tadd said. "We ain't for wasting our money on stuff like that. We'll go ashore, but if the bugs are bad, we'll climb back on our raft and moor out aways. They ain't never as bad out on the water like they are on land."

"Good idea," I said that for want of something better to say.

Our chitchat bogged down again like walking in knee-deep mud with shoes and stockings on. Slow going for sure.

"What time is it, Gandhi?"

"I ain't got no watch, Tadd. Didn't you bring yours?"

"Oh, yeah, I forgot," Tadd remembered. "Look in my clothes roll, will you, and feel in my long pants pocket for my watch and see what time it is."

"Sure will," I said, ducking my head under the lean-to, finding his pants and pulling out the watch. "Quarter to six," I called out after scrutinizing Mickey Mouse's hands.

"It's about time we pulled in." The way Tadd always cocked his head in conversation lent a frisky air to every word he spoke and made it sound reckless.

I grabbed the pole and dipped it in the water, pushing us towards shore. It was slow going and it seemed the bottom was awfully muddy.

"There's Hayes Landing dead ahead, Gandhi. Let's move up close to there."

We took turns at the pole, pushing the raft toward the landing. I pushed awhile and Tadd steered. Then he pushed awhile and I manned the rudder. After working up a good sweat, we beached our raft. As usual, Skipper was the first off and darted for the nearest tree. I was next with a line in my hand and secured the raft to the same tree that Skipper christened 'cause it was the closest one. Tadd and I stretched our legs and stalked about the tree-covered shore like we were pilgrims setting foot on undiscovered land. But that wasn't really the case, for Hayes Landing was a sandy spot where folks came with their boats to go out on the bay for fishing, clamming, and crabbing.

"What do you want for supper, Tadd? Spam or potted meat?"

"Let's fry us up some Spam and taters. And you might as well open a can of them baked beans. We sure are loaded with them, so let's eat 'em." Tadd's voice was blunt with no spark in it.

"How's about you making the fire, and I'll get the vittles ready?" I ventured a directive to Tadd, wondering how he would take it, since he was the captain of our expedition.

"Will do," he answered, snapping to it like a hunter who cocks his gun with his bead on a running rabbit. I felt tremendously pleased with myself for making that suggestion, although I don't know why.

The food was tangy and tasty, even though I do say so myself. We ate out of our cooking pans and when we were finished, we washed them in the crick. We didn't say anything for a long spell; we just lay there savoring the joy of our adventure. Then Tadd thought of something.

"Gandhi, 'member that night we went out to that old graveyard in the woods back of the Camp Grounds?"

"Yeah, that was something wasn't it?" I chuckled as I spoke.

"Sure was," Tadd said. "Remember how I tore my pants the time I went there first by myself?"

"Sure do," I said and to make it more convincing I continued, "Didn't I see where you tore 'em clean down to your underwear?"

"Yep," Tadd agreed with me shaking his head. "Well, I never told you, but I went back there again even after you and me had been there."

"At night time?" was my surprised question.

"Nope," Tadd said. "Day time. And I spied a loose brick near the ladder. Now, that's how come I done tore my pants. My hip pocket got caught in that brick and when I put the pressure on to jump out of there, I ripped my pants."

"Well, I'll be a stinking polecat," was my flabbergasted reply. "And all the time we thought it was a ghost."

"Now, mind you. I ain't sure," Tadd wasn't for taking all the mystery out of our escapade. "I say, *maybe* that's what happened. I ain't sure 'cause I know there's a monster that lives in that tomb. We seen his bed, didn't we?"

I looked around me to make sure there weren't any monsters lurking in the shadows that were closing in on us quick-like. "Yep, we sure did see it." I thought a minute and said, "Tadd, let's talk about something else."

"You ain't skeered, are you?" Tadd was sneering at me now.

"Not exactly, but it ain't no use talking about ghosts and things when we're down here in these weeds by ourselves, is it?"

Tadd's face began to show that he wasn't too happy about the subject we were pursuing either.

"Let's put an extra line on our raft before we turn in, Gandhi. No telling how strong the current is here. Can't be too careful, you know."

I was glad Tadd began talking about something else, and I jumped right up and went to our raft. I secured a second line to the stern and tied it to another tree close by. Tadd came over to inspect and said, "That ought to do it." He took two blankets from the lean-to and walked over to our campsite.

"We gonna keep the fire going all night?" This was my idea.

"Ain't no use for that," Tadd assured me. "We'll be asleep before long and won't see it no how."

"You're right," I said. "Let's bed down and snatch some shut-eye so's we can get up early tomorrow and be on our way."

We rolled up in our blankets, but found it was too hot to have anything over us, so we just lay there in our shorts with no covering but the green treetops and the dark, soft night. I loved nighttime. It wrapped you in a mysterious glow and your imagination ran wild.

I soon discovered that sleep was slow in coming, "Tadd," I whispered, "are you asleep?"

"No," he whispered back, "and I ain't going to sleep if you keep working your jaws. Now, hush, and go to sleep."

I lay there with my eyes wide open, hoping against hope that I could go to sleep with them open. Suddenly, I heard a screech that sounded like a woman being murdered. I reached out my hand to touch Tadd, and when I did he jumped six inches from the ground. I supposed I startled him. I didn't mean to.

"Gandhi," he whispered louder, "don't do that. What do you want?"

"Didn't you hear it?" I asked in a low whisper.

"Sure I did. Ain't you never heard an owl before?"

"Oh."

"Go to sleep."

I tried to sleep, but my eyelids wouldn't shut. If I had some adhesive tape handy, I would have stuck them down on my cheekbones. But there weren't any, and my eyes were just like the ends of two coke bottles with the caps lost. After awhile I dropped off to sleep to be suddenly awaked with Tadd stomping about and yelling. I was on my feet before I could blink another eye.

"What in the tarnation, Tadd?"

"A poison snake!" he yelled. "Grab a stick!"

"Where is it?" I yelled.

"Coming right at you," he pointed to it.

My feet and legs filled up with lead, and I couldn't move them. Tadd smashed it with a small tree limb he'd found, and the snake wiggled and twisted and hissed. I finally got the lead out and found me a stick. I joined Tadd in hitting and lambasting that snake until he stopped wiggling.

"What'll we do with it?" I pondered.

"Bury it," Tadd spoke in no uncertain terms.

"Bury it? What for?"

"If we don't, it'll rain and rain for who knows how many days. Ain't you never heard that? If you kill a poisonous snake, it'll rain. That's how farmers cause it to rain on their crops. Come on. Let's bury it 'cause we don't want no rain tomorrow."

We used our sticks for shovels and dug a deep hole to bury the snake. Afterwards, we sat back down on our blankets. The black velvet darkness enveloped us. The woods seemed full of summer noises, and I didn't like the nighttime as much as I did before.

"I'm sure glad you woke up in time to spy that there snake, Tadd."

"Me, too," was his answer.

A few minutes slipped by and then I said, "Maybe we'd better turn in again. We want to be in good shape for tomorrow."

Tadd brushed some sand over the remaining live embers and said, "Good night, Gandhi."

"Night," I said and got in a fetal position to try to sleep again.

I guess I must have fallen to sleep again for the next thing I knew my nose was full of the pungent smell of breakfast. When I opened my eyes, it was daylight. I saw Tadd bending over a small fire. I appreciatively sniffed the delicious odor of brewing coffee. I looked beyond him and saw a small tree branch being carried by the strange, forever flowing of the creek out to sea. Then I saw our raft. I rubbed my eyes again to make doubly sure my vision was unclouded. No, it wasn't there. I leaped from my blanket, lamenting as I stood, "Tadd, our skiff! Where'd you tie it?"

Tadd whirled around and spoke all at the same time, "I ain't touched it. Now, Gandhi Reed, it's too doggone early to be playing jokes. Did you sneak up last night while I was asleep and hide 'er?"

"I wouldn't do a thing like that."

"Yes, you would. In fun, I mean."

"I ain't funning, Tadd. No sir, not this dang early in the morning." I quickly assured him, running down to our raft. Tadd joined me and I could tell he was really concerned by the look on his face. His face always told on him how he was feeling at any particular time, whether he was happy, sad or scared. His face didn't lie. I could tell he was scared.

I scratched my head and said, "Can't understand that. I done tied a double half hitch in that there line."

"Are you sure?" Tadd was talking like he doubted my word.

"Sure, I'm sure."

"Well," Tadd drawled, "she ain't here now. I've heard being up the crick without a paddle, but this is a new one—being up the crick without a boat."

I became argumentative. "Well, Tadd Tobin, we got our raft, ain't we?"

"Yeah, but we sure as shooting need our skiff for emergency purposes. Just in case. Let's look around."

We forgot about our coffee and began searching the shoreline, hoping to see our skiff beached nearby. We looked a long time, but there was no skiff in sight. We tramped back to our campsite. Our coffee had boiled away, and Tadd started all over again making us some fresh brew. I meandered down to the raft and checked the lines. They were all secure. I jumped on board and examined the piece of line on the stern where our boat was tied. "Looky here, Tadd." I held up the piece of line.

"What?" he called out, not leaving the coffee this time.

I untied the remaining piece of line from the stern of the raft and brought it to Tadd for his inspection. He took it and scrutinized it thoroughly.

"Tarnation, you say." Tadd pressed his lips together like he was biting them to keep from saying any bad words.

"Yep," I said, shaking my head. "It's been cut all right. I knew I tied that line secure. Somebody was around here last night. I just knew I heard something out here last night moving around. Why, it ain't even safe for a body to leave town."

Tadd didn't say anything, so I kept on talking. "What do you think?"

"It was cut by a knife. That's for sure." Tadd was still holding the line and looking at it. "Well, we know what we got to do from here on out." He continued.

"What's that?"

"Sleep on our raft." And then he added, "We'll probably have to post a watch during the night. 'Specially if we're close to shore."

He poured our coffee into the two tin mugs we brought along. We sipped. It was hot, black, and strong—just the way Capt'n Lacey had taught us to drink it.

"Tadd?"

"Yeah?"

"How about Skipper?" I asked.

"What about him?" Then he shook his head fast like the light of my question was turning on in his brain. "Yeah, what about him? Where in the tarnation was he when that thieving skunk was here stealing our boat?"

"He coulda been out hunting," I was trying to find a good excuse for Skipper because I didn't want to think he wasn't a good watchdog. "You know he's run a rabbit before now."

"Yeah, but it ain't likely he'd be out running rabbits in the middle of the night."

"Well, he could have."

"Maybe." The wheels in Tadd's head were churning. I could almost hear them. "Maybe the thief come up here in another boat, real quiet-like and snuck away without making any noise. Or he could have swum up here and done it. And Skipper didn't catch his scent."

"Yeah," I said sounding more enthusiastic than I wanted to for I had no desire to lay the blame of losing our boat on Skipper. That's just what happened; I know it 'cause Skipper's got a good nose on 'im. He can smell a rat a mile away."

"Well, there's one thing for certain," Tadd said.

"What's that?" I said while I was taking a sip of coffee.

"We ain't got no boat now. We'll just have to make the best of it."

"Maybe we'll find 'er downstream." I tried to sound consoling.

"Maybe," Tadd answered with no assurance in his voice. He stood. "Let's start packing."

"Right," I agreed standing with the coffee tin in my hand and reaching for my blanket with the other hand.

Before you could spell Mispillion Lighthouse, we were packed and on our raft and shoved off. I stored our gear in the lean-to. Skipper was in his favorite spot, forward. Tadd and I stayed aft, checking the current and wondering if the wind was stiff enough to hoist sail.

"Let's try the sail, Gandhi."

I untied the boom from the spar and hoisted sail. There was just enough breeze from the northwest to fill the sail like a pair of big bloomers full of air fluttering on a clothesline. Tadd manned the tiller, and we glided noiselessly downstream, leaving the tree covered banks and our campsite behind us. We were underway, sailing for an unknown port. The morning sunlight was dancing on the ripples of the moving water, and we forgot all about losing our boat. The restless waters possessed form and movement, expressive, and admirable. It was a delightful morning full of expectation. We always wore an optimistic mood because we were grateful for every day of our life. We felt it was a gift from God just to live in His miraculous creation. It seemed to us that life was always full of surprises.

Soon we saw a burst of marsh grass peppered with white and purple flowers, which blossomed bright with summer in their veins. And over yonder we could see the thin vapor, stealing skyward from the low grounds. All in all, it was a glorious morning.

We sailed at a snail's pace for I don't know how long, and then the wind died down to nothing. I furled the sail and tied it and the boom to the mast. We decided to let the tide take us.

Tadd looked over the side and then to the borders of grown weeds along the banks. "Seems to me the tide's coming in."

I looked closer, squinting my eyes to get a better look. "Yep, sure does. What do you say?"

"I say it's time for a swim. That sun is shimmering hot."

I stood up and pointed while asking Tadd, "How about that bank over there to the port?" Looks like a likely place to hole up."

"Let's steer there. Here, Gandhi, you take the helm."

I took over the steering, and Tadd manned the long pole and began pushing our raft in the direction that I pointed to. It was slow going because the pole was sticking in the brown oozing mud below. We didn't care, though, since time was our richest commodity. Tadd continued to push on the pole with as much strength as he could muster, and we made slow headway toward our destination. At last, we reached land. Tadd's face looked strained. I guess it was from his tired muscles. His condition always showed up in his face.

Tadd said, "I got an idea. See that tree limb hanging out over the water?" He pointed to a long, leaning bough of a huge pine tree jetting out over the creek. "Let's tie a rope over it and then swing out into the crick. We can stand on that bank there and take a real good ride."

"Ain't you the smart one?" I said in admiration. "Boy, I've got to give it to you. You've got a head on your shoulders."

We took the rope, found a short piece of tree limb about a foot long, tied one end of the rope around it, and holding onto the other end, threw the short piece of limb over the big bough hanging out over the water. We eased our end of the rope up and up until the piece with the little limb tied on it came within our reach. Then we tied the two ends of rope together.

"You first," I said. "It was your idea."

Tadd asked, "How's about giving me a push, Gandhi?"

"Sure enough," I answered pulling him back toward me and then running with all my might and pushing him high over my head. He sailed way out, twenty feet or more over the water. I expected him to jump, but he didn't.

"What's the matter?" I sang out.

"Nothing," he called back, "just checking."

"You gonna jump?" I yelled.

"Keep your shirt on, will ya?"

When he swayed back to the bank, he jumped off. I grabbed the rope.

"How about me trying, Tadd?"

"Be my guest," he said with a smile, and made a slight bow.

I placed my foot in the rope. "Gimme a push, Tadd."

Tadd drew me back and gave me a running push, high above his head. When I swung out over the water and looked down, I knew why Tadd didn't jump. It looked to be a hundred feet or more down there. A body could get killed doing a fool thing like that.

"Jump!" Tadd called out.

I still hung on and swayed back toward him on the bank. He grabbed my feet and began running and gave me an extra hard push. And out I sailed over the water again.

I heard Tadd yell, "Chicken!"

That made me mad and I jumped. I hit the water "kasplash" like a ton of bricks. I thought that all the wind I had in my lungs would squeeze right out through my nose. I sank to the slimy bottom of the crick in short order. My bottom mingled soundly with the muddy creek bed. I was thankful for one thing—where I landed was no oyster bed for it if had been one, my bottom would have resembled the red and white stripes on the flag. I gave a push all the while kicking to the top. It wasn't too deep; maybe twelve feet or more. I came up spitting water like Old Faithful coughs up steam. I climbed the bank like an almost drowned dog clambering to get out of his beckoning grave. Still out of wind, I puffed out the words to Tadd, "It's your turn."

"I don't think I want to jump. Not yet, anyhow."

"Aw, go on," I urged. "You ain't chicken, are you Tadd?" I taunted.

"No, I ain't chicken, Gandhi Reed, and you'd better not call me chicken." Tadd was getting his dander up, but I didn't care. He called me chicken and I jumped. Now, I wanted to see him jump.

I stood there just looking at him with pleading eyes. My body was glistening from the water drops on me.

He stalked over and took the rope in his hand. "All right, dadgumit. If I get killed, I get killed. And you'll have to meander back to town the best way you can."

Maybe he expected me to tell him not to do it, but I didn't. He looked at me for a minute, his eyes pleading with me to tell him I was fooling, but I spoke not a word.

"Gimme a push," he mumbled.

"Gladly," I said and pulled him back to me. I ran and pushed him out over the water with all the savage vigor I could muster up.

He smacked that water like a fat man taking a belly whopper. When he came up, he too, was spitting water, and it was my turn to laugh. It was a real funny sight. He came ashore and his belly was as red as a beet.

"That weren't such a good idea, after all, was it, Gandhi?" he finally said to me after he caught his breath and sat down.

"No, it weren't," I agreed, "but we gave 'er a try, didn't we, buddy?"

He looked at me and saw me smiling, and he smiled and said, "Let's take a swim."

We piled overboard and swam around for quite a spell, enjoying the cool water. Skipper decided to join us and waded in and swam out to us. Tadd was floating on his back when he called out to me, "What time do you suppose it is?"

I shaded my eyes with my left hand and looked up at the sun, "Don't know, but that sun is pretty high and hot. Must be around noon or better."

"Let's eat," Tadd suggested. My tongue was hunger glazed, so I quickly agreed with him.

We swam to shore. Within a matter of minutes, we were dried off from the sun after we had wiped our bodies with our hands. We put on our shorts. Against the sun, our bodies threw a rumpled, black shadow on the ground.

"How's about some potted meat?" I called out.

"Is that all we got?"

"Nope. But it's convenient."

"Let's have it then."

"Okay."

After lunch, we sprawled on the sand. The sun blazed savagely white and steamy hot. We laid down and tucked ourselves comfortably in a trough of ground. The next thing I knew, Tadd was shaking me. I was a bit startled. I sat up and asked, "What's wrong, What's the matter?"

Tadd smiled, "We both went to sleep. Must not have been long, though, 'cause the sun is still high. Come on. Let's move out."

Back on the raft, I hoisted the sail, although the breeze wasn't enough to blow out a match, it was that weak. Anyway, I left the sail hoisted. It looked good even if it didn't amount to a hill of rotten beans.

WE DRIFTED SLOWLY FOR A LONG SPACE OF TIME, not making much headway at all. Suddenly, I looked to the starboard side and called out, "Look out, Tadd. Turn 'er to port."

I grabbed the pole and began pushing with all my might to the port.

"What is it?" Tadd inquired.

"Look at that," I said.

"Gosh, I'd forgot about that, hadn't you?"

"Yep, I sure had," I said, heaving a sigh of relief. "Boy, that old sunken hull has been there a long time. You can't see it too well at high tide, but she sure would have given us a peck of trouble if we hit 'er. Might of tore our raft to pieces. We've been down this crick enough times to know that old hull was here on this point. Ain't this Parrott's Point, Tadd?"

"Yeah, sure is. Guess we ain't being careful enough, Gandhi, in our navigating. We better perk up now and remember what Capt'n Lacey told us," Tadd said fiercely.

Right then and there, we began keeping our eyes peeled and on the lookout to make sure that we didn't run into anything, especially any sunken object hiding under water. We took turns at the rudder, all the while making slow progress because of the still wind.

Tadd spoke to me while I was standing trick at the tiller. "We gotta be on the lookout for Brickhouse Bar. If we get stuck on that, we'll be there 'til the tide comes in."

"Right," I said in my captain voice. "You look and I'll keep an eye peeled, too."

"Gandhi, if we're lucky, we might make Crab Alley Landing by night. There's a little cover right around there that will make a nice mooring place for us."

"Yeah," I answered as another thought flicked on in my mind, "ain't that where the old deserted Dickerson House is?"

"Yeah, believe it is," Tadd said, "but nobody messes around there no more. They say it's covered with poison oak, and besides it's supposed to be haunted, like all old, deserted houses are. I guess the ghosts hate to give up the place like real live people hate to give up anything they got, 'specially if they like it. I've heard tell that old man Dickerson was a rich man that never married. They say he killed himself by running a pitch fork clean though his body and he died really slow by bleeding to death."

"Think that's the truth?" I asked.

"Sure as shooting. Tales such as that usually carry no lies," Tadd assured me. "And besides, why should some terrible thing like being killed on a pitch fork be told 'bout you if it weren't true?"

"I guess you're right, Tadd. Say, ain't that a fresh wind blowing up?"

"You bet. We'll make Crab Alley Landing easy now. There's Brickhouse Bar. Steer to the left of it."

It was a pleasure to guide that raft, especially when there was enough wind to fill her sails. I felt kind of important handling that tiller and feeling the raft move in the direction that I wanted 'er to. I mused how strange it was that a little piece of wood we used as a rudder could cause our heavy raft to sail in any direction we desired just by pushing on it. When I pressed the rudder to the right, the raft immediately responded and moved to the left. When I put pressure on the rudder to the left, she moved toward the starboard.

"What in the tarnation are you doing, Gandhi Reed? First, we are heading port and then we're heading starboard. Can't you make up your mind which side of the crick you want to be on?" Tadd spoke in words dripping with disgust.

"Naw," I replied, "I was just thinking."

"What?"

"About that little rudder."

"What about it?"

"Nothing."

"Aw, come on, tell me. What are you thinking about?"

"Well," I began, "ain't it funny that that little sliver of wood can guide us the way we're going?"

"Ain't never give it no thought," Tadd spoke, "but since you mentioned it, it is kinda odd, ain't it? How about them big ocean liners? They weigh millions of tons, and I 'spect their rudder don't weigh more than fifty pounds, if that. And it steers a big ship loaded to 'er portholes."

"Yeah, that's something, ain't it?" I said, marveling at the thought of it all. "Hey, Tadd, a real bright idea lit up inside me, how about Niter?"

"Gosh dash, Gandhi," Tadd scratched his head, speaking to me all at the same time, "you think more different thoughts faster than a grasshopper can jump. What about Niter?"

"Well, we're talking about rudders, ain't we? What about a bridle and bit?"

Tadd caught on right away. "Yeah," he said slow-like and full of admiration. "Compared to a horse, it's kinda small, ain't it?"

"Same difference what we're talking about, ain't it?"

"Sure is," he answered, shaking his head.

"Ain't that Crab Alley Landing?" I pointed in the direction that I was speaking.

"That's it," Tadd said with lines of satisfaction scratched on his face like he was a cat licking his chops after eating a fat mouse. "Head 'er in, Gandhi. See that cove to your starboard? What do you say we moor there for the night? But, let's beach 'er for now, and cook up something to eat.

"Aye, aye, Captain," I said and there wasn't a trace of malice in my voice.

No sooner did our raft touch the soft sandy shore than Skipper alighted to start his sniffing and lifting his leg. I guess that's doglike so we paid him no mind but concerned ourselves in securing our raft to a tree and getting some food on shore for supper.

CHAPTER 9

Supper was over, and we were safely moored in the cove at Crab Alley Landing. The velocity of the wind increased considerably, and we detected thunder rumbling in the distance followed by heat lightning. Skipper inched closer to my side as if he sniffed danger in the air.

Tadd spoke in subdued tones, "Gandhi, did you notice that sunrise this morning?"

"Didn't pay it much mind. "Why?"

"Well, I seen it," Tadd was electrified with excited anxiety. He carefully picked his words. "And it didn't look good. 'Member how the Capt'n used to have us read the weather by looking at the sky? He said them weather fellers didn't know how to predict the weather with all their highfalutin' instruments."

"Yeah, I 'member," I interrupted Tadd as I jogged my thoughts.

"This morning the sky was a deep Indian red, and I 'spected we'd have rain and maybe a storm, but I didn't say nothing."

"Think we ought to stay here or camp on shore?" I asked.

Before Tadd could answer, the darkness was ripped open by jagged streaks of lightning, trailed by a clap of thunder that rumbled angrily like an earthquake. Tadd hadn't answered me. He didn't have to for both of us pushed on the pole to get our raft into shore and quick. It hadn't started to rain yet. I always felt better during a storm if it was raining for it gave me the feeling of being wrapped in a blanket of security. In very short order, we were back on shore and our raft securely beached. The lightning streaked sharper, and the thunder roared louder. But still no rain. We tied everything down on our raft. We had run it on the beach as far out of the water as we could. Then, we covered our raft completely with canvas and secured it. No rain, yet, but we knew that it would be coming.

Tadd spoke as we hugged our blankets under our arms. Skipper was right under my feet. I couldn't walk unless I stepped over him. "Gandhi, we're gonna have to sleep in the old Dickerson house."

I leaped with both feet off the ground at his words. Goose pimples covered my whole body like I had the measles and a good crop of spots they were. "No siree," I said loud and emphatic. "You ain't dragging me in that there haunted house tonight. I'll stay out here and get struck by lightning, but I ain't going in there and be skeered out of my skin."

"Aw, Gandhi, why not? Any port in a storm," Tadd replied, but I didn't detect any conviction in his voice. And his face showed apprehension as it always does when he has inner feelings. His face always showed his hidden thoughts.

"Just 'cause! That's why!" I minced no words. "You ain't, and nobody or nothing ain't gonna corral me in that house. I've heard too much about that place. I don't know why we ever stopped here for the night in the first place." For two cents I would lay right down on the soft kindly bosom of mother earth beneath my bare feet and cry. That's how bad I felt. Capt'n Lacey always said a man takes off his mask when he's alone. And right then I sure did feel alone, even though Tadd and Skipper were there. My whole body sunk under the heavy loneliness of the night.

Tadd was moved with sudden tenderness. He stepped toward me, put his right arm around my shoulders, and hugged me tight and said, "I'm skeered, too, Gandhi. Right to death."

Without warning, a streak of lightning lit up the sky like a Fourth of July night at the State Fair. There was a clap of thunder that sounded as of the biggest giant in the world was falling downstairs from heaven to earth. It seemed like every cloud in the sky emptied all its pockets at the same time. If it had continued to rain very long with all the force it was raining at that very minute, we would have been drowned on the spot.

I knew we were not thinking right because we darted straight for that old Dickerson house. We were soaked clean through before we reached the door stoop. Tadd and I and Skipper were as close together as we could get without being sewn to one another. I whispered, "Did you bring the flashlight?"

Tadd didn't answer, but reached into his left pants pocket, retrieved the flashlight, and flicked it on for me to see. He turned it off.

"Leave it on," I pleaded. "It won't hurt nothing, will it?"

"Guess not," his voice was muted. In fact, so was mine, and we were talking to each other like waves in motion with rising and falling tones.

As Tadd shined his flashlight inside the living room or what was left of it, we stepped across the threshold. It was a room of dark silence with a moldy breath. Crumpled sheets of aged newspaper lay near the blackened fireplace. Tadd moved the flashlight about the room, and the beam shot out through the hall door to the foot of the stairway. There were some bones of a cat or small dog laying there, which made us shiver. All the while we stood there, the thunder and lightning and rain continued at an awful pace with no let up. A celestial gale was blowing through the paneless windows of the old house. Our astonished eyes were seeing weird sights and our flesh dwelled in hope that we would live long enough to tell somebody about it, especially Capt'n Lacey.

At that very moment, we knew what harassed and haunted souls were like. Already, we had seen too much of this place. We heard a loud noise like the roof was caving in. Tadd and I at the same time experienced a sudden jolt, like missing the last stairstep we thought was there but wasn't. Outside the trees were straining in an east wind and some of them were smacking their limbs against the old house. Currents of thunderbolts exploded about us again and again and again. We were so scared that we thought we would die but hoped we wouldn't because nobody would ever find our bodies in that old deserted house. We stood still, paralyzed in fear. Our pulses quickened and muscles tensed at the prospect of imminent danger from the lurking shadows.

"Any sug—ges—tions?" I stammered to Tadd.

"Yeah."

"What?"

"Build a fire."

"Did you bring any mat—ch—es?" I was scared and cold and wished I were home.

"Yup, right here," Tadd answered as he drew a penny box of matches out of his pant's pocket.

"You fetch some boards of this here floor, Gandhi, and I'll light the paper." Suddenly, a lizard scurried across the rotten floorboards and was quickly swallowed into a dusty crevice.

I threw my arm around Tadd's neck in a vice-like grip and exclaimed, "No, you don't! Where you and that light go, I'm going. We'll gather the wood together, and we'll light that fire together."

"Fair enough," Tadd replied, releasing my arm from about his neck to keep me from choking him half to death.

We ripped up some of the rotten floorboards and took them over to the fireplace. The storm had subsided, but the rain continued to pour down like it must have done in Noah's Ark time.

All three of us sat down in front of the fire that was cracking and sputtering from the burning of the overly seasoned and downright rotten floorboards.

"Tadd," I said.

"Yeah?"

"Guess we didn't bury it deep enough" was my solemn statement.

"Gosh dash, Gandhi," Tadd sounded exasperated, "when you talk, why don't you say what you mean so's I can understand, too."

"Well, it was your idea, weren't it?" I whined in a wheedling voice.

"What tarnation idea?"

"About burying the snake," I reminded him in not too gentle tones. "You said if we didn't bury the snake, it would rain. Well, we buried him, but as I said before, I guess we didn't bury him deep enough, 'cause with all this here rain, I bet he's floating downstream toward us right now."

"Oh, that. Why didn't you say so in the first place?" Tadd had caught the drift of the conversation. "I suppose we didn't bury 'im deep enough. Anyway, if God wants it to rain, it'll rain, no matter if you bury snakes or not. He's the head of things down here on earth, and if He says rain, then rain it is. And He sure must have said it in a loud voice this time 'cause it's a real frog strangler."

"Sure is," I said. Then I thought aloud, "We gonna stay in here all night?"

"We ain't got much choice," Tadd sorrowfully reminded me.

"Well, I'll tell you one thing I ain't gonna do." I remonstrated.

"I ain't gonna go to sleep."

"Nobody said you had to, did they?" Tadd replied.

"Nope. And it wouldn't make any difference if they had." There was smugness in my voice now for I was defiant and meant what I said.

Night sounds echoed through the cathedral gloom—eerie, distant, and hollow. Silence was what we didn't want so we talked on and on, saying anything and nothing. Mostly, we talked to keep ourselves awake. And there was no let up in the downpour rain. Finally, fatigue overtook us. We sat back to back with Skipper near us. For a split second, both of us must have closed our eyes and snatched a few winks when we were startled by a low, moaning cry.

I whispered to Tadd without moving my position. I had goose pimples on my goose pimples. "Did you hear that cry?"

"Yeah," Tadd whispered back to me, and he seemed to hunch his shoulders up over his ears to shut out the pitiful sound.

"What did it sound like to you?" I whispered.

"The same as it sounded to you," was his reply.

I continued to whisper my questions because I didn't want whomever was crying to hear us. "I mean what does it sound like? A woman? A man? Or what?"

"Sounds like a baby," was Tadd's low tone answer.

"Does to me, too." I answered back, my voice almost inaudible.

"There it goes again," Tadd said. "Do you suppose it was crying when we came in here, but we didn't hear it until we got quiet and stopped talking?"

"Suppose so," I said.

Moments of silence slipped by which seemed like an eternity to me and Tadd. Somehow, it was always me that broke the silence, but I couldn't help it. I am not one for keeping quiet and especially in our deplorable plight. That baby's cry was inexpressibly menacing and soulful and frightening.

"Tadd?"

"Yeah."

We still held our positions, back to back, talking to one another over our shoulders in that sinister atmosphere. "Suppose somebody done dropped that baby off here to die and it's crying 'cause it's hungry or something?" I was wondering out loud and speaking off the top of my head.

"Could be," Tadd mused along with me. Then he added, "Reckon it wants some milk or something. We oughta go take a look."

I was silent for a minute before I answered then I spoke, "Guess a little baby can't hurt us. Besides, if he's hungry we ought to give 'im something to eat...some potted meat or baked beans, maybe. We got plenty and could spare some. I'm sure if Rev. Thompson were here he'd say it was our Christian duty to help a body in need. Right, Tadd?"

"Right. We can't let no little innocent baby suffer when we're around." Slowly, Tadd began to get up and I did, too. "Let's take a look." He flicked on his flashlight. Skipper was right at my heels, and I was so close to Tadd that if his pants had been four sizes larger we could have worn them together.

We sneaked barefooted into what was the dining room. Tadd flashed his light over the gutted room with only its ribs showing, or so it seemed, for the plaster had all fallen from the lathes that had held it secure. It was a spooky sight.

"There it goes again," I whispered. And every time I heard that baby cry, I got goose pimples all over, even in my hair for I felt them there. I thought my hair was standing straight up.

"Shh," Tadd said putting his right index finger over his lips. "Let's listen real good and when he cries again, we'll follow the sound."

We remained mum as a wooden Indian, but we could still hear one another breathing. We clung close to one another. "There it goes again," Tadd said. "Sounded like in the hall to me. Didn't it to you?"

"Yeah," I said moving right in Tadd's footsteps as he made his way back into the living room and through the door which led into the hall. Darkness rushed into the room from out of the corners as the flowing embers faded and died from our fire in the fireplace. It grew black as pitch except for the ribbon of light from Tadd's flashlight. It wasn't raining as hard as before but kept falling at a steady pace.

When we emerged into the hall, we stood near the foot of the staircase. Tadd took another step and yelled, "What's that?" He flashed his light toward his bare feet. It was the bony carcass of the cat that we had seen when we first flashed our light in there.

We waited. Tadd whispered to me. He didn't have to whisper loud because my body was right up close against his. I intended for it to stay that way as long as we were in that terrible house. Tadd spoke with bated breath, "Have you heard it again?"

I listened for a brief spell before I whispered, "Nope. Nary a cry."

We waited and listened and listened and waited, not moving out of our tracks. Then we heard it, more mournful than before as if that baby knew we were there and he was crying for help.

"What do you say?" Tadd asked me in a muted sigh.

"I didn't say nothing," I assured him feebly.

"I mean, where do you say it's coming from now?" Tadd spoke right into my ear, which was next to his mouth.

I turned my head and spoke in his ear, "Well, to tell you the truth, it sounded like it was coming from upstairs. But I ain't for going up there. Leastwise, not now. Let's wait 'til morning. We can see better then."

Tadd must have been mulling my words over in his mind for he didn't speak for a few minutes. Then he said, "Supposing that baby has been here for a long time and is starving to death? If we don't get it some food tonight, maybe it'll die. Do you want that on your conscience the rest of your born days?"

I thought on his words before I answered, all the while trying to dredge up my courage. "If you're gonna put it that way, there ain't nothing else to do but go upstairs and find it and feed it."

"That's right," Tadd agreed and at the same time reached out to hold me close to him as he proceeded up the stairs. It wasn't necessary for him to do that, though, since he couldn't have pried me away from him that night with a ten foot steel bar. Skipper silently stayed at our heels.

We climbed the deserted stairway slow and easy and fragile like. And every step we took, it seemed there were louder and longer creaks and squeaks from stepping on each stair step. At last, we reached the top of the stairs. Tadd slashed his light around in the upstairs hallway. Plaster had come loose from the wall, and it all looked bare and skeleton-looking, like the dining room below. There hadn't been anybody living in that house for a long, long time by the look of things. Cobwebs hung from every available spot. I had the weakest feeling in the pit of my stomach. I thought I would throw up before I took another step. We didn't move from the top of the staircase. We waited and waited. It seemed an hour or more. Silence weighed heavily on us and our breathing was labored. Our eyes scanned every nook and cranny around us.

There it was—the most mournful, low, sad cry that I had every heard a baby cry. It was clear enough and coming from the back bedroom to our left.

"It's from in there," I said pointing to the back bedroom.

We moved in a fresh spasm of energy through the low hanging cobwebs, brushing them out of our eyes as we walked along. We didn't even hesitate as we reached the back bedroom, but walked right in. We were determined to pick up the baby and take it back downstairs and give it something to eat.

Tadd flashed his light around the bedroom, which was filled with cobwebs, as well and hanging plaster with old faded flower designed paper clinging to it.

After Tadd had scanned the room with the pencil of light from his flashlight, he muttered, "Hmmm, guess I missed 'im."

"Ain't that small, is he?" I asked.

"No, he ain't that small. It's just that I missed seeing 'im the first time I looked," Tadd whispered.

Slowly, Tadd flashed a steady skein of light along every inch of the bedroom floor. We knew that the baby wouldn't be hanging from the ceiling or the wall, so we searched the floor. We saw nothing but little piles of plaster and some yellowish wallpaper that was showing many years of wear, especially around its dark brown stained edges.

"I'd swear that he was in this room. Wouldn't you, Gandhi?"

"Yep, it sure sounded like that cry was coming from in here," I agreed.

We turned and re-entered the hall. As we made our way to the other bedroom, we heard the cry clearer than ever. It was the kind of pathetic, doleful cry that tightened your skin and pinched it with millions of goose pimples that gave you the shivers all over. The cry came from the bedroom that we had just left. There was no mistake about that.

Tadd turned to me and I was close by his side, looking him right in the face. We suffered a moment of blind despair. "What do you suppose? We just came out of that room, and gosh darn, it sure sounded like he was in there, didn't it?"

"Yeah, but he ain't," I said. "Let's look in this bedroom. Maybe he's in there."

We entered the other bedroom, which was a carbon copy of the one we had just forsaken except it appeared to have more plaster and faded paper on the walls. It was full of cobwebs dangling down like shredded lace curtains, up and down the room, Tadd flashed a finger of light. Not a trace of the baby. We didn't say a word for we were dumfounded.

"What now?" I asked right in Tadd's ear since I was pressing next to him. He whispered back, "There's two more bedrooms, ain't there?" Might as well inspect them. He's got to be in one of 'em."

We worked our way out of the bedroom, ducking the cobwebs as we went but getting them caught in our hair and face all the same.

In the third bedroom, we were flanked by gutted walls. The windows rattled; the shutters clattered; our knees knocked. This was the north side of the house, which took the brunt of all storms. Slower now, Tadd began to search every board of the floor when we again heard that distinct, piteous painful cry of the baby that brought goose pimples from the bottom of our feet up to the top of our ears. We froze stiff in the positions we were holding, and our hearts felt like wax melting down inside us.

When Tadd sucked some spit back into his dry mouth, he whispered, "He ain't in here. That's for certain."

Out in the hall we waited. I thought to myself that if our going back and forth kept up, it would soon be daylight. And I for one was ready for the morning to come. But so far, it was pitch-black out with a steady, soaking, falling rain. During this troubled hour, hope and fear were blended in our faces while dark doubts licked our hearts.

It seemed an hour or two, but no cry. "Maybe he's gone to sleep?" I whispered in Tadd's ear.

He leaned close to me and said, "Or maybe he's dead."

I felt a sensation shoot through my body that almost dislocated my ribs from my skin. I kept my mouth shut to keep from saying more than I should.

We waited. And lingered. Still no sound.

"Let's go down," I suggested.

"Okay," was Tadd's two-syllable reply.

Just as we were about to descend the rickety steps, we heard it. As clear as a crystal bell, the baby gave out the most blood-curdling cry that I had ever heard in all my life. I do believe that if I had felt my head at that moment, my hair would have been standing on its end. I got a sickening feeling deep in my bowels.

Tadd sounded full of cold fury. "Now, gosh darn it, I knowed that baby was crying from that back bedroom, the one we went into the first time. Come on, Gandhi. I'm tired of this here messing around." Tadd didn't whisper any longer but spoke out loud.

We marched back to the bedroom on the left, the very first one we examined. Tadd was more deliberate in flashing his light around this time. He seemed to be shoving the beam of light into every little crack in the decaying floor. His eyes were as unflinching as a hawk's. Determination flashed in his every blink, and he jutted out his chin to prove it.

Tadd left nothing to chance in our continued search for the baby. He flashed the light along the walls, up around the plaster fallen ceiling. Still, we saw no baby. Suddenly, the baby cried out again. We jumped and bumped into one another and stayed close all at the same time. Skipper apparently grew tired of it all right at that very minute, for he scampered out of that room, and we heard his toenails tapping each step of the staircase as he trotted down.

"Are you thinking what I'm thinking?" Tadd whispered in my ear, his lips touching my ear lobes, yet I could hardly hear him; he was speaking so low.

I turned my head and spoke right back in his ear in the same tone he used, "I don't know, but it sounded like it was coming from that wall over yonder. Do you suppose it could have got caught in there? Or...?" I didn't finish.

Tadd whispered back, "Yeah, you're right. It's coming from that wall. I bet his mother put him there to die."

I cringed at Tadd's words and leaned closer to whisper to him, "Don't keep talking 'bout him dying, Tadd. He ain't dead yet, 'cause we can hear 'im, can't we? What'll we do? How we gonna retrieve him out of the wall?"

Tadd reflected for a moment and whispered to me, who was closer to him than a loose sweater could ever be. "Let's put our ear against the wall there and listen. When we find the exact spot, we'll tear it off with our hands and take the baby downstairs and give it some food."

"Yeah," I whispered back, "but could be he's messed his pants.

The Good Ol' Days

You know, babies don't wait to go to the toilet 'cause they just let it fly. That's why you have to have a pile of diapers when babies are around."

"Then you can clean 'im," Tadd bolted out.

"No, you don't shove that job off on me, Tadd Tobin," I weighed a thought and said, "We'll both clean 'im."

Tadd nodded his head in the affirmative, all the while moving over closer to the wall and sticking his ear far out so that his body wouldn't be touching the wall—only his ear. I fixed myself close to him. Finally, his ear was against the wall. He pulled me toward him and whispered, "You listen, too. Put your ear against the wall near me. And listen."

We stood there for many prolonged anxious moments, holding our ears against the wall and not hearing a sound. We were transfixed by this baffling obstacle. Slowly, a low, sorrowful moan came right through that wall into our ears. If my eyeballs had not been fastened in their sockets, I am sure they would have popped right out of my head when I heard that glum moan. It was a sound like I had never heard before. I waited for Tadd to make the next suggestion since I was too scared stiff to move or talk. In fact, I was trembling inside. It seemed that everything I had inside me had come loose and was just floating around.

"Start ripping right there, Gandhi," Tadd said, pointing to the spot he wanted me to pull out from the wall with my hands. All I could do was shake my head in the negative. Somehow, my voice had escaped me.

"All right," Tadd said in disgust, "here, you hold the light for me. I'll do it. Can't leave a little baby in there to die, even if his mother could."

Tadd wrapped his fingers around some loose plaster down from the spot where he pointed for me to pull. He yanked hard and a big slab of plaster fell to the floor. He took the light from my hand and shone it on the jagged shapes of the ripped open wall. There was nothing. He returned the light to me and grasped both hands around more plaster and braced himself with his right foot against the wall. He yanked with all his might. The remaining plaster on that side of the wall broke loose and cascaded to the floor, causing a small dust cloud. And with all of this Tadd lost his balance and fell to the floor along with the useless plaster. I shone the light on him and helped him to his feet. He snatched the light out my hand and said, "Let's take a look."

He directed the beam of his flashlight into the spot where he pulled the plaster loose. He held the light on what we saw. We couldn't believe our eyes. Maybe we were having a nightmare or something because what we saw was not real. It just was not true at all! We were dumbstruck, speechless, and aghast. We became like marble pillars and the beam of Tadd's flashlight froze like an icicle on the very spot where it shone.

An eternity of time passed over our lives as we became sealed on the very site where we stood. We were transfixed there and our minds were full of wonderment. Our thoughts floated on the wings of our fanciful ideas that could have been true.

Tadd was the first one, this time, to shatter the silence that hung heavy around us. "Gandhi, nobody in the whole wide world is gonna believe this. It ain't gonna be any use to even tell it."

My eyes were still glued on the sight before me, which was illuminated by the flashlight. There lodged between the outside weather boarding of the house and the inside wall and cradled on an unplanned board secured in the space between the wall and the outer boards was a skeleton of a baby which would measure about two feet long. We looked and nothing apparently was missing from the skeleton. The skull, backbone, ribs, both arm bones, and both leg bones were all intact. It seemed like acid had eaten the flesh clean from the bones of the skeleton. It was a gruesome sight and I couldn't for the life of me keep back the tears that coursed down my cheeks. I stole a glance at Tadd, and I wouldn't swear to it, but it looked like tears spilling down his cheeks, too.

I didn't answer Tadd because for the first time in my life I had no desire to talk. I just felt all silent and loose inside me. I believe all my energy had taken flight. He didn't look toward me when he spoke but said, "Let's go back downstairs. There ain't nothing we can do here now."

The Good Ol' Days

Tadd moved slowly to the door, and I was right beside him and somehow I wasn't scared anymore. I just felt all lonely inside and running over with sadness. It was an empty feeling, full of loose connections, like you wanted desperately to do something to help, but you couldn't get your hands or feet or anything working together. I felt like I was coming all unglued.

We sat down in front of the fireplace. Skipper lay near by. The fire had long ago burned out and nothing but ashes remained. We kept the flashlight on and turned toward the fireplace. Without a word, we pondered over our nightmare of darkness punctured with fear and sadness.

Dim light at first began to splash noiselessly into the living room where we sat and suddenly, the room was overflowing with daylight, tinctured with red that reminded me, at least, of spilled blood that should never have been shed in the first place. I was still thinking of what we saw upstairs. A little innocent baby nailed up in the wall of a god-forsaken house, left there to die for no reason except maybe because of the sin of his mother. It was a shameful, horrible discovery which stirred an unholy turbulence within us. I was haunted with grief.

I turned to Tadd and said, "I'm sure glad that the Lord decided to have night and day when He made this ol' earth, 'cause I'd hate to go on living only in the night time.

"Me, too," Tadd added reflectively.

More silence between us. I looked out the window and there in the east settled low on the horizon was the sun, blood red, looking like a ball of fire. The rain had stopped sometime between midnight and morning, but we had forgotten all about that.

Tadd interrupted my reverie, "Gandhi, what are we gonna do 'bout them bones up there?"

I was taken back by his question. "What are we gonna do 'bout 'em? Why nothing. There ain't nothing we ought to do except let him alone in peace. Maybe our opening them boards allowed his spirit to escape and go to heaven."

"Did you notice something while we been sitting here all this time? Tadd asked.

"No, I ain't."
"You mean to tell me you ain't noticed nothing?"
"Nope."
"Well, you dumb bunny," Tadd began and I knew then he was going to lay me out for doing something I shouldn't or not doing something I ought to have done. "You ain't noticed nothing, huh?" He continued, "How 'bout them baby cries we heard? No, don't say you didn't hear 'em 'cause we both did. No use saying it was our imagination 'cause it weren't. We done heard 'em all right, and we went from room to room to hear 'em. Right?"

"You're right, all right," I had to agree.

"Ain't it strange since we done opened that wall up that we ain't heard no more crying?" Tadd was full of questions.

I agreed by shaking my head more than once.

"Do you suppose that since we opened that wall and freed 'im from his prison he ain't gonna cry no more?"

I sat there and for the life of me I just couldn't come up with any answer.

"Well," Tadd spoke loud and clear, "you ain't answered my question."

"Which one?" I asked in real honesty.

"About them bones! What are we gonna do with 'em?" Tadd was persistent.

"Don't know. What do you say?" I was fishing for his answer.

"I reckon we ought to bury 'em. You suppose if Rev. Thompson was here he'd agree?" Tadd was thinking real serious thoughts.

"Reckon so," I said, then added quick-like, "but who's gonna handle them bones up there? I just don't think I could touch 'em."

"I will," Tadd said. There was no getting around it; Tadd was the braver of the two of us.

"All right," I said leaping to my feet. "Let's do it and be long gone from this place. I don't care if I ever see it again."

Tadd was on his feet and his eyes were surveying the room where we were. He started moving about. I followed him. He found a little wooden box in the kitchen that looked like a box that once a long time ago housed gun shells 'cause it had Remington arms printed on the side of it. But the printing was real faded.

"This oughta do," he commented and led the way upstairs.

We entered the back bedroom and walked over to the spot where the skeleton was.

"Gosh darn!" Tadd exclaimed in a loud scream.

I moved closer and looked and only the board was held secure from the nails to the studding. It was clean as a whistle. Not a bone was in sight as if they had evaporated in thin air. We dared to inch nearer to get a closer look. Tadd even reached out his hand and felt the boards. There was nothing on it. Nothing! I stretched forth my hand in a slow motion and gently rubbed that board where I had seen with my own eyes the full skeleton of a baby. It was as bare as Mother Hubbard's cupboard.

Being at wits end, I looked at Tadd. His eyes were bigger than saucers. All at once, he quickly dropped the box he was holding and ran out of the bedroom and down the stairs and out the front door. I was hot on his heels as we both fled from there, with Skipper close behind.

At the beach, Tadd united the bowline to our raft and I untied the stern line and we shoved off together. Skipper leaped on the raft as we moved from shore.

"Hoist that sail, Gandhi! Quick! Let's navigate from this place!" Tadd was pushing with furious energy on the pole and moving us out in midstream. A gentle morning breeze filled our sails and not fast enough for us. The old Dickerson house shrank in the distance as we shot glances at it over our shoulders from time to time.

WHEN THE HOUSE WAS COMPLETELY OUT OF SIGHT and we couldn't see any trace of it, I reminded Tadd, "We ain't had no breakfast yet."

"Well, I weren't for eating back there. Were you?"

"Nope. That's a fact. I don't believe I coulda swallowed nothing 'cause my throat was so shrunk up. To tell you the truth, I couldn't even talk there for awhile," I honestly confessed to Tadd.

"Me neither," was his honest answer back to me.

"I'll tell you what," I said.

"What?"

"Let's try to catch some fish for breakfast. That'd be a change of pace for us, wouldn't it?"

"Sure would," Tadd was in agreement. "Grab our lines out of the box, Gandhi. We'll try our luck."

I snapped to it and rummaged our lines from the stowage. In the meanwhile, Tadd steered our raft toward the marshy banks on our port. In no time at all, we had half a can full of worms. Back in midstream again, after baiting our hooks, we dipped our lines overboard.

"What'll you expect we'll catch, Tadd?"

"We oughta snag a bass or two. Maybe some perch," was Tadd's cocksure reply.

"Hope you're right," I said.

There we were, two buddies, in love with pleasure and having sublime faith in luck. And we weren't disappointed. We caught five small perch. Finding a sandy spot of beach, we landed, built a fire, and cooked our fish. It was a delicious breakfast. After we had washed our pots and pans, we sat down for a rest.

Tadd started sharing his inner thoughts with me. "Gandhi," he began, "I ain't ever, ever gonna tell anybody 'bout what happened last night. They'd swear we'd gone loony and probably put us in the bug house for crazy people for the rest of our lives."

I shuddered at his words. "Right, Tadd. I can't hardly believe it myself. And if somebody else had done told me what we seen, I'd more than likely call 'em a liar. Wouldn't you?"

"Yep. It just don't make sense. Now, we heard that crying. That's for sure. We saw them bones. That's for certain. But that empty board..." His thoughts became fences instead of gates, and he was hemmed in.

The Good Ol' Days

"You felt the board, Tadd. And there weren't nothing on it. What else do you want for proof?" I asked him.

"Yeah I know all that, but it just ain't right, somehow."

I suggested to him, "Maybe God was waiting for somebody to come along and pull that plaster away so's He could take them bones up to heaven with Him. And that's why we kept hearing that crying. That's 'cause God wanted somebody to hear and open up an escape for the baby 'cause all babies go to heaven, don't they?"

Tadd never spoke for a long drawn out full minute. He looked me square in the eyes and said, "Gandhi, I bet you're right. I guess God was causing us to do something for Him, and I always thought that God was only supposed to do stuff for us. It's a funny world and mysterious like, ain't it?"

"Sure is," I said having no argument with him on that score.

"Well," Tadd spoke getting up, "let's head on up the crick. We got more seafaring to do today. Right, buddy?"

"Right, buddy," I answered with my words brimming full of admiration and affection for Tadd.

I manned the pole pushing us out in the midstream while Tadd handled the tiller. That morning brewed a strong, southwestern breeze that both veered and strengthened. I unfurled the sail and hoisted it to the top of our mast. The wind coming in on us from the stern filled the sail like a paper bag blown up with air and about to burst. Our raft began making swift headway, and we were extremely happy. Skipper was lying in his usual spot forward where the greenish waters creamed joyously under our bow. We sensed a strange spiritual peace.

"Remember the tale Capt'n Lacey used to tell us 'bout that British sloop of war which sank out in the breakwaters during colonial times?" Tadd asked.

"Sure do," I replied without hesitation. "She was full of gold, weren't she?"

"Yeah," Tadd nodded his head as he spoke. "She had millions and millions of dollars of gold in her hull. Boy, Gandhi, suppose we could dive over and find all that gold?"

"Yep, that would be something, all right." I thought about it for a minute and then added, "It sure would!"

Tadd skippered the raft well, and we were sailing at a good clip. He said, "You know what I'd do, Gandhi, if we found a mess of money?"

"Build the biggest candy store in the whole world?" I suggested.

"No, you dumb bunny," Tadd answered laughing. "I'd go to New York and buy my passage on a ship going 'round the world."

"That sounds swell, Tadd. Could I go with you?" I pleaded as if we had found the gold already.

"Sure you could. We're buddies, ain't we? We'd leave at nighttime. And when we woke up the next morning, we'd be way out to sea with no land in sight. Just the sea and sky touching each other way out there all around us. It'd be like we was the only people in the world alive, and we'd have all the world to ourselves. Wouldn't that be something?"

"Yeah," I said in a whisper because I imagined myself right there on the ship that Tadd was describing.

"And we'd keep right on sailing down to Bermuda and on through the Panama Canal. We'd stop off at Mexico awhile and then on to California. After our fill of California, we'd head for Hawaii. I 'spect we ought to stay there a whole year. But if we liked it a whole lot, why not stay there the rest of our lives?"

"Why not?" I asked agreeing with every word.

"But if we wanted to see more," he added, "we'd have to go on to Australia, then up to China and Japan and back down to India and up to the Suez Canal."

I interrupted, "How's about stopping off to see them sphinxes or whatever they are in Egypt?"

"If you want, we could stop off there for a spell and look around. When you've got a million dollars of gold, you can stop off anywhere you like and stay as long as you want, can't you?" Tadd sure had reasoning power.

"You're absolutely right," I affirmed.

"When we got tired of Egypt and Africa," Tadd continued, "we'd go up to Rome and have a look. Then we'd go to that place in Italy where they use boats for cars."

"Where's that?" was my question.

"I don't exactly know, but we'd find it. Right?" Tadd assured.

"Right," I shot back to him with my approval.

"Then we'd go ashore at the Rock of Gibraltar and see all them monkeys," Tadd remarked.

I scratched my head and asked, "Tadd, how come you know all about these here places we're gonna stop off at?"

"You dumb bunny, ain't you read no geography? That's where I done learned about all them places." Tadd was beginning to show his intelligence.

"Go on. Where are we goin' next?" I asked.

"Let's see. Where are we?" Tadd screwed up his face in a thinking manner.

"There with them monkeys on some kind of a rock," I reminded him.

"Oh, yeah. Rock of Gibraltar," he spit that name out distinct enough for me to hear. "Then we'd go on up to Paris, France. From there, we'd go to England and see where the pilgrims came from. And then back to New York."

"How long do you 'spect it'll take us to do all that, Tadd?"

Tadd looked at me direct in the eyes and answered, "If we could find the gold and if we could sneak off without being caught and if we could find a ship going to all those places, I 'spect it'd take five or ten years."

I stretched out a moment before I answered for I was thinking about what he said. "That's a mess of ifs!"

"Sure are," Tadd said, "but it could happen."

"Sure could." And then after a short space of silence, I said, "Wish it would."

Tadd broke up our daydreaming by asking, "About time for lunch, ain't it? That sun seems mighty high."

"Reckon it is." I kinda felt disappointed because I wanted to talk about our going around the world more than eating at that particular moment.

Being surrounded by marsh, there wasn't any fit place to beach our raft, so we decided right then and there to throw out anchor.

"Let's take a swim." With that remark, Tadd dove overboard and Skipper was right behind him. I lost no time in joining them both. The water felt refreshing to our sweat-stained bodies. We didn't talk now, just swam around, and enjoyed the rapture of being in the water. It was a time of relaxation, and we were relaxing to the fullest.

After awhile, I climbed back on the raft. Skipper swam over to me, and I helped him up 'cause he never could make it by himself. Tadd joined us.

We made sandwiches of potted meat and crackers. The crackers were beginning to taste a bit rubbery even though we were keeping them in a tin can shut tight. Salt air played havoc with food on board, but we didn't mind since that same air boosted our spirits higher and higher each day. And when your spirits are soaring high, who cares about the taste of food? We were gripped with the weakness of thinking we could do anything we put our minds to.

"Where do you think we'll hole up tonight?" I wanted to make conversation.

"If this wind holds out, we oughta make Parson's Island," Tadd figured.

"That's close to the bay, ain't it?" was my inquiry.

"Yep. When we reach there, the bay is right 'round the bend," Tadd was speaking like an old salt who had plied the waters for fifty years or more.

"We going out in the bay?" I was fearful of that thought.

"Don't see why not," Tadd said. "This ain't no adventure here in the crick. Any baby could go down this here crick. You got any objections about going out in the bay?"

"I don't think so." Tadd was not going to have me admit that I would be scared to go there, but I did slip him a precaution, "But you 'member what Capt'n Lacey said, don't you?"

"Yeah," Tadd was quick to assure me. "He said the current was mighty strong, 'specially near the breakwater at Hell's Point. Now, nobody with the sense that God gave a goose would go near the breakwater in a craft like ours."

I heaved a sight of relief at Tadd's answer and said, "No sir, nobody would do that."

We sailed for two or three more hours. We forgot to check the time, but, in fact, we didn't care what time it was or for that matter even what day it was.

"There she be," Tadd pointed to a meager patch of land hugged all about by water with its interior full of dwarfed trees. The island appeared like a piney desolation, yet it was also a place of lonely beauty. A strong joy surged through our hearts as we beheld the sight that arrested and pleased our eyes. We yearned to breathe in the woodsy scent.

"I'll tell you what, Tadd."

"What?"

"Let's pretend that we're discovering this land. And Injuns are there. And we're just touching land for the first time in months, 'cause we just sailed in from England."

"Yeah," Tadd was willing to go along with my play-acting. "Let's do that. Hey, Gandhi, how's about taking our pole and tie a blanket on it? That'll be our flag to plant in the new country we'll discover."

"Good idea. And let's pretend our supper is like the one the Pilgrims ate with the Injuns on the first Thanksgiving Day." For some reason, I was full of ideas, like a jar stuffed with Heinz pickles.

Tadd didn't seem to warm up to that idea. "What's the matter?" I asked him.

"Your idea is all right, Gandhi," Tadd began slowly, "but trying to pretend that Spam tastes like turkey is gonna be pretty hard to do. I don't know whether I can stretch my imagination that far or not."

"Well, let's try, anyhow. Okay?" I begged.

"Okay."

Before too long, we sailed up on shore of Parson's Island. I had tied my blanket on the pole. When Tadd beached our raft, I leaped off on land and almost fell down over Skipper, who had the same idea of getting on land as quickly as possible, but for a different reason than we did. I caught my balance and held onto the pole with the blanket dangling. Lifting my other hand like Rev. Thompson does every Sunday at the end of the service to bless us, I said, "Peace, Big Chief of the Nanticoke Tribe. Mr. Big White Father come from across the water to smoke peace pipe with you."

Tadd began to laugh and he jumped on shore from the raft and said, "That's a good idea, Gandhi."

I turned to Tadd with deepening disgust and said, "Aw, come on, Tadd. Are you gonna play or not? Come on, now, be a sport."

"Well," Tadd began to give in, "how's about me being the chief?"

"Good idea," I agreed still standing there holding the pole with the blanket draped and twisted around it.

Tadd jumped in front of me, stretched out his hand the same as mine and grunted, "Ugh, Me, Big Chief White Eagle. What you do on my land?"

"Me, White Father from way off land. Bring you gifts. Me give you much gold for your land so my people can come here and live in freedom."

Tadd was quick on the trigger and asked, "Why you come to our shores in the first place? Are you all jailbirds?"

"Tadd," I said interrupting our pretending, "you know them Injuns didn't know nothing about jailbirds."

"Who's not acting out now?" Tadd asked in a teasing voice.

"Aw, baloney," I said, dropping the pole with the blanket curled around it. "Doggone it. Let's eat."

Tadd laughed, walked over to me, slung his arm about my shoulder and mimicked, "Okay, White Father. Let's eat that turkey."

I laughed with him and we went to the raft to get some stores, namely Spam and a can of baked beans—the same vittles we'd been eating since the beginning of our trip.

"For a change," I suggested, "let's fry the Spam and warm up the beans. Okay?"

"Sounds fitting," Tadd called out as he began picking up some dry wood to get the fire started.

After supper, we lay down near the fire. By and by, Tadd spoke through the merging shadows, "Gandhi, we've only been gone three days and, boy, they've been filled with excitement, ain't they?"

"Sure have. First the snake and then the baby be…" I didn't finish the sentence because we said we'd never talk about it again. And besides, it was not the time to talk about it, anyway, since the sun had dipped behind the woods casting long, foreboding shadows of dark shades.

Tadd steered our conversation to another course, quicklike. "You ain't seen nothing yet, Gandhi."

"What do you mean?"

"I mean, 'bout fishing. Catching them perch today weren't nothing. Wait 'til we reach Bloody Point Light. Boy, they say you can catch 'em that long." Tadd stretched his arms as far apart as he could reach.

"Aw, go on," I countered, "You ain't gonna make me believe that you can catch fish that long."

"Honest, Gandhi," Tadd seemed to be speaking the truth or at least he was believing himself.

"We'll see."

We stopped talking for a minute. I leaned back and inhaled the scents of Parson's Island. The strong smells reminded me of home and Saturday night and a bath because the pine scent was mighty strong, just like the soap that Mom made me wash with.

"Ain't it nice?" I said, "being out here away from home and not having to take a bath or dress up or nothing? I hope this here adventure don't ever end. Don't you, Tadd?"

"Yeah, I know what you mean. But we'll probably have to head back sometime. It ain't a pretty thought, is it?"

"Sure ain't." I said, yawning all at the same time.

"Sleepy?" Tadd asked.

"Guess so," I answered feeling suddenly tired. "Shall we turn in?"

"Might as well. Morning will be here before you know it, and we're gonna have a rip snorting time tomorrow. I just know it." Tadd's words were electric with excitement. We rolled up in our blankets.

"Night," I said to Tadd.

"Night."

The full moon threw a gentle glow over the stark, lonely landscape, which was a moment of beauty and breathtaking delight. The black trunks of the somber line of trees looked like rolled lumps of stone through the thin mist. We were lying on a crop of sharp spears of grass, tender and green. I looked up and saw the Little Dipper shimmering steadily above us while the sleepy water lazily lapped the wet edge of the beach. In that hushed, delightful atmosphere, we slept sound as a log and dreamed delicious dreams.

CHAPTER 10

Since we had left Lewiston, nine whole days and eight nights had now sped by like an arrow shot from a thirty pound bow. Days of happy memories stacked high, one on top of the other, and they were never to be forgotten, never in a million years. We knew the sights and smells and sounds of summer would linger in our hearts until we drew our last breath. There we were, young creatures appealing in simplicity and single heartedness, knowing that every day is a new life, a fresh experience, ripe and ready for our first touch. Our eyes were open to God's garden all about us, and we loved every inch of it and desired nothing to be changed. The edge of night drew closer around us.

At last, we moved from the narrow sleeve of the creek to the wider domain of the bay. Our raft was safely beached, clean out of the water. Supper was over and it was the same thing we had been eating for the past nine days, but we weren't complaining. No sir, not one bit.

As we walked the moonlit bay shore line and the cool night wind whipped across our sunburned faces, Tadd said, "Gandhi, ain't this the livingest life you've ever lived?"

"It sure is," I agreed with all my heart and added, "If it stayed this nice all year long, wouldn't it be fun to sail from beach to beach and explore? Who knows, we might dig up a chest of silver that was buried by pirates a long time ago."

Underfoot, the ground was soft and spongy. Tadd was dragging his toes in the sugar-colored sand beneath our feet as we walked along. Skipper scouted about ahead of us but steered clear of any king crab

The Good Ol' Days

that might be alive to bite off his nose if he sniffed too close. Tadd was bubbling with impish wit.

He said, "Yeah, I sure would like to dig up a trunk full of gold or silver. Betcha them pirates lived a rip snorting life. Just sailed the seas and robbed other ships and got fat and rich. Do you believe you would like to have been a pirate, Gandhi?"

"Yep, I believe I would, 'cause it sure was an exciting life. Weren't no dull moments on a pirate ship. Why, there's always something going on like walking the plank or whippings at the mast or men being cast in the hole to be eaten up alive by rats and.... You know, Tadd, come to think of it, I ain't so sure I would like to be a pirate after all...."

"Aw, Gandhi," Tadd looked at me sideways as he spoke and laughed.

We continued our stroll down the deserted beach and not a house or person was in sight. No one ever came down that far on the beach, and that's why we stopped there for the night. We sat down on a large piece of driftwood to watch the ships silently passing the inlet's mouth as they moved into the deep channel's bed. By now, they had surely picked up their pilot out by the breakwater and were probably headed for Philadelphia. We sat there in peaceable solitude and watched the ships fading lights as we tried to trace their far off patterns.

Tadd broke the silence, "Gandhi, what'cha going to be when you grow up?"

"I don't know. Ain't give it much thought," I answered truthfully.

And then I asked, "What you going to be when you grow up?"

Quick as a fish disengaging himself from a bent hook, Tadd shot back. "I ain't never going to grow up."

"You ain't never going to grow up?" I was surprised at his answer. I continued, "Well, how in the world are you gonna keep from doing that 'cause everybody grows up whether they want to or not."

"I'm gonna discover a drug that'll keep me a boy always, and I'll never, never grow up 'cause grownups are forever fuming and fussing and worrying and don't know how to enjoy every new day."

"You're right. But how in the name of God's green earth are you going to get the stuff to keep you a boy all the time?"

"There's a way."

"Name one." I was persistent in making this discovery for myself.

"Don't exactly know yet. But I'll find out. I'll ask old Doc Starkey when we're back in town if he has any drugs that can do such a thing. Have you ever seen all that different colored medicine he has in them tall, slim, funny-looking jugs in the back room? Why he's got enough of 'em to kill or cure the whole town of Lewiston from whatever ails it."

"Yeah, I've seen 'em."

We didn't say anything for a spell; then I ventured to ask, "Tadd, supposing…now, I say, supposing you do find a concoction to keep you from growing up…would you give me some, too?"

Tadd turned toward me, sliding around on the seat of his britches like he was sitting on a swivel chair and confided, "Now, buddy, you know I would."

"Thanks, Tadd," I affirmed with a satisfaction inside me that somehow made me feel like I was never going to grow up. And I was real happy. Tadd had a way about him to make a fellow feel real good about himself. I guess he ought to be a doctor 'cause at times he could make one feel good all over.

We continued to sit there looking out over the expanse of the bay that spilled right into the mouth of the Atlantic Ocean. The continuous wash of the water's edge made by the splashing of the endless waves as they pounded the beach in musical rhythm was music to our ears. The moonbeams danced on the restless white top rollers like elves and fairies running over a hot, spotlighted mirror. It was a place of solitude there on the sandy bay shore that had slept for centuries in the warm Atlantic sun—serene, content and full of long memories.

I cut the curtain of silence between us with the question, "Tadd, if somebody else wanted to drink some of that stuff you're gonna make to stay a boy, would you give it to 'em?"

"Like who?"

"Like Pete and Levin and Hunt and Burrous."

"Yeah, I'd give it to 'em, but I wouldn't give it to everybody—only to the ones that would appreciate it and knowed how to use it 'cause there ain't everybody who knows how to be a boy all his life."

"Do you, Tadd?" I asked.

"Yeah, I think so," was his answer.

As I dreamed about the fun we'd have as boys forever, I glanced over at Tadd. I could tell that his thoughts were a million miles away and I, for one, was not going to disturb him.

We sat there on that driftwood seat of ours, enjoying the splashing seclusion and breathing the fragrance of salt air slow and deep. It was a placid night, and the clean barrenness of the deserted beach deepened our electrified adventure. Capt'n Lacey told us that memories were our mental pockets to carry important collateral in, and from the way things had been happening, we were going to be rich. We sat down near the shoreline and marveled at the cobwebbed designs accidentally manufactured by the sprawling sand fleas.

"Gandhi," Tadd began, "tomorrow we'll do some real fishing. Bloody Point Light is right out yonder." He pointed in the direction of a faint dark glow.

I looked and saw a spasmodic flicker of light come skimming across the water back toward us at regular intervals as the salty breakers rolled slowly against the sandy shore. I was delighted with our adventure thus far and was eagerly looking forward to many more happy moments. I cherished this moment, "Is that it way out there?" I was squinting my eyes to make doubly sure I was seeing right.

"Yep, that's it. But it's further than you'd think." Tadd spoke in a nonchalant, all-knowing manner. He got that way once in a while, talking like he knew anything and everything. He wanted to give the impression that he knew what he was talking about. He did that not only in front of me, but when anybody was present.

I was putting him to the test when I asked him, "How far off?"

"Offhand, I'd say three miles," Tadd ventured a guess as he often did.

"That so," I said not knowing why I had put him to the test because I didn't know any more now than I did then. Oh well, it didn't matter.

"What kinda bait are we gonna use?"

Tadd was quick on the trigger to answer that question. "Peelers," he said. "We'll catch 'em real early tomorrow morning. They's the best bait there is for trout and perch and maybe blues."

"Guess we ain't gonna do no chumming?" I asked.

"Naw," Tadd retorted, "it's too stinking messy. And besides we'd have to go up to the clam house and buy some minnows. And money we ain't got. And we'd have to have a bucket or something to bust 'em up in and then throw the mess out on the water. It ain't worth it. Let's catch some peeler crabs tomorrow and that oughta do it. What do you say?"

"I'd say that sounds like the best idea. Chumming is a good way to fish, but it sure is expensive. Maybe there'll be some boats out there tomorrow, and we can pull in fairly close to 'em. Now, they ain't gonna catch all the fish in the bay. Right?"

"Right," Tadd nodded vigorously.

"We ought to turn in."

"Guess so. Tomorrow will be here before you know it."

We got up and trod back to our raft and campsite. I guess we had been sitting there so long that we both moved like we had dry joints. Skipper trotted ahead of us enjoying the feel of the sand under his paws as we moved in the pale radiance of the seascape. It was a God-created night, and His creation enveloped us like being snuggled in our mother's arms. I had warm feelings tingling my body.

Before you could say Mispillion Lighthouse, Tadd and I curled up in our blankets and went fast asleep right out there on the moon-soaked bay shore, unaware of the night sea fog that fumed over the glazed sand of the beach.

NEXT MORNING AFTER BREAKFAST, WE WADED ALONG THE SHORE, searching for peeler crabs that we would use for bait. It didn't take long until we had about a dozen peelers.

Navigating our raft out in the water was a peck of trouble. We had beached it high and dry, and now we were struggling to push it back into the water. The constant roll of the waves made our launching a tough job. If we hadn't floated out past the breakers pretty quickly, everything we had on board, including our food, would have been sopping wet. Finally, we made it, and Tadd I were soaked through to the skin. We didn't mind, though, for the day was going to be a beauty. The sun was already high and hot. Many sea gulls had left their morning autographs all over the sand. By just listening to the waves lapping the shore, we could imagine we heard the splash of leaping trout. Some flying gulls were whirling down from the upper air and catching their morning meal of small fish swimming too close to the surface of the water. Skipper barked intermittently at the diving gulls, which paid him no attention as they flew in the glint of the sun on the whitecaps.

Tadd and I were busy pushing with all our might on the long pole to get us away from the undercurrent of the incoming waves. Tadd was almost out of wind as he spoke, "Gandhi, how's about hoisting the sail while I try to keep 'er from heading to shore? If we can move further from shore, it won't be so bad."

He manned the pole by himself, while I quickly unfurled the sail and hoisted it to the top of the mast. Tadd put all his strength to the pole to keep us from being washed into shore. I handled the tiller, and after a few stretched moments of time, our sail bellied full. We were finally underway by the silent strength of the unseen wind while tumbling billows of restless sand stirred on the beach behind us.

A smile creased Tadd's face; he was bubbling over with inner joy and excitement. I grinned a big smile back at him, which seemed to seal our bonded friendship that I prayed would last into eternity.

The salt spray caused by our raft cutting through the bay's small swells sprinkled our faces. I licked my lips to taste the salt for I loved to be out on the water as did Tadd and Skipper. I guess you could call us old salts. Nothing is more peaceful and relaxing and invigorating than being out on the water, inhaling that refreshing salt air, being warmed by the sun and cooled off by the balmy sea breezes. It was a truly a doggone great experience.

We had a goal in mind that morning of reaching Bloody Point Light. Usually we traveled at a leisurely pace, stopping to take a swim or just drifting about to enjoy the newborn day. Today was different. We were going to do some real fishing. Tadd was cutting the peelers into fine chunks of bait while I held our raft steady toward Bloody Point Light. Because of the sun's glare, I lost sight of the Light now and again, but by squinting and shading my eyes, I got it in focus and headed straight toward it.

"You know something, Gandhi?" Tadd didn't look up at me but continued to cut bait.

"What?" I called back to him.

"We're going to the hottest fishing hole 'round these parts. I've heard plenty of tales 'bout fishing around Bloody Point Light. If we strike the tide right, we'll catch more fish than we can keep on board. We'll have to throw some back, that is, the ones we can't use. Right?"

"Right!" And now it was me not looking at Tadd for I had a bead on that bobbing red object out there on the water, which I supposed was Bloody Point Light, and I wasn't for losing it.

The sun appeared like it was lit with fire against the heavens still and tense, which caused us to lose so much sweat that I thought we would dissolve on the very spot where we sat. We were stripped down to our shorts and still were hotter than the inside of a kitchen range burning bright with kindling wood. It was so hot the breeze didn't have enough energy to blow. We just bobbed around on the water like a cork from the top of a medicine bottle that had been pushed down inside the bottle. Our sail gave the appearance of a used dishrag hanging inside a cabinet door. It was disgusting, knowing we had a destination and no wind to take us there.

I looked at Tadd as if to say, "What shall we do?"

Tadd shot his lower lip over his upper lip to get moisture for speech. "Ain't nothing we can do 'bout this," he finally spoke.

Long ago, I had stopped manning the tiller. Now, I let the sail down and furled it around the boom and lashed all of it to the spar. As

I worked, I called back across my shoulder to Tadd, "How deep do you suppose it is here?"

"Soon find out," Tadd said taking a coil of line from the deck of the raft, all the while taping a lead sinker on one end and measuring the length of line around his elbow, forearm and hand. "There's twenty-four feet. Let's try that."

He dropped the line overboard and let it down slowly and finally felt the sudden thump of the sinker hitting the solid bottom. He guessed at the remaining line out of water. "I'd say it's 'bout eighteen or nineteen feet. Let's take a swim."

I threw the anchor out and secured the line. Tadd dove overboard; I was right behind him. And Skipper plowed into the water, too. He sure was hot because he was panting with heavy heaves. We swam about, floated around, and held onto the edge of the raft for a long time. The water was a refreshing relief to our hot, sun-stained bodies. I helped Skipper back on board and pulled myself up. I stretched out my hand to Tadd. He grabbed it and as I began to stand to help him aboard, he gave a sudden pull and I fell headlong back into the water. I came up out of the water spitting and sputtering, vowing to get him back for his foul play, and he laughed and said that I was a good sport. We both jumped on the raft at about the same time.

"I'm hungry. What do you say let's eat?"

Tadd agreed. He clamored over to the lean-to and fetched us some potted meat and crackers. We ate in silence, each thinking that the crackers and potted meat were getting to be stale fare. We were looking for the day when we would have a good cooked meal by our moms once again.

Tadd looked at me. "Do you feel it?"

"What?"

"That breeze."

"Ain't much of a breeze."

"Well, it's some breeze," Tadd assured me. "Let's hoist sail. We'll never make it with our anchor out."

He pulled in the anchor. I untied the boom and sail from the mast and raised the sail to the top of the mast and secured the halyard to it. It just fluttered in the breeze, but at least there was some air stirring. Maybe it would pick up and move us on out to the Light. We stared hopefully at our wind-ruffled sail. We crept along on the water's surface at a snail's pace, but at least we were finally moving. I was standing a trick at the tiller.

Tadd spoke, "Gandhi, I don't see a fishing boat in sight. Suppose we're hitting here at the wrong time. If the tide ain't right, we ain't going to do a thing."

"Aw, we got plenty of time. If the tide ain't right, we'll wait for it. There's one thing for sure, that tide don't never stand still, right?" I asked.

A few moments of silence skipped between us and then Tadd threw a curve of a question, "Suppose we get out here and can't get back in 'fore night?"

If he had hit me square in the belly with all his might, I wouldn't have experienced a more cutting pain. My voice came back up in my throat out of the pit of my stomach. "I never once gave that a thought. What do you think, Tadd? 'Spect we oughta turn the raft 'round right now and head for shore?"

Tadd laughed at my split second fright. "Naw, Gandhi. I just said that to get your goat. You know there's always a breeze blowing on the bay, 'specially in late afternoon. Never seen it to fail."

I wasn't too sure about that, but I kept my doubts in the closet of my mind. The door wouldn't stay shut though, and those fears just kept walking all around in my head. Tadd must have noticed the expression on my face.

"Gandhi," his voice was soothing-like. "Forget what I said 'bout not getting back. Honest, I was only fooling. You don't 'spect for a minute that if I thought we couldn't make it back to shore that I'd be wanting to go on to the Light, do you? No, siree. Why, if I thought that, why we'd hightail it right back to the beach now. Aw, come on Gandhi, forget it. I was funning with you."

I guessed he was at that. Tadd always did have persuading powers.

I looked him square in the eyes and smiled away every doubt I had in my mind. "That's all right, buddy. I knowed all along you were kidding."

Tadd looked forward. "There she be. Won't be long now."

I peered ahead and there was Bloody Point Light swaying to and fro ever so slow and blinking her light like a one-eyed skeleton. It was much bigger than it appeared from land when you got close to it. I glanced back to shore over my shoulder. It didn't seem too far away. If we had to, I knew we could paddle to shore, although it would take a long time to do it.

"Head 'er in," Tadd called back to me. He had grabbed a line and was standing on the bow with Skipper.

"How's that?" I asked as I steered straight for the buoy.

"Good," Tadd hollered back as he tied the line from our raft to one of the steel girders of the buoy. "We made it, ol' buddy. Grab your line and let's fish."

"Right," I called back, thrilled at the thought that at last we had reached our destination.

As we stretched out on the deck of our raft, the line from our fishing poles swayed lazily with the rise and fall of the plastic water beneath us. A soothing calm caressed us as we were cradled in the lap of the sun-splashed water sparkling like little diamonds in the sun's rays.

Tadd spoke to me without turning his head as his eyes followed the massive clouds overhead, "You know what I wish?"

"What?"

"I wish I had an ice cream cone right now."

"Oh, for Pete's sake," I said. "Shut up, will you? You'll have us hankering for something we can't have. Can't you think of something else to talk about?"

"Mind you," Tadd continued, "I don't care if I can have any ice cream or not. I was just thinking how nice it would be if we could."

"Yeah," I agreed. "All the same, let's steer our minds on something else."

A light wind licked our exposed bodies. The high summer sun

warmed us all over. So far, neither one of us had had a strike. It was a lazy, hot afternoon. I heard a stir beside me and looked over. Tadd had wedged his pole between the boards of our raft and turned on his side. Within a few minutes, he was making a nasal sound that assured me he was deeply asleep. I remained on my back with my fishing pole resting over my body so that I could feel the slightest nudge if a fish down there wanted to take a nibble at my bait. I would have him for sure since my right hand gripped the pole and was ready to jerk the line at the slightest pull. The sun's incessant heat bathed me with delicious delight and I felt bone lazy.

I SUDDENLY HEARD THE BROKEN BARKING OF A DOG. It sounded afar off. And then I realized I had been asleep for an unknown time. It was Skipper barking. I spoke to him. "Skipper, what ails you? Hush! You'll scare the fish away."

Tadd looked toward me and then beyond me. "Gosh darn, Gandhi, we've done broke loose!"

I looked behind me. There was no light buoy, no boats, and no land...nothing was in sight, but long rolling swells. I sensed a panicky motion inside me. For the first time in my life, at least in front of Tadd, I began to cry. Tears streamed down my face as I wailed, "Tadd, you know what's happened?" We done come untied and drifted into the ocean. We're done for now. We're all gonna be killed."

I became hysterical. I stood up and screamed, "Why, oh, why did we ever go out to that Bloody Point Light in the first place? It's all your fault. You was the one who wanted to come, not me. You are the one who didn't tie that line secure. This is all your fault. You murderer!" I vaulted on Tadd with all my strength. My fingers were about his throat closing tighter and tighter. Suddenly, my jaw ached and smarted and stung all a the same time. I touched my lips with my fingers. I saw red, rich blood on them. I looked at Tadd, stunned, wondering what was happening. My thoughts flew off in ridiculous directions. I was stunned in silence.

Tadd spoke, his two hands holding my arms close to my side,

"Gandhi, ol' buddy. I had to hit you. I'm sorry. I didn't mean to strike you so hard, but you was acting crazy-like. I ain't never seen you like that before. Now, simmer down. We got to pull our wits together and head back to shore." He released his grip on my arms, and said, "Are you all right now?"

I wiped my mouth with the back of my hand I looked at the bloody streaks on it, and answered, "Yeah, guess so." I sat down on the raft. "Sorry, Tadd," I said, not looking up at him. "Don't know what got in me."

"That's all right," Tadd assured me, reaching down for my hand and helping me to my feet. "We ain't got no time for chit chatting now. Look at that sun." He pointed to the sun, which had already gone to rest, and it reflected a faint lavender sky with high blue above the clouds. This was a sure sign of good weather, but brought a chill of alarm to our spines since night would fall quickly.

"Hoist sail, Gandhi," Tadd commanded. Skipper whined, which didn't make matters any better, and I wondered if that was his way of brooding over our despairing plight. I knew that dogs had a sixth sense or something that was foreboding and maybe he knew something that we didn't. I believe that God endowed animals with this extra sense.

Tadd was at the tiller squinting out over the horizon. "Ain't that Mispillion Lighthouse? There to the west?" He pointed with his arm fully extended.

I moved toward him and wrinkled up my face to scrutinize the direction he pointed. It did seem like a faint light, flickering over the water's surface and I answered, "Yeah, it 'pears like it could be. We can sail toward it anyways. You know it must be coming from land."

"Yeah," was Tadd's fainthearted reply.

"Tadd?"

"Yep?"

"Are you skeered?"

"Ain't no use lying Gandhi. I'm plenty skeered, but it ain't gonna help matters to lay down and cry about 'em. We've got to do something about or predicament, and that's what I aim to do. Namely, head for that light. I'm almost certain that's Mispillion Lighthouse."

"I'm real skeered, too." I said in a pleading tone, wanting some assurance from someone somewhere.

"Don't fret now, Gandhi," Tadd spoke in a soothing voice. "We'll make it back. We know our directions. Why," his voice sounded a bit cheerier, "don't we know which way west is?"

"Yep," I said, forgetting my fear for the moment. I pointed in the direction of the flickering light. "There she be. Have you got her on beam, Tadd?"

"You bet I have. How's about rustling us up some grub? Do you know we ain't eaten yet, and it's about night?"

"Gosh, I plumb forgot about eating with us being lost and everything." I fell on my knees and crawled into the lean-to. I drew out of our food box a can of beans, a can of Spam and a can of Red Heart dog food for Skipper.

"Guess we'll have to eat it cold. Okay?"

"That won't hurt nothing as long as it's something to eat. I'm plenty hungry."

I worked the can opener of my scout knife real vigorous-like, gashing the top of that can of beans with a ragged, piecrust edge. I opened the can of Spam and then the dog food. I spooned the dog food right out on the deck of the raft and Skipper gulped it down with quick rapid-fire bites like he was starved to death.

Night crashed silently about us. Being adrift on that raft at night chewed away every ounce of baby fat we had left in us. From that moment on, we were grown boys and we knew it. For the first time in our lives, we had discovered misery and dead hope. Our hearts shivered with loneliness, and our aching cheeks longed for our mother's caresses. We yearned for relief from our physical distress and somehow felt reinforced by God's unseen, but fulfilling, supplies. I didn't tell Tadd 'cause I didn't know what he would think, but I was praying as hard as I could that God would protect us and lead us back to shore. I just felt in my heart that He would. I always talked to God, not regular, but often, and I believed without a doubt that He answered prayers. I trusted God and I just felt assured that He would not fail us. I began to feel a little bit better and not quite so scared.

Tadd tried to crack the wall of fear around us by telling a joke. He asked me, "Gandhi, why did the little moron jump off the Empire State Building?"

At that moment, I could have cared less. I answered, "Don't know, why?"

Tadd cackled his answer, "To try out his new spring pants."

I smiled across the evening shadows to him, but it was too dark to see my face. The ocean became a mirror of stars. A half moon, the color of fresh milk, made its appearance in the star-studded sky. Somehow, seeing the familiar moon and stars gave us solace we desperately needed right then. It could have been my imagination, but as I looked out over the water, I saw ghostly shadows slip over the swells and hide behind every wave for the right moment to jump at us and destroy our raft. All my previous fear came back and overwhelmed me. I was poisoned with doubt. I was badgered with an electric activity down in the pit of my stomach and tried to imagine I heard the aching call of the gulls along the shore.

"What's the matter?" Tadd asked me through the darkness. "Didn't you like that joke? You ain't said nothing. What're you doing?"

"Nothing," I replied, "Just thinking."

"What about?"

"You 'member before we set out on this raft trip that we said something about kidnapping somebody to bring along with us? Well, we'd sure have 'em in a pickle barrel if they was with us now."

"Yeah," Tadd mused. "Good thing we didn't kidnap nobody. That's for certain."

A split second slipped by and Tadd spoke anxiously. "Hush, ain't that a boat?"

"What? Where?" I moved around on the seat of my pants, looking in all directions.

"I thought I heard a faint throbbing of her engines," Tadd said.

"Which way does it sound like?" I inquired.

"Northeast I'd say," was Tadd's remark and then, "Look Gandhi. Ain't that her?" Tadd was shouting. "Yep, it's her. Look can't you see her running lights? Ain't them red and green lights beautiful?"

I caught the excitement, especially when I spied the lights. "They sure are!" I exclaimed. "Tadd, turn on our flashlight so's they can see us. Better still, give it to me. I'll flash it off and on. That way, they'll think it's some code and come rescue us."

"The flashlight is in our food box, Gandhi. Give it to me and I'll start flashing it."

I scrambled into the lean-to on my hands and knees, fumbling in the dark for that flashlight like a drowning man grasping for a log floating by him. At last, I had my hand on it. I flicked the switch. It worked! Instantly, I was on my feet and gave it to Tadd. He flashed the light in the direction of the boat out there on the water. Off and on, off and on, he flicked the switch on the flashlight, which sent out splashes of light in the direction of the red and green lights of the passing boat. Slowly, the throb of the engines faded, and the red and green lights were extinguished like someone suddenly blowing out candles on their birthday cake. He switched off the flashlight. I do believe that my heart was resting near my kneecaps. Our pending danger broke like the dawn on my frantic mind. It was a desperate moment in our lives and we knew it. Hope springs eternal so we thought and prayed.

"That ain't the only boat that plies these waters," Tadd meant to sound cheerful and encouraging, but his words didn't cheer me one bit. All around us was glistening emptiness. I fought our dismal distress with a quiet fury within me. I was getting more scared by the minute and was wondering—suppose we drifted more out to sea and no one would see us and we would perish without ever being found. I was trembling inside myself.

I doubtfully inquired, "Tadd, do you still have your eye on the Mispillion Light?"

Like a sponge full of water, his voice contained dripping doubt, "I think so. Can't be too sure with all them stars out and twinkling, too. But I reckon we're on course."

"Sure hope so," I said with a sigh, not really believing him 'cause you really can't see at night any too good. In fact, you can't really see at all. I was praying for morning to come real fast, but I didn't say anything.

Tadd uttered with some semblance of assurance, "Come morning, we'll have a better sense of direction."

"Yeah," was my lone reply.

Tadd sounded electrified with lighted hope, "Say, Gandhi, did we bring a compass?"

"I didn't. Did you?"

Tadd was again despondent, "Nope. Didn't think we'd have need of one. 'Course, I don't own one no how, but if we'd knowed that something like this was gonna happen, we could have got one from somebody."

"I suppose we could have asked Capt'n Lacey. He probably has an extra one. Wonder why we didn't do that, but as you said, we never thought we would need one. Oh, well, that ain't doing us any good now to even think about it." I was utterly discouraged and afraid and down right put out.

Tadd spoke up, "Gandhi, it's no use both us losing sleep. I'll stand a trick at the tiller, and you try to sleep. Then you can stand watch and I'll try. Okay?"

"Okay," I called out and reached in the lean-to for my blanket.

It seemed I'd just slipped off to sleep when Tadd was calling for me to wake up. I stretched, yawned, and stood up. Our raft was gently rolling in the shallow swells of the ocean. It was like sitting in a big rocking chair and having someone slowly rock you to and fro. I moved toward Tadd at the tiller to stand my watch during the dead hours of darkness on what seemed like a moonless Halloween night.

"See that light blinking there?" He pointed in the direction dead ahead of our bow.

I took my sight down the length of his arm to see. "Yeah, I think I see her."

"You gotta do better than that," Tadd spoke wearily.

"What do you mean?"

"I mean you gotta do more than think you see her. You gotta actually see it and know for sure. Now look again." He pushed my head down almost to his arm.

"There she is. Ain't no doubt about it. I see her, Tadd," I spoke in full assurance. As I manned the tiller while Tadd slept, I conceived an idea of rescue that died stillborn. We stood two hour watches. Tadd slept two hours while I manned the tiller. Then I slept two hours, and Tadd manned the tiller.

Dawn broke suddenly in beautiful splendor. The sun burst forth over the horizon of the ocean like a house on fire. It was an awesome sight. The cloudless sky was streaked with bluish-red like the dark veins in a thin man's arm. Instead of a big red round ball, the sun seemed broken into many pieces like a smashed water pitcher of the color blood. And then, it began to take form as if some unseen sculptor molded it into a perfect sphere. The deep blue of the heavens accented the rich redness of the sun. I looked to what I thought to be the northwest and saw the half moon, still visible in the brilliant light of a fresh born day. That moon wasn't visible last night. I was so caught up in the beauty around me that I had not taken any bearings. I scanned the horizon and was jolted with a sharp pain of fear when I saw nothing but water and sky intermingled together and encircling us.

"Tadd, wake up. Let's make our bearings."

Tadd rubbed his eyes, stretched his arms above his head and yawned, which sounded more like a groan. He called out with a sleepy voice, "Can you still see Mispillion Light?"

"Nope."

He leaped to his feet. "Gash dash, Gandhi. How in the tarnation did you lose it? Have you done lost your eyesight?"

"Well, I was steering toward it all the while. Then when it come daylight, I couldn't see it no more."

Tadd relieved me of the tiller. He looked around all points of the compass that we did not have. "There's east," he said pointing to the sun. He pointed in the opposite direction.

"There's west but where in the Sam hill is north and south?"

"Which way are you gonna head, Tadd?"

"Well, it's for certain we ain't going east. Might wind up in France. We'll head west. That oughta take us inland...somewhere."

"Remember how Capt'n Lacey told us not to sail out past Hell's Point?"

Tadd shook his head and said, "Yeah, I 'member, but we sure as shooting done gone way past it. Right?"

"Right."

"Say, Gandhi, how's about some breakfast? What've we got to eat?" Tadd sounded hungry.

"Beans and Spam. That's all that's left," I answered.

"When we get back to Lewiston, I don't 'spect ever to eat another bean or even look at a piece of Spam."

"Well," I began, "It's better than nothing. Guess we can't heat 'em up 'cause we're out of sterno. Have to eat 'em cold."

"All right" was Tadd's despairing reply.

We ate in silence, not having much to talk about at that very minute. Our thoughts were jumbled up, and we anxiously picked one thought after another. The big question was: would we ever see land again and get home?

Tadd jumped to his feet and shouted in an excited voice, "Doggone, Gandhi! Did you see that?"

"What?"

"A shark!"

"Aw, Tadd, quit your kidding," I pleaded.

"No kidding," Tadd shook his head vigorously, "I seen it with my very own eyes."

"I hope we don't cut ourselves on these here cans or anything, 'cause blood draws sharks around you like honey draws bees. Let's be extra careful. All right, Tadd?"

"Sure enough" was Tadd's breathless reply. "Look!" he yelled, all the while pointing at a certain spot on the greenish rolling water.

I looked and saw the body of a shark about six feet long silhouetted by the sun's glare as he sped along, lacing the water's surface with his sharp fin.

"If there's one, there's bound to be more. I don't like the looks of

The Good Ol' Days

this at all, Tadd. Supposing if we throw our empty cans over that the shark will swallow it and cut his insides to pieces and die?"

"Let's try it," replied Tadd, willing to try anything for our safety.

We threw our empty cans of beans and Spam as far as we could away from our raft hoping against hope that the shark would swallow them and die.

Our raft was billowed by the slow rolling mass of waves and light, variable winds that propelled us in westerly direction for the wind was blowing with a soft energy and the promise to blow harder.

After a long silence, Tadd finally said, "You know what I've been thinking about, Gandhi?"

I spit into the ocean and answered, "Nope."

Tadd continued, "I've been wondering if some drops of this here ocean that we're floating around on ain't licked the hot sand of Brazil or Africa? Just think, Columbus and Magellan and even the Pilgrims sailed on these waters. Who knows, we could be plying the very droplets that floated the Mayflower!"

"Gosh, Tadd, I ain't never thought of it that way. You're right, could be we're sitting right on the very same drops of water that floated them ships. Wow! Ain't that something. Sure gives you the creeps when you think about it, though. Do you suppose drops of water can last that long?" At this point of our conversation, I was quite incredulous.

"Why sure they do," Tadd assured me. "If they didn't last, we'd have no ocean at all."

"Guess you're right, Tadd. Never thought of it that way. If them drops didn't hold out, why we'd be sitting on dry ground right now, wouldn't we?"

"Yeah, we'd be sitting on dry ground this very minute, and I wouldn't mind a bit. Would you, Gandhi?"

"Nope, not a darn bit." I was quick to assure him.

"How's about taking over for a spell?" Tadd asked me as he let go of the tiller for me to take a trick at the helm.

The sun-soaked water about us reflected splashes of green. And all that day we sailed due west without spotting a single ship or vessel of any kind, especially any fishing boats. In the throne room of our hearts, Tadd and I quivered with fear, but outside our faces shone with pretended bravery and courage. Although not a word was spoken by Tadd or me to reveal that we were scared, I believe that each of us had a feeling that Mr. Fear himself had stalked right through the door of our souls into our secret closet. We were saddled with the task of survival. It is no small undertaking and we knew it. We had many memories stored up which would fit into neat compartments of time slots, and we wanted to get to shore so that we could share them with somebody or anybody. We were a crew of three out on the ocean, longing to feast our eyes on the contour of the coast and feel the solid sand between our toes. This was our one tall unspoken desire!

Evening shadows of our second night at sea cascaded over us like a fisherman's net draped around our bodies, making us prisoners of night as we melted further out to sea.

THERE WAS A FULL MOON and the stars were as little white twinkling Christmas lights peppering a big black sheet. I turned to Tadd and asked, "Hey, what'll we steer by tonight?"

"What do you mean?"

"I mean there ain't no lighthouse. So, how do you know which way is shore?" I asked, scratching my head.

Tadd followed suit and scratched his head, and I could tell he was figuring real hard the answer to that question. "Well, let's locate the North Star. If we can find it, we'll take our bearing from it."

I looked overhead and commented, "There's a mess of stars up there. Which one do you suppose is the North Star?"

"Now, don't tell me, Gandhi, that you ain't never picked out the North Star before? You know that it's brighter than all the rest. Let's see." Tadd stretched his neck and tilted his head back to fully view the lighted heavens. He thrust his right arm out straight with his index finger pointing, "There she be. Do you see it?"

The Good Ol' Days

"Yeah," I said, but my voice didn't contain the excitement Tadd's did. I inquired further, "What'll we do now? We done found it, but we've been sailing due west all day. Are we gonna head north?"

"We'll sail north by northwest," Tadd spoke in a seafaring manner.

"Doggone it, Tadd. How do you know which way is northwest?"

"Gandhi, you ask too many questions. We'll head her north by that star and keep her well to the port. That oughta be west."

Tadd seemed upset by my questions so I decided to change the course of our conversation. "Tadd, when we get back home we'll have to take ol' Niter out for a run. I bet your Uncle Scank ain't even had him out of the stable. We could take him out by the Camp Grounds and cut him loose. What do you say?"

"Sounds great, Gandhi. We'll let him fly. Give him full rein. Say, ain't that wind coming up a bit?"

I turned my face toward the bow. "Yeah, believe so. Seems the swells are growing bigger. What do you think?"

"I think we'd better tie down all our gear. You'd better put a line 'round Skipper...just in case."

"Do you think we're gonna have a storm?" my voice quaked.

"Naw," Tadd seemed sure of his answer, "We ain't gonna have no storm. Why the moon and stars are out bright as day. I believe the wind is gonna blow a bit more stuff. That's all."

Our raft began to roll violently in the white-capped swells. Everything on board was latched secure. Thank goodness. Otherwise, it would have been washed overboard. Tadd manned the tiller. The timber of our raft grew rough from the incessant salt spray.

"Gandhi, we'd better take in sail," Tadd called out.

I furled the sail and tied both the sail and boom to the mast against the hissing torrent of water. There were whitecaps aplenty. I had a queasy feeling in my stomach.

"Throw out the anchor."

"What for?" I asked. "We ain't got enough line to reach bottom."

"Throw it out anyway," Tadd called back to me. "It may keep 'er steady."

I threw out the anchor and gave it all the line that was tied to it. I didn't see any difference it made.

"Gandhi," Tadd was speaking again. "Grab this here tiller. Keep her steady as you go. Do you hear?"

I made my way slowly to the tiller for it wasn't easy walking on the raft that was rolling and sliding over the swells. I had secured a line to Skipper and tied it to the mast. Occasionally, waves would splash over us like sprays of water from a fire hose. The clouds above seemed to be booming across the sky, pushed by strong winds.

"Where's the North Star, Tadd?"

He yelled at me, "Forget the North Star. Just try to stay on the backside of them waves." Silence. Then minutes later, "Hey, Gandhi, where's that galvanized bucket?"

"Under the lean-to, tied to the food box," I hollered back as I tried to din the fact of our distress in Tadd's mind.

Tadd moved in a lively fashion, tying a piece of line to the handle of the bucket. I would guess the line was about twenty-five feet long. Pessimistic gloom clouded my thoughts. The sea spray over the port bow soaked us through to the skin.

"Whatcha doing?"

"Making a sea anchor," he called back to me without looking up.

"What's a sea anchor?"

Tadd didn't seem to mind my question. "It's to keep us from going too fast in these swells. It oughta keep our bow from dipping in the water."

"Where in the tarnation did you ever hear about that, Tadd?"

"From Capt'n Lacey. Heard him talk about it many a time."

"Where you gonna ply it out from? Bow or stern?"

"You ask the darnedest questions, Gandhi. I'm gonna let it out from the stern."

"Are you sure that's the right way?"

"No, I ain't sure," Tadd confessed, "but it seems to me that if you want to slow down, you'd put the brakes on from the rear. Right?"

"Sounds logical to me, Tadd."

The Good Ol' Days

"Well, then," Tadd said as he played out the line while the bucket swallowed water and sunk out of sight.

We rolled and tossed in those swells for hours and then there came a throbbing calm over us. The swells were back to normal and rocked our raft gently like sliding down a miniature roller coaster.

"Say, Tadd," I said sitting cross-legged on deck on looking up at him, "You know what?"

"What?"

"We've got only four cans of beans left and two cans of Spam."

"How's the water holding out?" Tadd asked.

I flooded the two-gallon water jugs with the beam of the flashlight. "One's empty; the other looks like it might have a quart in it."

Tadd didn't answer. Finally, he said, "Here Gandhi, take over for awhile."

"Whatcha gonna do?"

"I'm gonna pull in our sea anchor." He spoke in an unsteady voice, and I detected a quiver in his speech. Could he be getting scared for our lives? I was getting more scared, too. I was wondering if Tadd suspected anything that he hadn't told me about—like as not being found, running out of food and starving to death. But that wasn't like Tadd because he was the bravest boy I knew. Why, we could catch fish and live off them for weeks and weeks until we were rescued.

Tadd grunted and groaned and pulled. "Oh, we ain't gonna pull that sunken bucket in."

"Well, there's one thing for certain. We ain't gonna travel very far with that thing dragging. What do you aim to do, Tadd?"

"I'll show you," Tadd pulled out his pocketknife and sawed the line in two. "There, that does it." He folded his knife, put it back in his pocket and sat down on deck.

Neither of us spoke for quite a while for our minds were hosts to sad thoughts. Finally, I ripped the silent sheet between us. "Do you suppose that they miss us back home?"

"Naw, I don't reckon so. We done told 'em we'd be gone about two weeks," Then he said, "Gandhi, how's about you handling the tiller for a spell? I'll try to snatch some shut-eye. You call me after awhile and I'll relieve you. Okay?"

"Okay," I assured him.

We got very little sleep that night. The next day was a carbon copy of the day before except there were no high winds, for which we were thankful. A thin beam of watery sunshine broke through the clouds. We rationed our water supply by taking only small sips of it at a time. Even Skipper was limited to a few laps of the precious substance. That night an avalanche of darkness fell on us as we each stood two hour watches as before.

The next day broke silently while the sea and sky seemed to meet in impenetrable blue. Our conversation had worn thin, and we spoke very little. The water supply was exhausted. Our lips were parched and the moisture in our mouth turned to drought. By now we had lost all sense of direction, and we didn't even bother to unfurl our sail. We drifted aimlessly about, and we no longer seemed to care. We laid on the raft and would sleep or else just look at one another or at the sky or the somber green monotony of water. We had spotted no craft of any kind in more than three days. From time to time, Skipper would sit up on his haunches and let out a mournful howl. I sensed our mortal danger, and it gnawed at my bowels. Our energy began to flag, and we became aglow with despondency.

Tadd leaned toward me and said in a weak voice, "Do you know what that's the sign of?"

"What's what the sign of?" I didn't understand his question.

"Skipper's howling. Ain't you never heard that before? That when a dog howls, somebody is gonna die."

"No, I ain't never heard that before." I told Tadd. "Is it true?"

"Sure, it's true. I've heard folks tell about it, and they say it never misses. Especially when a dog howls under somebody's window, they die...usually right away.

"Boy, I'm glad we're out here, then." I replied.

"What do you mean?" Tadd asked with painful streaks covering his face. We both felt awfully weak, but somehow we yearned to talk.

"I mean there ain't no window out here so neither one of us is gonna die," I said with some relief in my voice.

"Guess you're right," Tadd answered in a matter-of-fact tone lacking any enthusiasm.

It was yesterday, or was it the day before, that we began to lose track of time. To tell the truth, we didn't rightly know how many days we had been at sea. We knew for sure that our water was gone, and we had one can of beans left in the food box. We just lay there on our backs and looked up at the sky, too weak to even sit up. Skipper whined and his eyes were glassy looking. Our hope for rescue was exhausted.

I FELT LIKE I WAS DRIFTING OFF TO SLEEP, but my eyes were wide open. Tadd's voice sounded far off, but I guess that was because he was so weak. "Gandhi, listen! Am I hearing things?" Ain't that a drone of a motor?"

I strained to listen but heard nothing.

"Listen!" he said, I turned slowly toward him. A tear from each corner of his eyes trickled down his sunbeaten freckled cheeks.

I listened hard. Yes, maybe, I could hear the throb of a motor. In a weak manner, I stretched forth my hand and held on to Tadd's hand. "Thank God," I cried.

"Say a prayer, Gandhi," Tadd whispered.

"I don't know none, 'cept the Lord's Prayer."

"Let's say that, then," Tadd's cheeks were wet with tears. And so were mine. And then he added, "We're just like all the rest of the folks in the world, ain't we?"

"What do you mean?"

"Well," Tadd continued feebly, "we wait 'til we're at our wits end before we call on God for help."

"Yeah, guess you're right," was my weak reply, but I didn't say anything about my praying all the days previously that God would save us somehow.

"Do you know what I wish, Gandhi?"

"No."

"That we could get a whiff of God's breath."

"Maybe we have," I said.

We kept our prone positions then we joined together in whispering the Lord's Prayer: "Our Father, who are in heaven. Hallowed be Thy name. Thy kingdom come, Thy will be done. On earth as it is in heaven. Give us this day our daily bread. And forgive us our trespasses as we forgive them that trespass against us. And lead us not into temptation but deliver us from evil. For Thine is the kingdom, and the power and the glory for ever and ever. In Jesus' name. Amen."

We lay there holding hands, too weak and haggard to move. The motor droned louder and louder, but we didn't have the strength to stand up and see if the boat was coming toward us or away from us. We could only hope and pray that they had spied us and would come and save us.

After that, I don't recall what happened. The next thing we knew someone had jumped onto our raft. He was wearing blue denims and a blue shirt and a little white round hat. He lifted Tadd into the arms of another man on board the boat along side, then he hoisted me up in the waiting arms. "What about Skipper?" I asked in a childish voice of the man who held me.

"Don't worry, sonny. We'll bring him aboard," was his consoling reply.

We were carried below and heard the voice of a man whom we dearly loved.

"Dear God! You're safe, boys. You're safe. How in the tarnation did you ever get out to sea?" It was Capt'n Lacey. His eyes were full of water, and he looked like he needed a shave badly. He was a brooding figure with lines of wear and wisdom etched on his leathery cheeks.

I tried to answer him, but my words wouldn't take shape in my mouth. I heard someone tell the Captain, "Better let them rest. We'll try to get them to eat. We can talk later."

Someone put us in soft bunks and wrapped us in warm blankets. I felt honest to goodness water without the taste of salt on my lips. I stretched my tongue to lick some into my parched insides.

The Good Ol' Days

THE NEXT DAY WE AWOKE IN the Ocean City, Maryland Coast Guard Station located about twenty miles due south of Mispillion Lighthouse. We had slept through a whole day and night.

I opened my eyes. "Where are we?" I wailed.

"You're safe, son," was the pleasant well-known voice of Capt'n Lacey. "You boys had quite a turn, didn't you?"

"Is that you, Capt'n?" Tadd was awake and heard Capt'n Lacey talking.

"Yes, Tadd, it's me. I was just telling Gandhi that you boys had some experience. You've worried the daylights out of all of us. Why, we've been out looking for you for days now. John Northam saw me in town about a week ago. He said he'd been out the crick and in the bay fishing. I asked him if he had seen you boys in his travels. He said he hadn't seen hide nor hair of you. That got me to thinking and worrying. Thank God you're gonna be all right." The Captain patted our heads.

"Did they save Skipper, Capt'n?" I asked.

"You bet they did. He's gonna be fine, too."

"What about our raft?" Tadd asked.

"Well, we didn't salvage that," the Captain drawled. "But, we saved your gear. That is, what little you had left. You can always make another raft," he said, looking at us and leaning forward to catch our reaction to his last words.

"Don't believe we'll be building another raft anytime soon, Captain. Right, Gandhi?" Tadd said.

"The way I feel now," I confessed, "I don't care if I never see another raft."

Silence. Then Tadd inquired, sheepishly, "Have you seen our moms and pops, Captain?"

"No, I ain't," Capt'n Lacey said, puffing out dense climbing gray columns of swirling smoke.

"I guess we'll be in for one of the greatest thrashings we've ever had when we get back home," Tadd said with a sigh.

"Oh, I don't know about that," Capt'n Lacey was speaking philosophically. "I 'spect they'll be so glad to see you that they'll forget about the spanking."

"Hope you're right, Capt'n," was my wishful reply.

"When are we going home?" Tadd asked.

"Today, if the doc says it's okay."

"How we gonna get there?" I asked.

"I have the Marie Tomas tied up to the dock of this here station. When they say it's all right for you to go home, we'll go back to Lewiston in her. How does that sound to you?" the Captain asked.

"Swell!" I assured him.

The Coast Guard doctor came in later that morning to examine us. He smiled and said, "You boys had quite an ordeal, but you are none the worse for it. I'm discharging you into the care of Capt'n Lacey."

"Thank you, Doc, and everybody here," said Tadd. "We're sorry we put you to so much trouble."

"You're welcome, sonny," the doctor replied.

We bade goodbye to the sailors at the Coast Guard Station, boarded the Marie Tomas and set out on the shallow Assawoman Bay. This would empty us into Rehoboth Bay and up Lewes Canal that wound around the mouth of Elk River into Lewiston.

CHAPTER 11

With Capt'n Lacey at the helm of the Marie Tomas, the ride back to Lewiston, especially up that winding creek, struck happy chords on the strings of our hearts as we cashed in on the luxury of the familiar sights pinpointed on sharply brooded banks.

"What time do you think we'll hit Lewiston?" Tadd was anxious to know.

"About an hour," said Capt'n Lacey. Now more than ever, his speech was as brief and emphatic as the crack of a rifle. There was something about Capt'n Lacey that made me think the last furrow in the old sod of his character had been turned. He appeared different. There was a certain air about him that led me to believe that he would never become overheated by alcohol again. This made me happy inside.

There was silence for awhile since our rescue put a new feeling in all of us. The Captain was more pensive, and Tadd and me were rejoicing inside but subdued on the outside because there were jumbled feelings in all three of us. I finally spoke after a prolonged space of silence, "You know something, Capt'n Lacey?"

"What?"

"You and the Coast Guard finding us and everything is the greatest thing that's happened to us since the discovery of whipped cream. Right, Tadd?"

"Right," was Tadd's reply. Brevity was his refuge and strength—sometimes, that is.

Silence again. Only the purr of the motor with its chug-chug punctuated the morning stillness.

Capt'n Lacey spoke. "Boys, sooner or later, every man sits down to dine on the fruits of his deeds." He seemed to be measuring his thoughts with slow, staggering words. This lively teller of wonder tales whom we loved was sharing tidbits of wisdom with us. We held him in high respect and honored his deep insights. He continued, "I suppose through carelessness or maybe through no fault of your own, you boys done caused a lot of folks in town to worry over you with much concern."

"But—" Tadd interrupted.

Capt'n Lacey didn't let him finish. "However, people are not better than the air they breathe. What I'm trying to say, boys, is this: I ain't certain what kind of reception you're going to have. There may be some harsh words spoken to you, not only by your parents, but other town folks as well. I want you to take your licking in whatever form like a man."

"But—" Tadd interrupted again. The Captain let him finish, "We ain't done no real wrong, Capt'n, against nobody but ourselves. Why should everybody be mad at us?" He desired to evade difficulty as well as I did.

"Well," Capt'n Lacey drawled, "when we live together as town folks, whatever happens to one or more of us seems to affect all of us in a round about way. You boys are a part of our town. When you cause grief or concern to your parents, it spreads to everybody in town in a sense. If there is sadness in your home, then that sadness seeps into others' homes. We are each born to be a child of the human family, and the family is not complete without the child. Do you understand?"

"Guess so," Tadd replied in a low breath, and he looked at me for my answer, wondering if I understood the Captain anymore than he did.

"Yeah, guess so." I answered almost in a whisper.

Conversation this day seemed pulled out of us like chunks of meat going through a sausage grinder. Usually when we were together, words rushed out of our mouths to one another like a fast flowing stream. I guess it was the tension of the hour and not knowing what awaited us when we reached Lewiston that strained our communications.

I was sitting on the stern of the boat looking across to the creek's banks noticing the many scattered wet stones, which reminded me of frosty crystals. I was just thinking to myself, and most of my thoughts were like a trail of cobwebs. In fact, my thoughts were so skinny and downright skeleton-like that I shivered at the sight of all those bare bones in my mind. Skipper snatched me back into reality by fighting the fleas lodged behind his ear. His right hind leg was moving like the flywheel on a gasoline engine, making an itchy scratching sound. Tadd was standing beside Capt'n Lacey at the wheel and his sleep-swollen face looked with fondness at the familiar sights around him, especially aboard the Marie Tomas. The huge quietness of the town water tower came into full view, and I knew that Lewiston was just around the bend.

Tadd called out in a loud voice after we made our turn, "What in the tarnation is all them folks doing down there?"

"Looks like the whole town's come out to greet you," Capt'n Lacey concluded.

I stood up to get a better view and saw ant-like humans swarming all over the wharf. Tadd's words gave currency to waves of pain inside me. I had a thousand butterflies in my stomach that began to fly around all at the same time. I moved in quick steps closer to Capt'n Lacey and Tadd.

"I know my pop is there. I can't see him, but sure as shooting he's there. Do you think he'll thrash me right in front of all them people, Capt'n, or wait 'til he gets me home?" I was worried.

"Don't know."

"Well, I wish we'd get there quick and have it over with. This waiting and wondering is bearing me down. How about you, Tadd?"

"I ain't too worried. And besides, Gandhi, do you really think your pop will whip you in front of the whole town? I don't think so. Neither will my pop. I'm pretty sure of that. I'm thinking they'll be so glad to see us that they'll forget all about whipping us...leastwise, that's what I think."

"Maybe, you're right, Tadd." These were the first real comforting words Tadd spoke since we had been on board.

We were moving closer now and the ant-like humans were taking form, and by looking into their faces I could tell who each one was. As Capt'n Lacey brought the Marie Tomas in, Tadd manned the bowline and I the stern line. Just at the right moment, the Captain put the engine in reverse to stop the boat and maneuvered her into her berth.

Rev. Thompson, his face wreathed in smiles, appeared as the spokesman for the town. He stepped forward on the wharf, and the people jelled like a huge body in behind him.

"Tadd and Marshall," Rev. Thompson began, "you are both safe. Thank God! You gave us all quite a fright. And Capt'n Lacey, we owe you a great debt of gratitude for your unceasing efforts in behalf of these boys. When we hadn't heard from you, Captain, in over two days, I frankly confess to you that my soul went through a dark night. I had all kinds of ideas of what might have happened to the boys. Not until this morning when I received a call from the Coast Guard Station were my fearful ideas blown sky high. Thank God, you are all back home safely."

Tadd, Skipper and I climbed up on the dock. At that moment, we were the real recipients of benevolence. Tadd's mom rushed toward him and smothered him with kisses and admonitions. His pop was there by his side and seemed awkward and at a loss for what to say or do. He rubbed his head and disheveled hair and said, "You little stinker. You had us all worried. But you're back now and that's what's important."

My mom flung her arms around my neck and just cried, saying nothing. My pop was there and he was sober. He looked at me and said, "Wait 'til I get you home." Then I knew what was in store for me, and I could feel my behind tingling.

And there was Miss Bloomery, a woman bluntly built in body and mind. Her tongue was still loose on both ends. "You boys ought to be ashamed of yourselves causing your parents and the whole town to worry like this. The sooner you boys learn to behave yourselves and act like little gentlemen, the better." She reminded us of what we already knew, and I guess that is what has to be done from generation to generation. But she still reminded me of someone who had been pierced with a phonograph needle.

I turned my head toward Capt'n Lacey, and he was looking at the people gathered there on the dock. If I didn't know the Captain better, I would have sworn that he had tears in his eyes.

Hunt and Pete and Levin and Burrous came up to Tadd and me. All four were grinning from ear to ear. Hunt spoke first, "Welcome back home, boys."

Pete added, "Yeah, glad you're back. We've been thinking about you."

Levin joined in, "Sure have. You had us skeered there for a minute."

Burrous asked, "When we going to have a meeting of the Wandering Knights, Tadd?"

"Real soon," Tadd replied, smiling.

And then, who pops up right at the side of Tadd but Jeanne Adaire? To make matters really embarrassing, she ups and kisses Tadd on the cheek in front of everybody. Tadd's face turned the color of an overripe apple. Most of the town folks laughed except me. I didn't see anything funny about that display. I thought it was awful and was glad no girl kissed me, although I did wonder what it might feel like to have a girl kiss you. Then I spied Louise. She was staring at me with glassy eyes. I didn't know what she might be up to so I said to Tadd, "We'd better be going home but quick!"

I believe Tadd understood for he said, "Yeah, let's go."

As our folks, Tadd, Skipper, and I made our way out to Main Street, some of the town folks patted us on the back and said how glad they were to see us safely back home.

THE NEXT DAY WE MET AT THE TOP OF THE HILL in front of the church, and Tadd greeted me with the question, "Did you get it?'

"Nope," I answered, "Did you?"

"Nope. I guess they was so glad to see us that they thought it weren't no use to whip us. What did you have for supper last night?"

I licked my lips before answering and rubbing my stomach I said, "Umm, it was something. Mom really splurged last night. We had pork chops and thick gravy, turnip greens, mashed potatoes and garden peas, and fresh yeast rolls and guess what?"

"What?"

"Ice cream."

"So did we. Boy, it sure did taste good, didn't it?" Tadd wet his lips and with his tongue like he could still taste the rich delicious flavor of chocolate ice cream.

"What'll we do today?" I asked.

"Don't you 'member?"

"What?"

"Boy, your memory is 'bout as short as a green pea." Tadd seemed disgusted with me. He continued, "Don't you 'member we said that when we got back we'd go riding on Niter?"

"Oh yeah, sure. I forgot there for a minute."

"Let's go." Tadd said as he put his arm around my shoulder and moved me toward the end of the land.

Aunt Abigail told us how happy she was to see us and was thankful that God returned us safely. Yes, we could take Niter. She said Uncle Scank wouldn't mind one bit.

We put the bridle on Niter and rode him bareback toward the Camp Ground dirt road. He appeared to be in high spirits and happy to have us on his back. We never did run him while we were both on board. After crossing the millpond bridge, I slid off Niter's rump and gave him a good slap. He sailed off in a quick canter down the dirt road with Tadd crouched on his back and leaning forward with his face almost touching Niter's straining neck and flowing mane. Tadd galloped him back, slid off and said, handing me the reins, "Your turn."

Quick as a flea jumps into the forest of hair on a shaggy dog's

The Good Ol' Days

back, I was on Niter and cantering him down the road. Skipper was right at our heels. I loved to go horseback riding, especially on Niter. He was so strong and powerful and fast. I leaned forward and clucked into his ear. I pretended that I was a jockey and he was a thoroughbred, and we were in the Kentucky Derby. I pretended that Skipper was another fast horse. I looked behind me. The wind whistled through my shirt. Skipper was close by. I clucked to Niter and urged him on to greater speed. He moved out really fast, and his hooves pounded that dirt road so rapidly that it sounded like a whole herd of wild horses that had been stampeded. I looked again to see if Skipper was still close by. He was a good hundred yards behind and his tongue seemed to be stretching from his drooling mouth to the dry dusted road.

I reined Niter in and waited for Skipper to catch up. When he did, he flopped down and gulped air that rushed into his vacuum-like lungs. When Skipper seemed to slow down in his breathing, I turned Niter back toward the bridge and gave him full rein. He flew like the wind. I glanced over my shoulder to find Skipper. He was slowly trotting toward us. Before we got to the bridge, I pulled hard on the reins and Niter braced all four feet and we slid to a stop.

"Gandhi, you ain't using what little sense God gave you."

I slid off Niter's back to the ground, digging my bare feet into the cool sand. "What do you mean?" I asked, still holding onto the reins.

Tadd took the reins from my hands and realizing that he was not making himself clear to me, he restated he thoughts to speak more sharply. "I mean, if you ride Niter like that any more today, you may kill him or maybe give him heart trouble."

"I wouldn't do that for the world, Tadd, and you know it. I love Niter just as much as you do. I don't see where running wide open once in a while can hurt anything."

"Just the same, Gandhi, you ain't gonna run him no more like that. Do you hear?"

"Yeah, I hear."

We walked down the dirt road and met Skipper walking toward us. His tongue was coated with saliva. He appeared pooped as I reached down and patted his head while he joined us in our walk up toward the Camp Grounds.

I had rolled the words around in my head that Tadd spoke to me. Then I said, "Tadd, I'm sorry I did what I did. If I thought for one minute that I would have anything to do with hurting, Niter, why, I'd...I'd go jump in the lake."

Tadd turned in my direction, grinned a smile and said, "That's all right, Gandhi, buddy. I knew you wouldn't."

"Shall we climb aboard and ride through the woods?" I asked.

"Yeah, let's."

On board again, the four of us turned off into the wood's road adjoining the spot where the old faded yellow tabernacle was anchored securely.

"Remember...?"

"Remember..."

We both said the same thing at the same time. We laughed.

"Go ahead, you first," I said.

Tadd continued, "Remember when we came out here that night in search for that graveyard and house? You was gonna say the same thing, weren't you?"

"Yeah. Boy that was something, weren't it?"

"Let's go find it again and look around. Want to?"

"Okay," I agreed.

Before long, we spied the crumbling brick wall that hugged the cemetery. The old brick house was still there, and it silently reminded us of our chilling night's experience. We dismounted, tied Niter to the rusty eaten gate, and slowly walked toward the house. Tadd peered in, turned to me and said laughingly, "It's still dark in there."

I tried to hold tight to our mood and answered, "Yeah, guess they ain't got electricity yet."

We both laughed together and mounted Niter once again.

Tadd reined him back toward the tabernacle. We walked him all the way. Now and again we would bend down to miss having a young strong limb of a sapling whipping us across our face. Or, we would lift a shirt-covered arm to keep a holly branch from scratching our eyes out. We rode most of that day through the woods, enjoying ourselves and secretly thanking God that He was kind enough to get us back safely again to land. It was a good feeling being around familiar people and places. Before the sun slipped down over the western horizon, we rode Niter back to Uncle Scank's rubbed him down, gave him some water, and put him into his stall. We thanked Aunt Abigail and went home.

DAYS BEGAN TO PILE UP ON ONE ANOTHER, and when we checked the calendar, we discovered that school would reopen, much to our amazement, in just five more days. To stumble over this fact was a sad jolt indeed, and our spirits were lowered because we knew our days of freedom would be abruptly ended.

We met at the church corner that morning. Tadd called out to me as I moved quickly to join him, "Let's go see Capt'n Lacey."

"Okay," I said, falling in step with him.

"You know what?"

"What?" I asked.

"Before you know it, these here tree leaves will start turning the color of blood and the color of golden delicious apples and the color of pumpkins. And then, they'll fall to the ground dead. And before you can say Jack Robinson, them tree limbs will be shivering under a coat of sugar white snow."

"Brr," I said wrinkling up my shoulder blades, "you'll give me the chills 'fore it's time."

Tadd laughed at me as I pretended to be cold. I laughed as well.

Skipper arrived at the dock long before we did. He was sitting there waiting for us. The Marie Tomas floated gently on the placid creek waters. "Ahoy, Capt'n. Are you aboard?" Tadd called out with his hands cupped around his mouth.

No answer. I jumped on board. "Hey, Capt'n?" Are you here?"

No answer. "I guess he's gone downtown," I said as I climbed back on the wharf.

We sauntered down toward the Squire's office along the creek's bank behind the hardware store. When we reached Red Bridge, Old Squire Hazzard was sitting in an aged captain's chair and leaning back against the building; his hat slouched down covering his eyes. His black-rimmed glasses had slid to the outer ridge of his nose while he cleaned his fingernails with his pocketknife.

For want of anything better to do, we walked over toward him. "Hello, Squire." Tadd called the greeting.

Squire Hazzard never changed his position. "Howdy, boys. Too bad about the Captain, ain't it?"

"What 'bout the Captain?" Knots were in my stomach and goose pimples peppered my flesh. I had an awful feeling that something bad had happened to Capt'n Lacey. It's funny how you always think the worse when you hear half finished sentences, and right away you jump to conclusions. Usually bad ones.

"What do you mean, 'too bad'?" Tadd's voice was high pitched because he was anxious and worried all at the same time.

"You his best friends, and you don't know?" the Squire asked, letting himself go keypunch down on all four legs of the chair he was sitting in. He continued to speak while pushing his hat back on his bald head from off his eyes and still cleaning his fingernails, "Well, guess he ain't too bad. Old Doc Howell don't seem to know what ails him. Said it could be his liver. On the other hand, it could be ulcers. But he thought he could, maybe, had a heart attack."

"Heart attack!" I yelled with all my might.

"Now, don't go getting my words tangled up and go 'round town saying that I said the Captain had a heart attack. Now, hear me right, boys." Squire Hazzard shook his pocketknife in our faces. " I said the Doc don't know what ails him."

"Where is he now? Up in the Doc's office?" I asked.

"Nope," was Squire Hazzard's reply.

"Well, where is he, then?" I inquired.

"In the hospital," Squire Hazzard answered.

"In the hospital!" I exclaimed, "why he'll die for sure in there, 'cause folks only go there when they're gonna die." I had to fight back the tears for they were welling up in my eyes, and I couldn't do anything about it.

"Don't go fretting now," Squire Hazzard tried to console us. "The Captain is hard as nails. He'll pull through."

We didn't say anything for a short spell, then we said goodbye to the Squire and walked down the dirt road, shaded by weeping willow trees right past Chicken Johnson's house. Nothing seemed to faze us except our concerned thoughts about the Captain. We walked on toward the millpond.

Our hearts had tightened and swelled up in our throats for our sorrow was sharp. We swung our arms as we paced along the powdery road, thinking long thoughts and wondering if anything drastic was going to happen to Capt'n Lacey and praying that it wouldn't.

As we continued on our way toward the millpond, Tadd turned his body around toward me like tightening a screw and asked, "Do you think he'll die?" His arms clung to his side like some insect's spindling legs. His face was ravaged with deep lines of experience and thought. It was so hot that day that even the air stood still, and perspiration soaked through our clothes.

I surveyed Tadd out of the tail of my eye before I answered him. His birthmarked left leg shone round, brown, and ugly just above the bend of the knee. I wondered why some people had birthmarks and others did not. Could it be a curse God was punishing some people with? Naw, I decided, that's probably superstition.

Skipper sidled out from trailing at our heels and began a slow trot ahead of us, sniffing as he went, smelling for I don't know what.

"Well?" Tadd drawled.

"Well, what?"

"Ain't you going to answer my question?" Tadd seemed demanding an answer to his question about Capt'n Lacey dying.

"Oh, yeah," I said. "I ain't forgot your question. I was thinking. Well, it all depends. If he's got ulcers or liver trouble, he's bound to get over it. But if he's got heart trouble, I don't 'spect we'll ever see him again. He might die right down there in the hospital."

We drew closer to the edge of the millpond, but not a word fell from our lips. Arriving at the water's edge, we waded in, our bare feet feeling soothed and sustained by the cooling effect of the water, especially since we had been walking over a sun-baked dirt road. We spied minnows nearby that sprinkled the water like somebody had thrown a handful of buckshot into it. We watched their spinning patterns.

Tadd spoke, "How far is Houston from here?"

"I 'member somebody saying it's about seven miles."

"How far do you 'spose it'd be by walking the railroad track?" Tadd asked. I knew he was figuring something, but for the life of me, I didn't know what.

"Don't know," I said.

Tadd continued to think out loud. "I figure that if we took the railroad track, it might lop off a couple of miles, Right?"

"You could be right, Tadd," And then I added quickly. "Oh, I get you. You're planning on going down to see Capt'n Lacey in the hospital, ain't you?"

"Right," snapped Tadd. "You with me?"

"You know it," I assured him.

"What say we go tomorrow?" Tadd said and then he threw a joiner, "Early."

"All right with me." And then I shifted the course of our conversation. "What'll we do in the meantime?"

Tadd looked down at our feet in the water, smiled and said, "Let's go down to the swimming hole and take a dip. Want to?"

"Sure do," I said, joining him as he walked toward the mill dam.

As we walked past the huge corn cob pile, Tadd shot a sidewise glance at me, and I immediately thought of the rubber gunfight we had there, and I smiled and answered,

"Yeah. Some fight, weren't it?"

"Sure was," Tadd agreed.

We cut off the road through a sparse covering of a wooded thicket that hugged the millpond. We wound around the pond through the woods and arrived at the swimming hole at last. No one was there and this made it all the more private for Tadd and me to formulate our plans for visiting Capt'n Lacey at the Memorial Hospital in Houston.

The Good Ol' Days

We undressed quicker than you could peel a banana and hit the water. I floated on my back like a fountain spitting water that I had sucked in my mouth when I dove underwater. The spreading boughs of the pine trees appeared to be placed just right, not bunched together like clusters of grapes, but situated far apart as stately palm trees on some palatial estate. Away from the cleared area of our swimming hole were clogged clumps of vine clinging to the closely growing trees which seemed to serve as a protective fence for us to keep off eavesdroppers and snoopers.

"Hey, whatcha doing?" Tadd's brisk voice echoed across the bluish gray water to me.

I called back, "Nothing. Just thinking."

Tadd swam toward me and then he let his feet down. The water was deep enough to cover us up to our necks. We didn't notice the sun's rays that stained the shoreline were patterned with streaks of foreboding red.

Tadd spoke through his ever ready smile, "Think they'll let us in to see him?"

"I don't reckon they will. Seems to me I heared tell you have to be pretty old to enter a hospital, like being eighteen years old or something. That is, if you are going visiting. I 'spect they'd let you in if you were a baby, and if you were sick enough."

"Yeah, guess that's right. But we're going all the same, ain't we?"

"Sure," I said. "Who knows, we might just be able to sneak in and sit a spell with him."

Tadd swam with a breaststroke away from me toward shore. I dove underwater and pulled myself forward with long, strong strokes. We arrived on shore about the same time. Tadd ran back further in the woods, gathered an armful of pine chats, and I followed after him. He sprinkled them down on the sand near the water's edge. We made us a blanket of dried and green pine chats and stretched out on them. The sun was full and hot, and dried us quickly.

"Think we should take him any tobacco?" Tadd asked, his head cradled in his cupped hands.

"All right with me," I said getting settled down in a prone position next to Tadd. And then I sat up with a jolt, "Tadd, if he's got heart failure, they might not let us give him any tobacco. Ain't tobacco supposed to make you short-winded and be bad on your heart?"

"I've heared as much," Tadd spoke smugly, "but I don't pay any account to it. I've also heared that smoking stunts your growth. Well, that ain't so 'cause look at Capt'n Lacey. He's over six foot and strong as an ox, and he's been smoking since he was a young gun."

"Yeah, that's right. Never thought of that."

The incessant sun's rays beat down on us causing our perspiring nude bodies to glisten like quartz in the sun.

"Tadd?"

"What?"

"Let's take another swim. I'm hot as a fox, ain't you?"

"Yeah. That ain't a bad idea."

I looked up and saw buzzards soaring overhead, ravenous and parasitic, their naked red heads stuck out from their darkened feathers like a swollen thumb out of a sleeve. I asked myself why God made such ugly critters, all the while hoping that they wouldn't throw up on us. Then I decided that God made them to eat the dead animals that nobody cared to give a decent burial.

Tadd slapped my belly as he called to me, leaping to his feet, "Up and at 'em, Gandhi. Let's hit the water."

We ran headlong into the water, making a shallow dive and swimming with fierce energy underwater toward the New York stump. Tadd reached there first, which saved me from trying to find it with my toes.

We vowed then and there to go see Capt'n Lacey for he was our closest friend and we were not going to forsake him, especially since he was in the worst place in the whole world—a hospital.

I darted a glance at Tadd and saw his face screwed up in wrinkles that meant he had his thinking cap on real tight. "Whatcha thinking about, Tadd?"

"Well," he began, stretching out his thinking to get a better look at it, "I was figuring how in the tarnation are we going to see the

Captain after we reach the hospital. If they don't let boys in the hospital, we ain't going to stand much chance in seeing him."

"Maybe we could sneak in without them seeing us."

"I don't 'speck so. I betcha they keep close tabs on visitors 'specially. And who knows, if they caught us in there, they might keep us."

"Phew! I wouldn't want that, would you, Tadd?"

"Nope. That's for sure."

"Say, Tadd, we had better make tracks. Won't be long before supper."

"Yeah, let's go." Tadd replied and we shoved off from the New York stump and headed for shore.

We stood on the drying box of the big pine tree and dried off completely before we put our clothes on. Then we took a short cut through the woods out to the street and walked toward home.

Tadd turned into his driveway and said, "See you in the morning, bright and early."

"Yeah," I answered and then asked all in the same breath, "What time?"

"About eight o'clock."

"Right."

"See you," Tadd called to me over his shoulder.

"See you," I said as I broke into a trot. Skipper scooted ahead of me at a faster clip.

As we parted, rays of orange sunlight were scattered into the golden late afternoon while a copper colored haze caressed the treetops. I secretly yearned for the hastening of the next morning, and my heart swelled in the hope of seeing Capt'n Lacey.

SLOWLY DAWN SPREAD OVER THE COUNTRYSIDE of Lewiston and my wide-open eyes greeted it longingly as I leaped from my bed and got dressed with an expectant heart. A battery of summer noises, especially the cheerful chatter of the purple martins outside my open window, filled my ears and I was bubbling over with joy inside me. I felt good for I was thinking about seeing Capt'n Lacey.

Twenty minutes before eight o'clock. I was waiting on the church corner and hidden in my right hip pocket was a baloney sandwich wrapped in a wax paper Sunshine Bread wrapper. Tadd appeared, whistling a bright tune. He waved for Skipper and me to join him. We walked jauntily out toward the school and then headed for the railroad tracks.

As we walked past the school, I said, "Four more days and we'll be back in prison."

"Gandhi, you think of the darnedest things on the nicest of days. Here we're going to see our bestest of friends and you come up with that dadblame reminder." Tadd talked like I had just punctured his sails.

"Sorry," I said meekly.

We broke into a run with quick-legged steps for our bare feet ached to feel the roughness of the railroad ties. At last, we reached the railroad tracks.

"Let's try walking the rails," Tadd suggested.

"Ain't no problem," I said, balancing myself and walking the rail that felt cool to my feet.

"Bring anything to eat?" Tadd asked as he balanced himself precariously on the other rail.

"Yep," I said, patting my bulging right hip pocket.

"I did too," Tadd answered, not bothering to show me where his hidden lunch was stashed.

We thrashed things over and over for an hour or more while we made steady headway down the railroad tracks, first walking from tie to tie and then changing to walking on the track.

Ahead was the railroad trestle that spanned Louder's Stream, which wound around and eventually emptied into Elk Creek. In the distance we heard the mournful whistle of a slow oncoming freight.

Tadd looked at me with sparking eyes. "Gandhi," he cried out.

I was quite sure of what he was going to say. "Yeah," I answered.

"Let's hide under the trestle and let the train roll over us."

"That'd be fun," I said.

The Good Ol' Days

We ran to the trestle.

"I 'spect she's about at the railroad crossing in town, don't you think?" Tadd said.

"Sounded like it," I answered.

Skipper trotted down the bank and took a few laps of Louder's Stream. Tadd and I scampered to the trestle and swung ourselves down into the underpinning. Comfortably seated on the creosote piling we waited. Soon, we spied the train, coming down the track toward us, bare looking, and belching grayish black smoke out of its tubular stack.

"Here she blows, Gandhi. Hold on tight. Don't let the vibration throw you off," Tadd said, grinning from ear-to-ear.

I squeezed tight my hold on the sticky piling. When the engine reached the trestle and sped over the rails, it sounded like a thousand air hammers chewing the guts out of a steel roof. I couldn't cover my ears for fear of falling into the stream. I just gritted my teeth, squeezed my eyes tight, and held on for dear life. I do believe that it was the longest train that had ever rolled through those parts. I longed for it to pass over quickly. At last, the caboose wiggled over us, trailing the many boxcars.

"Phew!" Tadd said not letting go his grip, "I do believe that was the biggest train in the whole state."

"Yeah," I said, relaxing my hold on the gummy piling.

"What now?" asked Tadd.

I looked down into the stream. It didn't seem too great a distance. "Let's drop down into the stream."

Tadd peered over his shoulder to the stream. He looked hesitant and then said, "Okay, let's."

We jumped bent kneed into the shallow stream. I must have been a bit exhausted from clinging so tight to the piling for when I landed I was thrown off balance and fell into the stream, sandwich and all. My muscles ached, the day was growing hot, but I was happy except for my misfortune.

"You clumsy ox," Tadd called out. "Jump up. Do you want to get waterlogged?"

I scrambled to my feet and wailed, "Oh, Tadd, my sandwich." I pulled the squashy sandwich out of my hip pocket and unwrapped it. The wax bread wrapper wasn't leak proof and the bread was all soggy. I held the water-soaked sandwich in my hand and looked at it with a forlorn face. Then I called, "Here, Skipper. Here, boy. Come and get it."

Skipper ran toward me, wagging his tail and panting. I offered him my sandwich. He ate it with two slobbery bites. "There goes my lunch," I said in a dismal voice.

"Guess you can have half of mine," Tadd said consolingly.

"What now?" I asked Tadd, as I stood there dripping wet.

"Let's shove on," Tadd said, "You can dry off while you walk."

We clamored up on the bank and onto the railroad tracks. The track was slippery to my wet feet so I decided to walk the ties. Tadd, for some reason, was walking way ahead of me and for the life of me, I could not keep up.

I called after him, "Wait a sec, will you?"

"What ails you, slow poke?" Tadd said as he stopped to wait for me to catch up with him.

"I don't know," I said. When I reached him, I continued, "Don't feel right, walking in wet clothes. 'Spect we ought to rest awhile and give them a chance to dry?"

"Naw, they won't dry faster that away." Tadd assured me. "Let's keep walking but at a slower pace. Okay?"

"Okay," I said pulling at my clinging pant legs and then at my wet shirt.

"Say, Tadd."

"What?"

"You know where the hospital is in Houston?"

"Sure, been there once."

"When?"

"Don't 'member, but we'll find it."

"You're the engineer," I said, remembering we were still on the railroad tracks.

The Good Ol' Days

"And you're the caboose," admonished Tadd. "Come on."

I tried to hurry my steps, but my legs felt like they were filled with lead.

"Where does this track come out, Tadd?"

"Just above the C.C. Camp," was his quick retort.

"What's that?"

"It's where the men that ain't got nothing to do work." Tadd seemed to know all the answers.

"Oh," I said, not knowing anymore than I did before I asked.

"Tadd?"

"Yeah?"

"Let's rest a minute. I think I got a splinter in my foot."

"Gandhi, if you ain't the darnedest one. First, you fall into the stream and now a splinter. What next?" Tadd was agitated.

I sat down on the cool railroad track, and it felt good to my wet backside. I surveyed my left foot. It was blackened from walking on the creosoted ties, but I thought I spied the splinter. "Ain't that it?"

Tadd grew closer. "Don't know. Your foot's so black I can't tell." Tadd reached in his pocket and brought out his knife.

"You ain't gonna cut it out with that, are you?" I drew my foot closer to my body.

"No, I ain't gonna cut it out, I'll just pick it out with the point. Now hold still and let me see."

He began to scrape the bottom of my foot with the point of the knife. I cringed and jerked my foot away from him.

"Gandhi, I ain't gonna hurt you. Don't be such a baby."

I let him take my foot to begin his picking. I was determined not to move it even if he cut it off. I shut my eyes tight so I couldn't see and hoped that way I wouldn't faint. That would be awful for sure.

He picked and scraped for hours or so it seemed to me. Finally after many deep, gouging attempts, he said, "There she be. I got it." I opened my eyes and Tadd showed me the splinter fastened on the point of his shiny blade. "Foot better?"

I stood up so that my weight was on my lower belly and not all on my foot. After a few seconds, I said, "Yeah, it really does feel better."

"Okay then, let's go."

"Right," I said, but still cautious about putting my full weight on that foot just in case all the splinter wasn't out.

Finally, we reached the main road that led into Houston. We walked on the graveled edge of the concrete road until we came to the town limits where the sidewalk began. I limped purposely for I didn't want to injure my foot further and probably have to stay in the hospital to let those doctors cut off my foot just for practice. Thoughts jumped back and forth in my brain from thought pole to thought pole. I was electrified with thinking.

Before we knew it, the hospital loomed into full view, a big, white two-story concrete building with huge circular pillars in front holding up a skimpy roof. A large lantern-like electric light hung suspended by a long hanging chain secured to the underbelly of the skimpy roof. The opened windows appeared to me as hungry mouths waiting to gobble up anyone who walked close enough. The close-cropped lawn looked like it was manicured with neat, trimmed evergreen shrubbery flanking its outer edges. An ancient maple tree was anchored securely in the middle of the lawn with its branches interlocked to make a solid shadow on the rich, green, velvety grass floor. I could see that the sun had sucked all the dew out of the grass for it was dry and thirsty looking. The black dirt was sliced away from the rose plants that bordered the main entrance, and it appeared to me that fresh, warm manure blanketed the lower stems of the roses.

Reaching the brick walkway that led to the main entrance, Tadd swung into stride, marching in a hearty manner up to the large white doors. One of the doors was opened, and you could see right through the screen into the hall of hospital. There was a great churning bubbling in my stomach. Tadd was walking ahead of me, and I reached out to slow him down by pulling on the back of his shirt.

Tadd waved his right arm behind him to loosen my grip on his shirt. "Gandhi, what ails you?" Whatcha pulling on my shirt for?"

"Do you 'spose we ought to ask somebody before we go in if it's all right to go in?" I managed to stumble out the words.

The Good Ol' Days

Tadd shot me a glance dripping with pure disgust and said, "Come on."

Through the screen door we went. We looked at the ceiling, the walls, and the floor. My eyes went up to the wall again to verify what I thought I saw the first time. There it was, drippings of paint that had slipped down the wall, making a sloppy looking job. Right away, I decided that I didn't like this hospital. The hospital was overheated and bright inside. A small white desk was directly in front of us where a well-fed woman with white hair was seated, a little white hat cocked on the back of her head, wearing a white dress, white stockings, and white shoes. I supposed that they didn't know that there was any other color in the world but white. The walls and ceiling were painted white. The floor was the color of cork. I wondered why they hadn't painted it white, too.

Tadd and I sailed forth to the heavy-set woman in white seated in the white desk. Her static eyes sent out sparks as she spoke, and she seemed sore and grouchy, just seeing us in her clean, white, medicine-stinking hospital. I wanted to run out of there. I was glad we didn't let Skipper come in with us, which might have caused a stir. She looked annoyed at us.

"Yes, what are you boys doing in here? Don't you know you're not supposed to come in this hospital unless accompanied by your parents?" She peered over her black, horn-rimmed glasses and scanned us over, beginning with the top of our hair-tousled heads and going steadily down. She stood up and gasped when she saw our blackened feet, "Heavens to Betsy! Your feet are filthy. You have probably tracked in enough disease to infect this whole hospital. Get out! Get out!"

We scooted out the front door before we even were permitted to ask about Capt'n Lacey, and to tell the truth I felt like a skunk in a flower garden. The nurse called out to an orderly, "Sammy! Get a buck of lye water, quick! Scrub every barefoot print you see. Make it shine." She looked out toward the front door where we were standing, wondering what to do next. She called out to us, "You dirty little urchins, don't you ever come back in here again. Oh, me! Oh, my!" She held her gray head with her hands and went to her little white desk and sat down.

Tadd walked toward the big maple tree. Skipper and I followed. We sat down in the shadow of the leaves on the spreading boughs of the magnificent tree. Before we could speak, a man was approaching us wearing a white coat, white pants, and white shoes. We jumped up ready to run.

"Say, what are you boys doing down here?" His voice was pleasant, and friendly.

Tadd spoke, "Our good friend, Capt'n Lacey, is in there, and we came down to see him, but that woman chased us out. She said we was filthy urchins or something."

The man in white stooped down to talk to us. "She's not such a bad woman; in fact, she's a wonderful person when you get to know her. And she is one of the best nurses in this hospital. She probably has had a rough day. You just caught her in the wrong mood, that's all." He stroked his chin, "Hmm, Capt'n Lacey. Sounds familiar. Cirrhosis of the liver, I believe. You say, he's your friend?"

"Yes, sir," I said, "He's the bestest friend we got in the whole wide world."

"I believe I can arrange for you to see him."

"Oh, would you, sir?" Tadd pleaded.

"Yes, I think that I can" was the sturdy answer from the man in white.

He started toward the big white doors. We followed. He turned to us and said, "If you please, boys, wait here. I won't be gone long."

Inside we heard him speak to the woman in white, "Nurse Brown, may I please have Capt'n Lacey's chart?"

She handed him a wooden board with papers clipped to it. We could see everything for we both were peering through the screen door.

"Thank you," said the man in white.

He handed the wooden board contraption back to the nurse and strode toward us. We jumped back out of sight so he could not see us looking in on him.

He came through the door and closed it without letting it slam. "Boys, Capt'n Lacey is in Room 207." He stooped down again so that when he talked to us he was on our level, looking us right in the eye. Our hearts went out to this man who was befriending us.

"Walk around to your left here," he pointed where we should go. "Then about midway of the building, stop and look up to the second floor. You will get to see Capt'n Lacey. I'm sorry you can't come inside to visit with him, but it's against regulations."

"Thanks a million, mister," Tadd said.

"I'm Dr. Spence," the man in white said, smiling.

"Thanks a big million, Dr. Spence," I said gratefully.

"You are welcome, boys." As he stood about to re-enter the hospital, a thought flicked in my mind.

"Dr. Spence?" I called out.

"Yes?"

"Would you do us another favor?"

"If I can."

"Tadd, give it to him," I said to Tadd.

"Oh, yeah," Tadd said reaching in his hip pocket. He handed the tobacco tin of Prince Albert to the doctor.

"Would you please give that to Capt'n Lacey for us?" I asked.

"I will be most happy to. Now, you boys run around to the side, and you will get to see your Captain."

"Thanks again, Dr. Spence. We're much obliging." I said.

Tadd and I raced off in the direction the doctor indicated with Skipper fast at our heels.

We waited and looked into every second floor window but no Capt'n Lacey.

"What if they can't get him up?" Tadd asked.

I stretched my neck to afford a better view but saw no one. "If they can't get him up, then that's all there is to it. We'll just have to go back home," I said really disappointed. And then I added as an afterthought, "At least, we got him his tobacco. Right?"

"Right," Tadd answered without enthusiasm.

Donald O. Clendaniel

I still was scanning the windows, "Tadd, there he is! Look!" I was pointing and jumping up and down.

We ran closer to get a better look. A woman in white was standing close to Capt'n Lacey. She was prettier than the one we met in the hall, and she had black hair, too. Under each of Capt'n Lacey's eyes were quarter-sized loops of loose skin. We could see him plainly since the second story was not very high. The nurse kept the window closed and we couldn't talk, but we saw him sharp and clear. A smile creased his weather-beaten face, and he looked at us as if his eyes would pop out of the folded wrinkles in his face. And to us, he was a sight for sore eyes. I couldn't believe I felt warm tears spilling down my cheeks. It could have been my imagination, but I thought I saw the Captain's hairy nostrils quivering while his body began to shake. The nurse moved quickly, and we didn't see the Captain anymore. We stood still fastened to the spot where we were. We heard a window rise in a single gesture. We looked up and saw the nurse who was with Capt'n Lacey.

"Boys," she called down softly, "Capt'n Lacey is a bit tired. He must rest now. He is doing fine and he wanted me to tell you that he truly appreciated your visiting him. He said he shall never forget it." She turned her head inside toward the bed, getting a message from the Captain for then she said, "Oh, yes, he says to thank you very much for the Prince Albert."

Tadd called back, "Tell him that he is as welcome as the flowers in May."

"Goodbye, boys," the nurse called to us in a melodic voice.

"Bye," we said together as we turned and began to walk back toward the railroad crossing.

We didn't speak much as we walked out past the C.C. Camp, leaving the white hospital with all its white contents behind us. We hadn't walked far down the railroad tracks when Tadd said, "It's past noon, ain't it? Guess we oughta have a bite to eat."

I was hoping that he hadn't forgotten his promise to me about sharing his sandwich. Skipper came sniffing around. "Get away, Skip," Tadd said, "you've had your dinner."

Tadd unwrapped his sandwich and my mouth began to water just

The Good Ol' Days

looking at him. He lifted his eyebrows and eyes at me and handing me half of his sandwich, he said, "Here, buddy."

I grabbed the sandwich and said, "Thank you, ol' buddy."

We munched our sandwich slowly, deliciously, savoring each bite. When I had swallowed the last morsel, I said, "Tadd."

"Yeah?"

"Weren't that some experience we had on that raft?"

"Sure was," he sighed.

I rambled on, reminiscing, "I thought for sure our time on earth and sea was spent. Didn't you?"

"Yep," Tadd said.

Tadd continued, "I thought that when we drifted seaward, we had disappeared from this earth for certain. To tell you the truth, Gandhi, I thought we was done for. It's an experience that I don't want to go through ever again, how's about you?"

"That's for sure," I assured him. "It was a time that takes ten years off your growth. Right?"

We grew silent, mentally jotting down the outstanding highlights of our weird raft experience in a mosaic of indelible words that become fixed in our minds, permanently locked and sealed. Then we plunged into talking about the weather to shut off our grievous memories.

Tadd stood up. "Let's go," he said.

"Okay," I agreed.

Skipper was close by us, wagging his tail like he was eager to receive a last crumb we might throw to him. But there was none.

The railroad tracks skirted the woods as we walked on the ties that would eventually lead us to Lewiston. Soon, we saw the clear, clean fields that bordered the railroad track and the shucks of corn were in a line like ducks on a pond. My imagination was stirred and became a sigh that reminded me that the time was close at hand for us to return to school. I didn't say anything, though, for Tadd's memory didn't have to be jogged about that again.

The slender shape of the railroad tracks beckoned to our feet, and we both began to walk the rails. Skipper toed over the wooden trestles behind us. We walked in silence and drank in the silent beauty of the lush and ever green fields about us. I was thinking of our visit to the hospital and the experience with the nurse in white, and then I thought of the pretty nurse with the black hair and I felt real good inside again. I realized that there are some people in this world who are contrary and miserable and then there are others who are pleasant and nice and even pretty. I smiled a silent grin, satisfied with our journey and having the privilege of seeing our best friend, Capt'n Lacey. I knew he would get better because he had that pretty nurse taking good care of him. I was truly content.

CHAPTER 12

Back in Lewiston, we wended our way down the pavement on past the school toward home. As we were passing the parsonage, Rev. Thompson called out to us, "Say, boys, where in the world have you been hiding? I've looked high and low for you. Won't you please come in a minute?" He beckoned to us.

We looked down at our blackened feet, wondering if it would be all right to enter, dirty feet and all.

"Come on in," he said, probably reading our minds about our dirty feet, and he held open the screen door for us. He smiled and said, "You are fine, just fine."

He led us into his study and closed the door firmly. We sat down in the big, worn brown leather chairs in front of his desk, our feet dangling about six inches from the floor. Rev. Thompson sat in his overstuffed leather swivel chair behind the desk. He removed his brown speckled glasses, blew his breath on each lens and rubbed them vigorously with a big, white clean handkerchief. He put his glasses back on. Then, he allowed his long, lean right forefinger to encircle the inside of his immaculate white collar that was turned around backwards. Even though he was a Methodist, he always wore a clerical collar.

Rev. Thompson cleared his throat, like we had heard him do many times on a Sunday morning before he began to preach. "Boys," he began in an unsteady voice.

We leaned forward on the edge of our chairs, racking our brains, trying to figure out the reason why he had called us into his study. I concluded that he was going to read us out for our raft trip and the stir we had caused the town people.

"Boys," he repeated himself, "growing up can be a painful experience, just as life itself at times is a painful experience. But if you don't grow, you aren't alive for growth is just another word for life."

I wondered if he was just practicing his next sermon on us. He appeared to me to be roaming for words in the top shelf of his brain to bring down on our level.

He removed his glasses, placed them gently on the desktop, and began to thump the desk with his fingers like he was striking the white keys on a piano keyboard. Out of the corner of my eye, I spied the rubber plant tub standing stately in the corner of the study while I waited for Rev. Thompson to continue. His nervous fingers drummed unceasingly on the desktop. He seemed to be in a state of special pleading, why I didn't know.

Rev. Thompson paused, replaced his glasses and said, "Boys, Capt'n Lacey is dead."

My body stiffened like an image in stone. Tadd belted from his chair and raced to the window. We felt empty inside, lost, and separated from our best friend in the whole wide world, wondering how we would make it without his friendship and sound advice.

Tadd spoke in a broken voice, "He can't be, Rev. Thompson. We just left him a couple of hours ago. And the nurse said he was all right." Tadd kept his back to Rev. Thompson and me as he spoke, and I believe he was crying.

"Yes," Rev. Thompson began slowly, "I know you went to see him. That was a fine Christian act you boys did, and Capt'n Lacey was overwhelmed with gratitude. I drove down to see him and must have just missed you boys in my travels. I was with him when he died. He took a turn for the worse with some kind of complications, the doctor said, and he died quietly and without a struggle."

My heart filled my mouth and I couldn't speak for the life of me. Tears streamed down my cheeks, and I couldn't control them. Every fiber of my being ached, and I was sore and forlorn with sorrow. I wanted to say something but couldn't. I wanted to say how much I loved Capt'n Lacey and would miss him terribly. My jaws seemed locked.

Tadd asked, almost in a whisper, "Why Rev. Thompson, why did God let a good man like the Captain die? Don't God care?"

"Yes, Tadd," Rev. Thompson spoke softly and reassuringly. "God cares! He even cares if a bird falls out of its nest. That's the message of our Christian faith. He let His Son, Jesus, die on a cross so that by His love, He could raise Him from the dead and prove to all the world that He has power over death. For you see, if we truly believe in Jesus Christ, our faith will be the vehicle that will carry us beyond the grave and into the arms of God. Do you understand?"

Tadd and I remained silent, shocked, stunned, our hearts torn asunder. We were in a quandary, wondering what to do next. We had been given a hard blow to our lives, and it so shook us up that we were a mixture of scared, bewildered, and broken hearted.

Rev. Thompson paused before he spoke again. He removed his glasses and held them in his hand while he chewed one of the stems. I know he was feeling our sadness with us. We loved Rev. Thompson, too. He was really our friend. He spoke, "Tadd, Marshall, you remember hearing about Benjamin Franklin? Well, he said that life was a book which becomes worn with use and age, but death is like getting a new cover from God."

Tadd returned to his chair. Neither of us spoke. Rev. Thompson scanned our faces, fully aware of our sad despair, and I know he was grieving with us.

He continued, "Boys, birth, growth, and death are all part of the whole of life. No one escapes it. No one! But God has a plan, a purpose for each life. We may not see it or understand it, but this does not make it any the more untrue. Just as little Sammy's life was snuffed out in his childhood, his purpose, I believe, was fulfilled on this earth. And so with Capt'n Lacey. He had lived a good many years, and he certainly was a blessing to you two. His charted course was completed."

We were fixed immobile in the big, brown leather chairs without any desire to talk and I am sure that Rev. Thompson understood.

After an interlude of strained silence, Rev. Thompson asked, "Would you like to pray for the soul of Capt'n Lacey?"

We nodded our heads. In his prayer, he said something about people giving the victory to the strong, but that God gave victory to the weak. And then he asked God to receive the soul of Capt'n Lacey and somehow I felt a little better knowing that the Captain would be in God's hands. I believed that Capt'n Lacey deserved the very best.

Rev. Thompson arose from his knees and came to us and shook our hands. "Boys, the funeral will be the day after tomorrow in the church. I know that you will want to be there. It will probably be two o'clock. I'll see you and may God bless you both with a rich faith in His goodness."

At last my tongue began to work and I wrapped it around four words, speaking for both Tadd and me, "Thank you, Rev. Thompson."

We took our leave of Rev. Thompson and instead of going home as we had previously planned, our leaden feet and broken hearts caused us to shamble down the hill toward the pier.

Miss Bloomery spoke to us as we passed her on the street, "Well, what mischief have you boys been up today?"

Neither of us bothered to answer or look at her. In fact, we didn't care very much for her and didn't give her the time of day. She jerked her head and threw her peaked nose in the air like she would catch raindrops and snorted, "Humph, of all the impish brats, you two take the cake." And she strode away from us.

We sat down on the pier, our legs dangling over the boards. Skipper lay down close to me as if he sensed our tragic loss. The creek that floated the forsaken Marie Tomas was stained a metallic blue green. A small patch of shade fell over us caused by the sinking of the western sun. On the opposite bank of the creek was whitened, sun-baked mud. Somehow, just being there in repose brought us an unruffled tranquility. A large untidy man staggered by us without speaking, for which we were grateful. A small craft with two fishermen coursed downstream and vanished in the chill gray. Our desires were many, and our unspoken cries pitiful. A small turtle swam by, his craning neck affording him the view of the scenery in his passage. I scratched behind

Skipper's ear as we all three sat there in silence with a painful struggle to withhold our emotions, which overflowed inside us.

My thoughts switched back to the day that Capt'n Lacey brought us home from the Coast Guard Station and how all the town folks were out in the full array to greet us. I marveled how so much was done by so many for so few, just us two—Tadd and me. We were stout admirers of Capt'n Lacey and there was no getting away from it; we would pay him our respects.

Twilight encircled our gloom and Tadd was the first to speak, "Think we ought to be going?"

"Yeah," I answered, standing up, feeling lonely all over.

We made our weary way up the hill. I left Tadd at the church corner with the farewell, "See you tomorrow."

"See you," he called to me over his shoulder without turning about and headed straight for his home.

TADD AND I SPENT THE NEXT DAY IN GLOOM and misery, not doing anything in particular, just milling about the Camp Grounds, walking through the woods aimlessly. But somehow, our creative energy always placed us in the throbbing cadences of life's true rhythm, and we were like two germinated seeds craving to be planted and longing to grow. The Pilgrim Holiness minister and two men were placing chairs about in the old tabernacle. We sauntered over and offered to help. He seemed most grateful and we worked with him until it was about suppertime.

The next day spilled forth in a blaze of glory with a jagged brilliance. I dressed slowly in my bedroom, feeling all disconnected, haggard and worn. It was a feeling like a deformed creature must have when he sees himself in a looking glass and beholds his twisted body for the first time. My body seemed twisted and torn with grief. I had never in my life felt so despondent and out of sorts.

At one thirty, Tadd and I met on the church corner and walked with heavy feet into the church. Rev. Thompson and Mr. Harvey were the only ones there, with the body of Capt'n Lacey lying in a cheap, cloth coffin.

Rev. Thompson approached us and in a subdued voice intoned, "Boys, I think it would be most proper if you consent to help serve as pallbearers for Capt'n Lacey. Would you mind?"

Tadd looked at me. I stared back at him. He spoke for both of us when he replied, "Sure, we'll be glad to do it."

I looked at him wondering how he could speak so quickly and freely for me. I had never been a pallbearer in my life, and I was sure neither had Tadd. Could we lift the coffin high enough to carry it to the hearse? Would there be others to help us? There must be more than just two pallbearers. I answered Rev. Thompson, "Will there be others to help us carry the coffin?"

"Yes, of course. There are always six persons who serve as pallbearers," Rev. Thompson assured us.

We sat down in the back pew. A little later, Topsy came in and took her place in buzzard's row. I was told she never missed a funeral for anyone. Then, Mr. Mason walked in and sat down in a lonely pew near the front of the church. We heard a man puffing like he was under a strain. It was Squire Hazzard, and I suppose climbing the stairs up to the church sanctuary was an effort for his fat body. We waited and not another soul arrived. The only ones in attendance for Capt'n Lacey's funeral were the ones already mentioned. The church was dreary looking, especially with so few present. I asked myself how in the world could all the town people forget so quickly and so easily. It was Capt'n Lacey who saved the day for all of us during the flood, and just five adults and two kids were present to pay their last respects. I concluded that their memory must be short for most people.

Rev. Thompson mounted the chancel and stood behind the pulpit. He cleared his throat and began, "There is a divine purpose that binds together the scattered pages of all the universe into God's Holy Book. Capt'n Lacey's life was a page out of God's Book. This does not mean that the Captain was without sin or fault. No, he walked the way of all flesh, for Holy Scripture reveals to us that every life is sown in corruption and raised in incorruption by God's grace and love. St. Paul states that life is sown in dishonor, and it is raised in glory; it is sown in weakness, and it is raised in power. It is sown a natural body, and it is raised a spiritual body. There is a natural body, and there is a spiritual body. And as we have borne the image of the earth, we shall also bear the image of the heavenly."

Rev. Thompson paused and looked us all straight in the eye. He continued, "Capt'n Lacey was a seafaring man. He knew in his heart the call of the deep, and I am certain that he understood that death is a call of the deep from the deep. Listen to Psalm 107, verses 23-30.

> *They that go down to the sea in ships,*
> *that do business in great waters;*
> *These see the works of the Lord;*
> *and the wonders in the deep.*
> *For he commandeth and raiseth the*
> *stormy wind, which lifteth up the waves thereof.*
> *They mount up to the heaven,*
> *they go down again to the depths;*
> *Their soul is melted because of trouble.*
> *They reel to and fro, and stagger like a drunken man,*
> *and are at their wit's end.*
> *Then they cry unto the Lord in their trouble,*
> *And he bringeth them out of their distresses.*
> *He maketh the storm a calm, so that the waves*
> *Thereof are still. Then and they are glad because they be quiet;*
> *so he bringeth them unto their desired haven.*

Rev. Thompson coughed in his hand. He spoke further, "Capt'n Lacey, by the unseen eternal hand of heaven has been brought safely into his desired haven where he will be everlastingly anchored in the divine sea of God's life."

He read a few more passages from the Bible and pronounced the benediction with uplifted arms.

Mr. Harvey stood and said in his hollow voice, "Those who wish to view the body for the last time, please come forward."

Mr. Mason and Squire Hazzard moved slowly past the sunflower coffin and returned to their seats. Tadd and I shot a glance at Topsy to see if she were going forward. Her eyes were closed and her rotund frame swayed to and fro with her lips moving all the while without making a sound. We concluded she would not go up to see the Captain.

Tadd poked me with his elbow in my ribs and whispered, "Come on." I followed him without a murmur. Before the coffin, we stood for untold minutes, drinking in our last sight of the stilled form of our beloved friend, Capt'n Lacey. His face had a grayish color about it and he looked thinner. I yearned to throw my arms around his dead body and cry my heart out, but I knew that I could never give vent to such pent-up emotions. I held my ground, looked into the Captain's sleeping face and remembered all the cherished hours we had spent in his presence. I recalled, too, how he said that memory was like important collateral that could be spent over and over again.

Tadd and I looked behind us. It was Rev. Thompson who stood near us and placed his arm about the shoulders of Tadd and me. I felt salty, watery tears spilling into my open, speechless mouth. When Tadd saw me crying, we both at the same time buried our heads in Rev. Thompson's chest and cried and sobbed until there were no more tears left. Rev. Thompson walked with us to the back of the church.

When we were out of earshot of those present, Rev. Thompson said, "Tadd, Marshall, today you have become young men. I am depending on your assistance through the rest of this service. It won't be easy, but God never promised that life would be easy. Will you help me?"

We rubbed our eyes with our fists, straightened our backbone, determined to act like men, as Capt'n Lacey would want us to.

Rev. Thompson took hold of the coffin's handle at one end, Mr. Mason on the other end, Squire Hazzard on the other side, and Mr. Harvey at that end. Mr. Harvey said, "Marshall, you take hold in the middle there between the Reverend and Mr. Mason, and Tadd, you take hold between the Squire and me. Now, have you got a good hold? Let's go. It's gonna be a bit tricky going down these stairs. You on the front end, hold it high as we walk down. We want to keep the coffin straight as we can."

Slowly, we walked down the aisle, out into the vestibule, and down the steps. The hearse was parked out in the street next to the curb that led up to the church steps.

Rev. Thompson spoke, "Mr. Mason and Squire, you and the boys can ride to the cemetery with me. There is no need for you to drive."

We all nodded our heads.

At the graveside, Rev. Thompson solemnly intoned the committal, and we began to walk toward the car. I heard the gravediggers shovel the big clods of dirt on the vault and the loud thud seemed as if my heart had been thrown in there with it. I hated the sound of that dirt falling on the Captain. I cringed and wanted to run.

Rev. Thompson drove us back to the church and the two men got out of the vehicle, thanked the Reverend for the lift, and went to their separate cars. Tadd and I started to get out. "Just a minute, boys," Rev. Thompson detained us with his words. "Before the Captain died, he implicitly directed me in the presence of the nurse and the doctor that you were to be his heirs. So that means that after his funeral expenses are accounted for, you will receive everything that Capt'n Lacey owned. I don't know all the particulars of his estate or all that he had. He made me his executor and after I have settled the estate, I shall turn over everything that is left to you. He may have had some money in the bank. I don't know. But I am sure that at least the Marie Tomas will be yours."

We both said at the same time, "Thank you, Rev. Thompson."

I looked into the kindly face of Rev. Thompson and with a grateful heart said, "Thank you, Rev. Thompson for everything, especially the Psalm about men going down in ships and God getting them into harbor safe. It's comforting that Capt'n Lacey is on the leeward side of God's care. That's what you said, ain't it?"

"Yes, Marshall, I believe that with all my heart. Just before he died, the Captain put all his faith in the Admiral of souls. Goodbye boys, and thank you for your help."

"You're welcome, Reverend," Tadd said, sliding out of the seat and pushing me with him.

"Where to now?" I asked.

"Let's shove off down to the pier. Whatcha say? And see our boat?"

I looked at Tadd and grinned, realizing for the first time what he was saying about our boat and said, "Let's go."

I heard a dog bark. It was Skipper running toward us after waiting for us there at the church. We three walked down the hill and onto the pier. Tadd turned to me and asked, "Do you want to go on board our Marie Tomas and sit on the stern for a spell?"

"Yeah, it might make us feel just a little closer to Capt'n Lacey, don't you think?"

"Yeah, you're right," Tadd agreed.

Tadd, Skipper and I jumped on board our boat. It was a funny feeling knowing it was our boat for the very first time and wondering if we could keep it with all the expense involved in maintaining a boat. I knew then that we would take care of it somehow. God would provide. He had been so good to us all the while.

We were wearing our Sunday clothes, but we sat right down on the deck and bathed ourselves in the silence. I spoke remorsefully, "Day after tomorrow we start school again. It's awful, ain't it?"

Tadd said, "Don't mention it."

The exposed surface of our saddened hearts was no secret to either of us, and we shuddered as a small tuft of wind brushed against our faces. The upthrust of our grievous experience and personal loss weighed us down in a becalmed silence. We continued to sit in our places without speaking, for hours on end it seemed.

Intuitively, Tadd uttered from his heart of hearts, moving his head from side to side, his cheeks wet with tears, "He was a noble, generous man!"

I swallowed the lump in my throat as tears filled my eyes and spilled down all over my face and said, "Indeed, he was and I loved him very much and will miss him greatly. I will never forget him."

ABOUT THE AUTHOR

Dr. Donald O. Clendaniel was born in Milton, Delaware, and resides there today. He served in the United States Navy aboard the USS LST 389 in the European Theatre of Operations during World War II. He received his doctor of ministry degree from Drew University. He is the author of the following books: *God's Greatest Gamble, Six Spiritual Dynamics, Edge of Conflict* and *Success and Happiness*. He has two children and six grandchildren.